3 or 10

AnnetteKaye

Table of Contents

Dedication

Marnie, you helped me see wildflowers...

Thank You

"Some people could be given an entire field of roses and only see thorns in it.

Others could be given a single weed and only see the wildflowers in it.

Perception is a key to gratitude. And gratitude is a key component to joy".

Saige and Whisper; as we did this thing called life, we each had good days and bad. You both turned out well, strong, and dedicated, Thank You for taking this journey with me.

Bethanie and Daniel; you both were a huge part of my every day. Distance separated us, yet every moment we were separate, you were on my mind, in conversation, and in every tear.

You four are my reason for fighting, carrying on, and continuing, even in the moments I wanted to give up. Thank You!

Love Ma, Mama, MOM

Introduction

You are "Enough." Yes, you—just as you are. We all have more in common than we think.

I'm AnnetteKaye—my artistic name, not a pen name. It's the real me, forged in a simple yet profound act of self-discovery. My dad named me Annette, my mom added Kaye, and by age 13, as I signed my first artwork, AnnetteKaye was born. It became more than a signature—it became a declaration of identity.

For years, I let others define who I was. My true identity remained lost. Doctors prescribed pills and labeled me with diagnoses that seemed to define my personality rather than developing a true understanding of it. Yes, I was struggling—but not in the way they thought. It took years for me to realize that the path to healing wasn't in numbing myself with medication but in understanding and reclaiming my wholeness.

At 33, I was a mother of four; I realized that during each pregnancy, I had stopped taking medication, and yet, my life wasn't fundamentally different. It was a wake-up call! I stopped listening to professionals who didn't truly listen to me. I got rid of the psychiatrist, took control of my treatment plan, and demanded to be seen as more than a list of symptoms. After that, I became a whole new person.

My journey wasn't linear. I've been given more labels than most would think possible: PTSD, bipolar disorder, depression, anxiety, ADHD, borderline personality disorder, and many others. Each diagnosis came from a 15-minute consultation and a prescription. But those labels never captured my essence. They didn't explain the choices I made, the challenges I faced, or the victories I earned.

I vividly remember the turning points. At 31, I was prescribed lithium, which poisoned me, leaving me pleading with my doctor to stop the treatment. He dismissed my concerns until my body forced us both to listen. That time period of my life was horrifying. At 33, I found my footing, taking back my voice and focusing on the basics: addressing my sleep, balancing my hormones, and healing from the trauma that shaped so much of my life.

I owe much of my transformation to an extraordinary practitioner, Marnie, at a small family clinic who truly listened. With her guidance, I learned to trust my intuition and embrace a different kind of medicine: self-compassion, gratitude, and hope.

Gratitude became my lifeline. My doctor Marnie gave me a simple prescription—find three positive things each day and post them on Facebook. It felt ridiculous at first, but I tried. Slowly, those three positives and I added ten things I was grateful for, and the practice grew into a cornerstone of my healing. Gratitude shifted my focus from what was broken to what was whole.

My life isn't defined by the diagnoses that filled my medical chart but by the other facts that shape who I am. I earned a 3.8 GPA in college, raised incredible children, successfully ran businesses, paid off four homes, and published this book. I've lived in Europe, learned new languages, driven on the Autobahn, and cultivated relationships filled with love and authenticity.

This book isn't a replacement for medical care, and I'm not here to tell you to abandon your doctor. But I am here to tell you that healing is possible and that small, intentional changes can transform your life. We are all a little broken, but we're also resilient, capable of joy, and deserving of hope.

3 or 10 is my story, but more importantly, it's a story of possibility, a story that gives hope to all those who're lurking in the darkness. It is expanding thinking to see a multifaceted fact that makes us whole, a whole person. It's a reminder that you are not alone. You are normal. You are enough. And with each day, you can move closer to the life you deserve, one small step, one moment of gratitude at a time.

Let my journey inspire yours. Together, let's redefine what it means to heal.

Facing Fear

3 or 10 So, I've been complimented many times about my writing style. Thank you to everyone who has taken the time to boost my self-esteem. You are each a blessing. Mom always said I should be a journalist. Would CNN or The New York Times give me a shot?

My daughter recognized me as talented and made me send into a poetry contest!!! I'm published in a book!!! BOOYAH, did God give me a gift that I didn't recognize? WordSmith... what a title!! I've always been very proud of my writing, but I've never seen it as special. Can't everyone write it down? Well, I guess not. Finally, Keith had the straw that broke the camel's back. He said, "What a gift to give your kids," and "You can instill inspiration."

Jo and I have always encouraged each other to write; she uses 3 or 10 principles to help others. Kayleen always comments on my 3 or 10, making me feel good inside. And Marnie, who prescribed "3," must have known I just needed to be taught positive thinking.

3 or 10 I copied 328 pages of 3 or 10 into a book... I sat and designed the cover... now I just have to find the courage to find a publisher... scary for sure... what if they don't love me as much as my friends who are family do??? To not try would assure failure... I guess I need to try!!!

Notes;____

____

____

God
Jesus
The Bible

3 or 10 The book of Revelations always scares me. I spend my time with Job, Luke, and Psalms, but we must sometimes expand our knowledge. What is the "7 Bowls of the Wrath of God"? What is "The Mark of The Beast"? I have friends and family who believe we are at the end of times. Yet, they continue to build for the future. So, do they believe or wonder? I think we have a "wrath" and a "beast," but I see them both as living, breathing, and doing today. I'm very frustrated that church pastors are not actively "speaking the word" or "building the church." They seem consumed by helping the beast. They are on a perpetual "coffee break." Ya know, "idle hands." I've been in St Maries since 2015 and Emida since 2020. Not one church has actively introduced itself. I was actively going to one church, but when my Indy died, not one call, card, or casserole showed up. Nice "church" family to be a member of? NOT!!!

3 or 10: Am I doing what Jesus asks of me? I share the word. I pray for family, friends, and strangers. I pay 10% for tithing, both money and time. And I ponder what is wrong with America can all be solved by bringing more people to God and less playing with Satan... (greed, gossip, false witness, murder, slander, false idols, pettiness, stealing, etc.) Yes, I actively question and repent my sins. Yes, I actively preach the word. Yes, I raised my children up in The Lord. Yes, I actively praise God. Yes, when I sin, I accept Correction!! And Yes, through The Son, I know I get to go to heaven. Amen

Revelation 16:1-11

Then I heard a loud voice from the temple telling the seven angels, "Go and pour out on the earth the seven bowls of the wrath of God." So the first angel went and poured his bowl on the earth, and foul and evil sores came upon the men who bore the mark of the beast and worshiped its image. The second angel poured his bowl into the sea, and it became like the blood of a dead man, and every living thing died that was in the sea. The third angel poured his bowl into the rivers and the fountains of water, and they became blood. And I heard the angel of water say, "Just art thou in these thy judgments, thou who art and wast, O Holy One. For men have shed the blood of saints and prophets, and thou hast given them blood to drink. It is their due!" And I heard the altar cry, "Yea, Lord God the Almighty, true and just are thy judgments!" The fourth angel poured his bowl on the sun, and it was allowed to scorch men with fire; men were scorched by the fierce heat, and they cursed the name of God who had power over these plagues, and they did not repent and give him glory. The fifth angel poured his bowl on the throne of the beast, and its kingdom was in darkness; men gnawed their tongues in anguish and cursed the God of heaven for their pain and sores, and did not repent of their deeds.

Thoughts;____

____

____

Faith
Wisdom
Reflection

3 or 10 What is your foundation? Without a good foundation, a house crumbles. In the Bible, my body is called a temple. Temples crumble without a foundation. Am I crumbled? In life, I have, at times, crumbled. Health or mental, there are times I am a failure. I can wallow in that or rebuild the foundation so my life can stand tall, with fruits and vegetables, exercise, meditation, good night sleep, and God, faith, knowing I'll go to heaven, feeling forgiven. Without knowing what builds a good foundation, it will crumble. Good and bad behaviors. Taking care of ourselves with as much vigor as we do others. Being as honest as we hope others are. Integrity is not an on/off thing. Ya either have it or not. Being forgiven only comes after the epiphany of recognizing you did wrong and asking for forgiveness.

I know my 3 or 10 has been a lot of 2 sides of the coin lately; that is 2 fold.

1. Balance: no life is good without balance.

2. Reflection to create plans; reaching goals is what causes happiness and self-esteem.

3 or 10: On my feet to do good. Busy, busy, so I feel the foundation under my feet.

FOR,

GOD SO LOVED THE WORLD THAT HE GAVE HIS

ONLY BEGOTTEN

SON THAT WHOSOEVER BELIEVES IN HIM SHOULD NOT

PERISH BUT HAVE

EVERLASTING

LIFE

Thoughts;____

____

____

God
Prayer

3 or 10

We all have a higher power. That power is the 1st Step in AA and NA. Most of my friends and family call it God, yet some call it by other names. And lots of people (me included) have multiple names.

I see a parallel between Darwin and Creation. I 100% see prayer and manifestation as setting goals. The energy surrounding us needs a name as well. The Holy Spirit and quantum physics both seem to be electric.

This election has divided our country, friendships, and families. I am included in this because I feel as if this election was good versus evil. It's hard to feel warm and fuzzy toward people voting to destroy #myamerica. I have permitted myself to be separate, feel grief about hurting friendships, and give myself time to let my anger settle down so I don't say harsh things that I can't take back.

Watching the news yesterday, they talked about the feeling of relief that the election was over. I completely agree that this election was absolutely too heavy to carry alone. All the name-calling. Hitler, fascist, white supremacy, and "garbage". It's hard to blow off the hurtful names that MAGA was called. I am MAGA, so it was me, and they were degrading. This truly is a horrible situation that is abused by bullying. Being abused feeds my anger, and according to the news, I'm not alone. That relief has been helping me to settle down, feel the tension in my upper back and neck to relax a little, and move forward to forgive friends and family who hate America. I'm not there yet, but I am getting closer. I'm glad that before I said horrible things, I was smart enough, with self-awareness, to separate from the crowd.

I need to see "hating America" in a different light. To reconcile that is easier said than done. But I am gaining ground.

3 or 10

It is my responsibility to manifest happiness in my life. Along the way, it is good to acknowledge when I'm weak. That weakness is in no way a bad thing. No one is up, happy, loving, trustworthy, and whole all the time. It is my shattered pieces that, like a stained glass window, allow my sparkle to lay beautifully on the wall as the sun shines through. Yes, even in the brokenness, I sparkle. I don't hate my friends and family that I'm currently avoiding; I love them so much I don't want hard-core patriotism to brandish anger. I love my America; I voted against her death, and so did 76 million others.

Witches call it spells.

Christians call it prayer.

Spiritualists call it manifestation.

Atheists call it the placebo effect.

Scientists call it quantum physics.

Everyone's arguing over its name.

No one if denying its existence.

Thoughts;____

____

____

Grief

3 or 10 TALK IT OUT!!!

People try so hard to show their good side, a public personality, and happiness. Life is 50/50... yin/yang, good/evil..etc. We all need help, we all need tears, we all feel grief, sadness, and unhappiness, and it is in that fact that we can feel uplifted, peaceful, caring, and calm. I've been being really hard on myself for the whole Jake mess. Forty-two years, fifty years, eight weeks, five years, 5, 12, 26, 48 (Yep, that makes no sense to the reader) but represents a lifetime of Jake and I, A LIFETIME.

Grief, guilt, anger, sadness, UNANSWERED QUESTIONS!!! Things left unsaid... So I went to talk about all this. Talking about the last year of Jake being so sick and stubborn (refusing to go to the doctor) and my buying this house. A social worker said, "It sounds like caretaker fatigue."

OH!! My THANK YOU!!! Fatigue!!! It creates giving up! Throwing hands in the air. Hiding from people.

3 or 10: Sometimes, we need to talk it out to resolve feelings not understood. A second opinion or a fresh set of eyes. I look at the year before Jake's death and the year before Mom's. With Mom, we had a diagnosis, pain pills, and knowing we would say goodbye!!! With Jake, I hadn't!!!

No wonder mom died in my arms, Jake died with strangers.

I thought I was broken and needed fixing.

NOT TRUE!

I was hurt and needed healing, a completely different concept.

Thoughts;____

____

____

Grief
Death and Dying
Healing

3 or 10 Somehow, I injured my hand—probably broke my thumb—about four weeks ago. Then, on Sunday, I managed to hurt it even worse. It's so bad now that I can't sleep or even drive. So, what can you really do with no thumb and a useless right hand?

I can tell you what ya can't do, door knobs, turn off your phone, pick up a cup of coffee... ugh. So productivity, haha!!! When things go wrong, I always ask God, "What is the lesson?" Well, I'm not sure of his answer, but I can honestly say life is better.

A working thumb is definitely a blessing to be counted. Some days, it's essential to take stock of those "simple" blessings.

3 or 10: A simple blessing is still a blessing. Today, hot dish water feels really good.

The easiest way to organize your stuff is to get rid of most of it.

Thoughts;____

____

____

Bonding

3 or 10 Some blessings have a way of taking over a day. So yesterday, I planned for a completely ordinary, nothing-out-of-the-ordinary kind of day. But at 7:30, Whisper called me in tears after reading my "3 or 10" from the day before. I had moved her to happy tears. Then Saige called, and we spent an hour just chatting about life. My simple goal for the day was to vacuum and set up my vending machine. When I opened it, the vending machine that I paid $50 for was already full of money— $32.40! Yep, that really happened.

Planned is the keyword. A 1 o'clock flag ceremony was planned for our town of 45 people. Nope! Customers came in, so I missed it. But at 1:30, I got there and hugged my important peeps. At about 2:30, a pickup pulled in, and I greeted him as I do all the visitors. Oh my goodness, a funny guy, it was Stacy. I've been looking to reconnect for 20 years. K-Garten, a 4th-grade play, 9th-grade math. He used to stick his tongue out at me to bug me. We chatted for an hour or so over a cup of coffee. Catching up a little. Then, my foster parents (38 years now) dropped in with gifts and life-size seagulls that Karen made in the 70s.

Oh my God, they were beautiful. She made them way back then for her Mom. When cleaning out the estate, she thought of me. So we chatted about the recent passing and how much work and sadness it is to clean out a lifetime home. Bonding is sometimes unexpected.

I love birds... there was also a little box with a beautiful glass hand-blown cherub. Stunningly done, it will fit in perfectly with my 300+ angels that comfort me. A trailer pulled in with a donation to Roxboro. A hot tub with all the parts. BOOYAH! Randy thought of me.

3 or 10: Even crazy day BLESSINGS are blessings... Sometimes, we're just so caught up in the whirlwind that we forget to pause and count them.

Silence says a lot more than you think.

Thoughts;____
____
____

Grief
Healing
Anniversary

3 or 10

It always amazes me that our bodies know anniversaries that our minds would like to forget. I tossed and turned, telling myself to sleep. And then, a moment later, I did it again. I believe this exercise went on for an hour or so this morning. Yep, today is one of those days. The anniversary is one that changed my soul. I could hate this day, or I could celebrate living through this day. I did live through it, kicking and screaming. And this is eight years. And my body knew this before I woke. I could go to a pity party, but that will do me no good. So I'm gonna let this day wash over me. I'm not sure what that will look like. I won't hear from Saige today as she processes her thoughts. She is, in fact, stronger than me. Her wisdom was born in her. My old soul child. As she is silent, I "know" her pain. Not really, but it's true, and I understand it. I was robbed of a grandchild; she was robbed of a child. I remember trying to explain to Jake I was hurting for myself, but I was crushed for my daughter.

Time heals all wounds is a lie. Time is a calendar; some wounds never even scab over and are pure, raw, bloody, and broken. Time helps us with positive thoughts as our lives have been well added in. Yet, this day will forever be one of the worst things that will happen to this family. I'm supposed to find positive in it. I'm not that evolved. The only thing time has provided is "the shock" has worn off. And this creates a melancholy.

3 or 10

I know that one positive thing come out of Indy's death. I understand the pain of losing a child. When others tell me of their child or grand I "know" the heartbreaking, soul robbing, pure shock, and pain. I'm able to sit with them knowing they have no words. I'm able to feel the heaviness of visiting a headstone with only 1 year on it. "2016" while others get 50, 75, even 100, years. I may never know why God put this anniversary in my life, but my body reminds me of it before my eyes even open.

You will get there. But right now, you are here (And here is wonderful)

Thoughts;____
____
____

Growth

3 or 10 I woke up to an annoying alarm, freezing in my house. I hit the snooze button, which I rarely do, but of course, it went off again. So I told myself, "Alright, it's time to face the day… ugh." I got my coffee, turned on the news, and opened Facebook. My notifications were lit up. Click! Oh wow, someone said something nice. Thank you, Lisa—nice comments are the best!

Fact: most notifications are just tags filled with hate. Funny memes and positive thoughts, though? Now, those are a breath of fresh air. Positive thoughts are wonderful… repeat… positive thoughts are WONDERFUL. And when friends send those positive vibes your way? It's truly amazing.

Usually, I get tagged in posts hating on Trump, trying to make me deny God, or sharing awful news stories. But then, a different thought washed over me…

I CHALLENGE my friends to say 10 positive things about their peeps. I'll show you how... WE CAN CHANGE THE WORLD FOR GOOD!!!

☐ **Darin**, you are a wonderful, loving brother. THANK YOU!

☐ **Saige** and **Whisper**, I love you more than my own life.

☐ **Kayleen**, you always lift my spirits. THANK YOU!

☐ **James**, you have loved me for over 20 years. THANK YOU!

☐ **Jo**, I count on your soft-spoken love of God. THANK YOU!

☐ **Ben**, you rock, buddy! THANK YOU!

☐ **Trina**, you love our little town. BEAUTIFUL!

☐ **Marnie**, your dedication to mankind shines through in every word you speak. THANK YOU!

☐ **Russell**, your photography always lifts my heart to beauty. THANK YOU!

☐ **David**, your humor always makes me giggle. THANK YOU!

☐ **David**, your commitment to truth is inspiring. THANK YOU!

☐ **Monster, Indy, Butch**, you make my heart burst with joy.
AMAZING!

☐ **Joy**, you always find the most God-loving pictures. THANK YOU!

☐ **Mary**, you always share your love of the Bible. THANK YOU!

☐ **Jim**, your love of dogs is so perfect. THANK YOU!

☐ **Wendy**, you are a great aunt. THANK YOU!

OK PEEPS I CHALLENGE YOU!!!

Say 10 positive things today

Thoughts;____

____

____

AnneteKaye's Post

Lisa:

I just love your 3 or 10 posts! Can you please explain what 3 or 10 means? 🌼 🤍

AnneteKaye:

"3 or 10"

3 positive thoughts

Or

10 things to be grateful for

Thoughts;____
____
____

Loneliness

3 or 10 In my fifty-two years of cooking, I've never cooked for just one person! I'll be fifty-four soon, and life feels like an endless list of changes. Every life is just one new experience—good or bad—after another. Growing up, my mom always made big pots of stew, and my grandpa would cook enough "just in case" someone stopped by. My husband and I hosted all the holidays in Germany because he was an NCO, and then there were all those kids I had...

I have no one-person recipes. I've never cooked one steak, ten shrimp, or two pork chops. My pans are all family-size. A big huge freezer for a month of supplies... stands empty. A week of groceries $65... not $150. In fact, I don't even have to budget or clip coupons. And it's a fact this is bugging me in my soul. Empty nesting is the worst, but then I had Jake (who ate like a teenager).

Soul... how do we change what our soul desires? I'm waiting for the day I either have the drug rehabilitation set up... so I can cook or I adopt twenty kids, haha.

3 or 10: Some change is welcome, some not... but all come with the need for the soul to be satisfied!!!

If you ask The Universe for signs,

believe what shows up.

Thoughts;____

____

____

Hope
Self-Esteem

3 or 10 this morning, my nephew (who is 30 and knows better) told me to F-off. But him being rude is normal behavior for him, so it is just what it is. That is sad. Really sad. But when people behave like that, we are given choices. I could fight back. I can ignore him. I can put the facts in play. What did I do to be given so much disrespect? Nothing; well, I disagree with him!!!

Oh my God, I'm a criminal that deserves a foul mouth on my feed?? No!!! That's not it!!!

Oh, I should understand that he is perfect??? No!! That's not it.

I should cower under his manliness??? No!! That's not it.

So the only thing left is to recognize he is a punk with bad manners??? No!! That's not it.

3 or 10: The truth is, when others are unhappy with no self-esteem, they lash out to drag down others. That is truly SAD!!! I'm not going down today!!! I'm not fighting back. I'm not playing in his low self-esteem sandbox. He is 30, knows better, and chooses to be rude... I'm not. Yes!! That's it!!!

You did nothing wrong by asking to be treated right.

Thoughts;____

____

____

God
Wisdom
Beliefs

3 or 10 When I think about beliefs, I see they stem from experiences. Some say Jesus and the Holy Spirit can't be seen, but I'd argue otherwise—they show up in dreams, in that unexpected phone call from someone you were just thinking about, in a flower blooming among weeds, or the first breath of a newborn puppy. If we're open to it, we can find "our universe" and "our beliefs" at work all around us. For me, that presence is called "God." My experiences with God have been as profound as witnessing the first breath of my children and then their children, as simple as a Bible on a nightstand and the words reaching deep into my soul, as nurturing as planting a garden and watching it grow, as rewarding as hard work followed by peaceful rest, and as comforting as the warmth of the sun breaking through the cold.

The hard part about God and the universe is others' beliefs. Reincarnation: I can't prove or disprove, yet I have a belief. Psychic noise: I can't prove yet I know to be true. The soul mate theory is not pinpointed, but when seen, it is recognized.

3 or 10: "Others" beliefs are not mine to hold. Some say the Bible says astrology is wrong, yet the Bible talks about the stars. Some say talking to the dead is impossible, yet the Bible talks about the wisdom of generations. I always lie to therapists: "Do you hear voices?" Well, to admit that, yes, I hear my grandfather's wisdom in his voice repeated at times I need advice, it could label me with Schizophrenia (oh boy, that is a can of worms)

Haha, no, just a person with the gift!!! Intuitive or crazy, I see the signs and hear the words exactly when I am supposed to. And so do you!!! Pay attention. It is a beautiful gift to "SEE" God. The Holy Spirit is so beautiful.

The Universe will turn your whole life inside out to talk to you.

Thoughts;____
____
____

Tasks
Humor

3 or 10 Some days are tough. It's true—people don't wake up every morning feeling happy, motivated, or positive. Some days, we all struggle. We face feelings of embarrassment, shame, guilt, or even resentment. And that's okay—it's part of being human.

The reality is sometimes, the problems we face are bigger than ourselves. And sometimes, the overwhelming thing called life just kicks our butt. As we trip over our own plans, we fill life up with "ummm"? And that ummm interferes with happiness. I'm currently in a cycle of "Oh my god, the to-do list is longer than my arm." So I spin my wheels, not knowing what to do next. No task completed feeds overwhelm, making each task feel heavy. And everyone around says, "Finish one thing at a time."

3 or 10: A nap is indeed a task.

I said to myself, "Self." (And I knew it was me, cause I recognized my voice, and I was wearing my underwear)

"Today is going to be a good day!"

Thoughts;_______________________________________

____

____

A Break
Relaxation
Rest

3 or 10

I had some work I had to do yesterday at the casino. So after I got done, I went in to play $50 and eat dinner. I turned the $50 into $250, so that was nice. Dinner was horrible, but expected. My server was very busy watching videos on her phone, so I sat for ten minutes, waiting to be acknowledged. This has become the norm for customer service. This new generation has no shame. I'd be embarrassed if someone sat for ten minutes while I watched videos.

On my drive home, it was dark, so I was driving accordingly (missing a herd of elk), listening to the radio, and getting in my mindset. A song about regrets came on about doing things now because one day you won't be able to. "A Rain Check!!! Until you can't."

Of course, I call myself "middle-aged," which isn't true. American "middle" is 38, almost 20 years ago (sad face). But it struck me: "Until You Can't," a little tear welled up and a lump in my throat (I'm sure that is what the songwriter wanted), and I thought of my mom and my kids. My kids are young, so they don't "feel" such emotional pull yet. But they will. I've probably listened to that song 1,000 times, but it pulled on me last night.

3 or 10

Getting out of chaos, problems, and stress for a few hours is always good. It wasn't planned, so very organic. And very needed.

It's no secret it's just not your business

Thoughts;____

____

____

Spiritual
Heaven
Angels

3 or 10 Okay, okay, I get it—message received! So, today, I just had to sit and cry. Why? Well, since around March 2020, feathers have been appearing everywhere. Garrison and I talk a lot, and on his birthday last year, I asked him to send me a sign. Ever since then, the feathers keep showing up.

At Christmas, the casino was decorated with feathers, and I found myself telling Saige about the sign I had asked for and how it was answered. I shared with them that I've started collecting feathers now. Whisper wasn't there for this conversation. I asked Saige if she could find me some of the feather ornaments the casino used in their decorations.

Well, Mother's Day Whisper, of course, called and said she had sent me mail, a gift... So today I opened the gift... trifecta!!!! A gift for being a mother, my angels, and a FEATHER!!!

Okay, okay!!! We are all connected on this side and the other side.

3 or 10: Wait for it... seek... ask the universe... pray... wait... poof it will always show you the connection.

Whisper, I love it, thank you!!!

Steal feather wall-hanging

"Feathers appear when Angels are near."

Thoughts;____
____
____

Intuitions
Angels
Faith

3 or 10 Mostly, we all know there is a power bigger than ourselves. No matter what you believe about psychic ability, we all have those gut feelings, instincts, and intuition. And we all see "signs". My God is amazing and has proven that He is in every aspect of my life. But I was also provided a special gift that non-Christians didn't get. ANGELS!!!

Yep, heavenly hosts that come running when I call. Every answer from them comes from a "loving" place. Never have they told me to "do" from fear, guilt, or gossip. Never have they told me to hate, be resentful, or get even. Never have they intruded on my "free will" or even scolded me for "bad choices." Yet they always provide a "way out" of such shenanigans. They are a God-given gift to prayer, life path, and calm. Never have I regretted a moment spent with them.

Some call it "mindfulness." That quieting of the mind so that we may "hear." Sometimes, I lie down in my bed silently, with a mindset of relaxing, unwinding, making note of muscles being tense, and telling them to stop. Sometimes, I focus on a meal, each bite, and the flavors. Sometimes, I drive down the road focused on the song that was written to bring forth an emotion, a heartfelt message, or even a tear.

3 or 10: Today, I asked my angels for motivation to get tasks done. And they replied, "One task at a time." So I have a plan.

Visualize; Childlike Angel holding flowers

Thoughts;____

____

____

Trauma
Healing
Common Ground

3 or 10

I don't know a single person that isn't dealing with stuff. Some as no fault, the death of someone they love or a car accident. Some are as horrific as war or rape, child abuse, but also neglect by a school bully or abusive teacher. Everyone I know has "stuff". Everyone has some heavy-weight emotional blanketing of the psyche or heart.

We all have more common ground than not. But very few face that.

At 19, I was in a horrible motorcycle wreck. My injuries were many that would not be indeed known until age added arthritis. The trauma was dealt with early because I was the only one injured. When the motorcycle hit the car's back door, there was a cute blonde (5-8 year old) boy in the back seat watching in horror as the motorcycle driver and I flew over the car. Then, my mind went blank. The next memory I have was in the ER, ripping out an IV and screaming, "I'm allergic to penicillin."

I'm working on the introduction to my book. An "introductory letter" answering three questions. 1. Who am I? 2. Why did I write? 3. Who is my audience? With "How I hope to help?". This makes perfect sense, but it is hard and scattered as I write it. How much of me do I want to share with strangers? How will my family members "take" my words? Will they hurt, become angry, or start a feud? Or will it all be received as my journey?

3 or 10

We all know people have perceptions from their very personal experiences. Some are very grounded. Some are off the wall. Some are fueled by true reality facts. Some are fueled by drugs and drinking, and come with double vision or hallucinations. I certainly don't want to hurt anyone, but I know some won't read the meaning of my words. Maybe I should have written a novel. That isn't my style, as I have only read one college assignment novel in my 57 years. I've always been a self-growth or Biblical knowledge reader. At 57, I still don't grasp The Bible perfectly. So I'm not done yet. With these fears, I chatted with Whisper and Saige, and both gave me support! That feels amazing.

Nobody tells you how hard it is to rewire your brain so you can allow amazing things to happen to you after so much trauma or hurt. Blessings exist, good people exist, a softer life exists. Let it happen.

Thoughts;____

____

____

Joy in the Everyday

3 or 10 3 positive thoughts are the goal... 10 things I'm grateful for to know

1. It's cold but not freezing (wearing a coat cold)

2. My 3 or 10 helps focus me

3. Idaho is truly my home by choice

4. Coffee

5. Sleep

6. Family

7. My truck

8. The Community

9. God himself

10. Eyesight

11. Camera

12. Abbie, Secret, Port, Skiz, Stella, Ruby, Savage kisses!!! Slime from the boxers!!!

13. Paper towels to wipe off slime

Marnie, this is my best today!

I love talking to myself

She gets me

Thoughts;____

____

____

Mindfulness
Self-Acceptance

3 or 10 Lazy, overwhelmed, stressed, sleepless, broke... all common terms used in everyday life.

Why? Because they are predominate. Sadness or happiness is a step-by-step process. The way we speak to ourselves and others is the trick. But what we hear is also good or bad. We must be careful with words but more with tone. We must listen "outside the box". A therapist told me, "You don't have a happy face." WHAT?? Well, she is correct. My face is usually following my mind. Deep, concentrated thought doesn't look happy. I'm always focused on something. Doing life for me is a learning. I'm usually reading or talking to gain knowledge. And I'm always in thought, that's why I don't sleep. My mind is on an Indianapolis 500 24/7. How can I fix it? No!!! Why fix it? It's me; God-given... been this way all my life. So what to do? Accept the gift given!!!

3 or 10: I love this owl. He is adorable!! And he is checking up on me. He is PERFECT... yet another God-given gift.

A Photo of a small owl perched upside down on a tree branch. The owl has a round face with large, round eyes staring directly at the camera. Its feathers are predominantly brown with darker markings. The background is a bright blue sky with a few green leaves visible.

Thoughts;____

____

____

Spectrum of Relationships

3 or 10 Relationships change.... Relationships fail... Relationships blossom... WHY??? Because people change... People Blossom... People fail... there are hundreds of books about how to be a success... And 100's more about failure... So why not a couple about the middle of the road? I have a friend whose marriage is going through tough times, and he asked, "What do I do?"

Long before that question can be answered, he must ask, "What do I want?"

Relationships have two main parts... What do I get? What am I willing to give? Work-life is a perfect way to look at it... I'm willing to give 1 hour for this much money!!! I'm willing to give my all or just give half of my all. I want "these" benefits. I'm willing to be on time. I'm willing to stay late. I'm not willing to be abused or lied to. So then, what is the definition of what is abused? What is lied to? What is the "wage" this job is worth? Same with a marriage or friendship. What is my time worth? What do I get for "the wage"? What is abused? What is lied to? What makes me happy? Until he answers those questions for himself, he can not answer "what do I do?" And I'm certainly not capable of answering those questions for him.

3 or 10: I'm happy to announce that being single is my current choice. Not because I want to be alone. I'd love nothing more than coffee brought to me in bed or a person to scratch my back on demand. But I'm currently unwilling to "pay" the wages. Cooking him breakfast, sharing my home, shopping for his socks, or giving up my quiet time. I've got books to read, prayers to pray, work to do... grands to spoil, money to spend, and play dates to attend. And my dogs are asleep on the couch so really there is no place for him to sit anyway. Haha

Forgive those who don't know how to love you.

They were teaching you how to love yourself.

Ryan Elliot

Thoughts;____

____

____

Faith
Manifesting

3 or 10

It always amazes me when I send out prayers for stress relief or changes I need, and from out of nowhere, things, blessings, and solutions just walk right into my life. Because I talk about manifesting so often, my kids reach out and ask that I ask the universe for things, blessings, and solutions for their lives. I believe prayer is a list of goals; sending those goals to a higher power creates things to be moved out of the way.

Well, it happened in a big way yesterday. Crushed by some circumstances, not life-threatening, just not my best life, I cried out. I need a big change, as my world has hit an icky point. BOOYAH! I got a text message from a friend: SOLUTION! Not without hard work, but exactly what I told God I needed. He is always in charge of both the blessings and the timing.

The reason I'm so good at manifesting, I believe, is because I know 100% I believe 100% in the process. I know, without a doubt, that blessings come. Some quietly enter our lives; some come rolling in like a thunderstorm. This one is in between, pure relief; that is just a needed change in my life.

3 or 10

Manifesting change is an art that starts with a request. The way prayer works is in the "knowing", the answer will come, sometimes it is a "NO", and I really dislike the "oh hell no", yet; sometimes it is a yes. Sometimes a soft yes and sometimes a "YES" and once in a while it is a "Oh hell yeah". Even in the darkest hours of my life, I'm always taken care of. Sometimes it is clearly God, sometimes it is My Angels, and this one required help from a friend. So God stepped in and told a friend to reach out with "my solution". Amen

You can't change how people feel about you. So don't even try. Just live your life and be happy.

Thoughts;____

____

____

Moral Integrity

3 or 10 The moral fiber of the government is entirely off. The moral fiber of society is crazy. The moral code in the school system is outrageous. But the one that frustrates me is the moral fiber of family. I was having a call with one of my kids, saddened by the historical facts of people. My ex-son-in-law is whinny, a liar, a thief, abusive and controlling. Yep, an ugly human being. His mom and step mom run to defend him, which makes them ugly, too. Being a liar should not be defended. Being a thief should not be defended. Etc. and I'm told by family members "to get over it." I will never get over one person abusing his wife and children. I will continue to get pissed off and cry. Yes, I cry as I watch him hurting the people I love and protect. My mom raised two kids who have never had a drug or alcohol problem. How? She refused to tolerate those behaviors. Yes, I got drunk and smoked pot a few times. And I got grounded and the silent treatment. That silent treatment was the worst. My mother refused to talk to me, and I was absolutely crushed. At six, my mom marched my butt into Safeway and forced me to tell them I was a thief, return the gum, but it didn't stop there. When we got home, I had to call Grampa and tell him I was a thief. Crushed!!! Ashamed!!! Embarrassed!!! My ex-son-in-law has 2 moms, but no one loves him... and it shows. Thief, Liar, Abusive!!! Moral Fiber.... tolerating bad behavior is the least loving thing that can happen to another human.

3 or 10: Love me or hate me... if you're horrible, I'll call you out. Because "being ok" with immoral behaviors is not on my to-do list. I wish more people would "stand" for morals. The 11 Commandments is a pretty short list. My X son-in-law stole my daughter's dog and lied to my grandson about giving Knapper back to Saige... Lonnie, there are only 11 Commandments, but Monster will learn you are immoral... he is watching. Slow, festering hate is building. Sad that no one loved you enough to give you the silent treatment. But trust me, your boys will.

Kinda tired of being okay with things

I'm not okay with

Thoughts;____
____
____

Thank You
Appreciate

3 or 10

I'm a member of several coaching pages. It balances some of the negativity in the world with positive choices. At some point, they have all asked, "What could you teach or talk about for 30 minutes?" I know 30 minutes worth of many topics from faith, business, death and dying, birth and parenthood, psychology and mediumship, dogs and livestock, and land ownership, but my favorite is "The Art of a Thank You." Not only is thank you humbling, but it is also self-esteem-building. It creates positive feelings and reminders. If done correctly, it is to bring forward warm feelings that sometimes last a lifetime.

I use many tricks, habits, and gestures to say Thank You. For me, it is more than an off-the-cuff "thanks." It goes far deeper and is said far louder. For me, it is a thoughtful moment in time. One of the main self-esteem building in my life is "appreciation."

Years ago, my boyfriend, my teenage Whisper, and I traveled down a farmland road. We climbed a hill to the top, and the view was open and inviting; it was massive, reaching farther than the eye could see. Hand-painted fields in different colors, sizes, and shapes. The sun was causing a sunset of pure awesome inspiration at the moment in time. We also knew that this view would last only for a few moments and would never be seen again. And I said to my daughter, "Look, God hand-painted this just for you." The boyfriend squeezed my hand in a nonverbal approval. Later, alone, telling me, "You bring God to life; that is beautiful."

3 or 10

I hope every person feels the benefits of "The Art of a Thank You." Not just a gift, but the motivation it takes to create a thank you. We have a 100 times a day we can help others feel appreciated. This goes far beyond our human friends. It leaps forward into the blessing given by God, our very heartbeats in our chest, to the miracle of birth, from the morning coffee delivered to our bed to the approval in the squeeze of a hand to reminding ourselves of a moment we were acknowledged. All people enjoy feeling appreciated, and it can switch despair to hope, sadness to smiles, and just hanging on to the reason to hang on. Saying Thank You is free to use but the pay back is Priceless.

Thank You

Thoughts;____

____

____

Healing
Learning
Challenged

3 or 10

The words "I don't know how" is a cop-out. And one of my biggest
failures.

My son had a starter break on his car; as we were going through fixing
it, he said, "I don't know how," so being a "mom," I said open the box
and look at the starter, find it on your car, start with the bolt holes and
find and remove the bolts, carefully put each in the new starter in the
box, then remove the electric connector, the starter should fall away,
put the new one in place, bolts and then connect electric" he was
frustrated at me but did as it was suggested, BOOYAH his car was
fixed.

Years later, he said, "You taught me more about mechanical stuff than
Dad ever did." That comment said two things: 1. His dad was a bad
example, robbing him of knowledge and self-resilience, and 2. Children
need positive role models to create positive self-worth.

Sometimes, I'm a big fat failure using "I don't know how." I fluff
myself up with a list of things I'm good at, know about, or have
accomplished, yet I get frozen when it comes to new things.

The skill saw terrifies me, but if I would take time to learn it, the kick
back, measure once, measure twice, how a saw horses works, and when
the blade needs to be changed, my "self" would blossom into
"knowledge." Who on earth decides to build a house and not learn how
to use a saw? Me is the answer.

3 or 10

I need to take my own instructions and get on with it. Or do I need to
resign with "I hire people for that?' Neither is right, and neither is
wrong.

I know more about dogs (breeding, training, psychology) than most. I
know more about business (licensing, liability, and IRS) than most. I
know more about retail than most. I know most everything about
restaurants management. I completely understand the court system (not

law). Depending on the subject matter, I might have a Phd in failure or come back. So! Do I really need to learn skill saw skills?

"Healing is found in trusting the process, knowing that every step, no matter how uncertain, is leading you to wholeness."

Thoughts;____
____
____

Humor in Hardship

3 or 10 If you have been following my 3 or 10, you know I'm having a hard time in life right now. I've shared my hurt, grief, and have asked for prayers.

This morning, I called to make an appointment with a counselor. The receptionist asked, "If I was depressed?" I said, "Yes." She then asked, "If I feel hopeless?" I said, "Yes." Then she asked, "Why are you calling for an appointment?" I literally busted out laughing. Her attitude changed to an offended tone... so I asked, "Do a lot of people call your office because they don't like the color of their hair?" But I was still laughing.

Same medical office a couple of weeks ago: "Is Jake still your emergency contact?" I said, "No, he died." She said, "Is his address still..." I said, "No!!! He moved to the cemetery!!" The girl sitting next to her giggled, and then the girl asked, "Is his contact number...?" I literally said, "I don't think Heaven has a phone." The girl next to her AGAIN GIGGLED!!!

People get inside their own head and cannot hear!! I do it too, so it must be "normal," right??

3 or 10: My life right now is a Ron White tour... ya can't fix stupid!!! 1/2 of what is wrong with me is not being heard! A list of "I'm ok" with a sigh. I took Saige to dinner last night with the intent of crying it out. WE HAD A GREAT DINNER... at The Melting Pot... (fondue) I love the Wisconsin Cheddar part... we literally scraped every last bit of it out of the pan. And I might be addicted to pineapple dipped in melted chocolate... not sure about the addictive part... we will wait to see if I start Jones'n for more.

I showed my Facebook page to my psychiatrist

and she wants to talk to all of you

Thoughts;____

____

____

Calling Out Injustice

3 or 10 Stealing is WRONG!!!

Discrimination is WRONG!!!

I'm WHITE

Last night, I was at a meeting where entitled "white" men were discussing the fact that Natives have the right to hunt their land. (State law about the reservation)

First, the "WHITE" men "took" human rights away from the native people 1700's.

Then, the "white" man restricted the migration of the natives to reservations 1800's

THEN, the white man "deeded" the reservations for the white man to own the land. THEN AND STILL collecting property taxes to promote the "white" man's goals.

And last night, a group of "white" men were trying to assemble to prevent hunting on "STOLEN LAND."

I've lived on the reservation for 50 years, on and off, and never once have I seen Natives destroy land or fences. Yet, my property taxes keep being taken from the Natives.

ASHAMED!!! "White" man should be ashamed of their CONTINUED stealing and discrimination!!!! And MOVE OFF the reservation. Stealing is wrong!!!

Yes, I'm calling out the "white" men who believe STEALING AND DISCRIMINATION are their "right." You are nasty punks. And I say PUNK because the current law is Natives can hunt the reservation. A sov·er·eign NATION!!! That you!!! Yes, YOU... are violating their being by stealing and discrimination!!! I'll say it: YOU ARE A THIEF!!

3 or 10: It's a fact that the "white" man has treated, and continues to treat, Natives horribly. You should feel shame, guilt, and repent—then change your behavior.

Photo; "Silhouette of a Native Chief on horseback with a hawk flying over head, at sunset"

Thoughts;____

____

____

Honoring Life Beyond the Loss

3 or 10 I've been trying to figure out "Jake's" headstone. His family won't honor him, and knowing that cultural difference saddens me. No funeral for a life lived. What the hell is wrong with people? No celebration! No good bye! No prayer for his soul!! No wish that he Rest In Peace. But I did and do love him. And honored at times to be his wife. But it is a fact that Jake is the one that set this up. No family connection. No reaching out in the good or bad times. No check-in phone calls. No birthday cards.

Jake refused to love. He felt deeply, as his wife, I watched him not know what to do. I watched him struggle with the pain and guilt of his family culture.

Funerals and headstones cost money, and in his family, hoarding money is far more important than dinner to celebrate family. I hurt so bad for his kids. But instead of a funeral, they post pics of inheritance. They learned well the family rules.

3 or 10: I'm so blessed with a family that honors the very being of family and a soul blessed in being born. The knowing of what is going on in the lives of its members. The fact that if I needed, my brother would take his last dollars And give. The fights or fussing or celebrations each of us may have. My family shows me that I am important in the herd. That I am far more important than a savings account. I'm planning Jake's headstone to honor his being born and missed.

"Jake"

Bedwell

Brandon Milton

13 March 1964 ----

6 September 2020

Always Have

Always Will

Thoughts;____

____

____

When Strength Fades

3 or 10 Tears roll down my face. It is a fact we can't be strong all the time. Sometimes, acknowledging that is the first step. So I didn't know today would start with tears, but it did. Why? Because life is "off" right now. The list of "to do" is far longer than I can get a head of. People not keeping their word. Yea, that's a big problem. Set a goal to be let down by others. Oh, they always say "sorry" or "why didn't you ask," or they blow ya off because it's not important to them. This leaves people overwhelmed because goals aren't being reached. So tightening my goals is my only option. Lonely creeps in to do it all alone. Then the tears fall.

3 or 10: Prayers are needed. Yet, I never ask because I know I won't receive it. I do have people that check in on me. They are a treasure I hold dear. But mainly, life is a list of people by design who don't have time to keep their word. Today, Annette is sad, in tears, and lonely. Yep, it's true. But the reason I have 3 or 10 is simply to limit these kinds of days.

God Help Me Through This

Thoughts;____

____

____

Beauty in the Chaos

3 or 10 Surround yourself with beautiful things!!! Search for the elk grazing, a rainbow, breathe in the smell after the storm, a friend's complete hug. The mundane and life's stress will consume you if you let it. My problems are self-inflicted. Not all of them, death, divorce, cold weather, etc are not my responsibility to carry. The responsibility of marriage, kindness to the living, and purchasing a warm winter coat are mine to hold. With disaster in the world, my part is sorting it out and placing it where it belongs. My focus is my responsibility!!! My reactions are indeed mine to carry.

3 or 10: To see this beautiful bird brings a moment of bliss. His stunning feathers lead me to thank God for his artistic hand-painted works of perfect surrounding me. The gift of a camera allowed me to see things not from north Idaho. The photographer caught a moment to share with me what he had seen. The internet lets this bird travel the world in the time of a heartbeat. What is he thinking? Does he notice that, for a moment, he takes me from the mundane to standing in awesome glory? Thank You, little bird, for bringing me pure joy to reflect on.

Photo; "A finch with a blue head, yellow that turns to rainbow colors standing on a branch…. He is Gorgeous"

Thoughts;____
____
____

Choosing Between Satan and Jesus

3 or 10 Been pondering a lot about Satan and his reality. The Bible talks about the "big" sins. Murder, adultery, bearing false witness... but it is also clear about how he takes over the thoughts. Impure thoughts are talked about often in the Bible. What is an "impure" thought? Well, wishing someone dead would fit... but "I'm worthless" is just as damaging. Unforgivable is a little bit of Satan creeping in. Jesus says He can forgive any sin!!! Who is right? Satan or Jesus? When we get inside our own heads and say unloving things, we are indeed playing Satan's game. Buddha talks of "positive affirmation," and so does Jesus. Seek, and ye Shall Find!!! This is about a pay check, a house, or a promotion, yet it is also about happy or sad thoughts. "I'm never going to get caught up" or "Thank Heavens, I have plenty of work." "My house is a mess" or "my mess is home" Satan or Jesus?

3 or 10 Satan pushes on us. He lives in every thought we have. He lives in every relationship we have. He is one who chooses not to create roots in our lives. Jesus is alive and well and, through free will, is watching for us to brandish Satan. He waits for us to praise God!!! Affirmation of his presence in our lives. TAKE YOUR PICK... Satan or Jesus!!!

Success is nothing more than a few simple disciplines, practiced every day

Thoughts;____

____

____

Education
Personal Strength

3 or 10 People get lost, sometimes in a day or a month. The goals set get sidelined by the day. I have a clip board with pen and paper. I journal, and I list. Constantly!!! I flip pages, review, write, scribble, and check mark tasks complete. It's my system. It doesn't work for some, but I am a "mind mapper." It's God-given, and that's how my mind works.

I was in a college class that required notes be turned in, pictures of roses, smiley faces, a word or two, and big circles around numbers. My notes were given an F!!! So I asked the professor "why an F"? He told me those weren't "notes." I giggled and asked if we could go through them!! 22 circled... page number of book lecture was about... circle it was going to be on test... a star with a tail... President Lincoln! A smiley with a question mark the word slavery!!! Slaves set free when? I needed to look it up... 46 underlined 3 times... during the lecture, this was a big deal.. so the professor told me I needed to keep bullet notes.. again I giggled... and asked, "Are notes for me to learn or you to learn?"

For the next test,, I again turned in my notes but took time to list my explanation and attached an article about learning styles and "mind mapping." At the bottom, I, asked the question, "how did I score on my test?" When the notes came back,, they had "A-" the professor had me meet with him... he said "your notes have zero topics from the lecture, yet you ace your tests". "How do you do that"? I simply replied... "those notes are everything you lectured on".. "and in 5 years, I'll still look at those scribbles and hear your voice... "

3 or 10 The way I sort my life is great FOR ME!! It makes no sense to people looking into my life. Their perfectly organized notes make no sense to me. But a smiley face shooting star was part of the lecture.

"Told you so."
Sincerely,
Your Intuition.

Thoughts;____
____
____

America/Patriotism
Out Of Control
Depression

3 or 10 A friend called me yesterday; a loving, happy, hard-working, loves his success, wonderful man said he was feeling depressed and didn't know why, so we chatted, and I said "it's all the news media and horrible things going on with our nation". This nation is not what my grandfather fought in World War II for. Then we talked about Vietnam and all of the chaos going on at the border, the drugs and the gun control and the fact that our president is not capable of handling his job and the fact that it is a fact this election was stolen from Republicans when we got off the phone he promised me he would shut off the news and not feel so depressed.

The world around us and the crumbling of things we hold dear... feeds depression. But it's all out of our control. Having control over the environment is essential to happiness. So what do we do as we watch America be destroyed from within? And the name-calling, I was never a white supremacist or racist till I started supporting Trump. So, for 49 years, I was a kind, loving person, and boom, I'm a degrading individual from people I've never met. A funny thing is I come from a linage that worked the Underground Railroad, moving slaves from danger to safety.... but the Democrats have forgotten that piece of history!!! So daily, We, the People are completely degraded... WTHECK is going on?

3 or 10 internal anger is a fact, and controlling the personal environment is a needed reaction. I before E is a Dems rule!!! It makes no sense... it is a lie... it is clearly a lie, and it's a probable lie…

i before e

Except when your foreign neighbor Keith received eight counterfeit beige sleighs from feisty caffeinated weightlifters.

Weird

Thoughts;____
____
____

Family
Apologies
Self

3 or 10 We all make terrible mistakes in life. Some are little and overlooked; some are huge and leave a scare. They all have one thing in common: there are always three sides to forgiveness. Really, 4, but 3 here on earth. Self; The Other Person; and the other person forgiving you, then four is repent to Jesus. So the hardest of the 3 is self and receiving forgiveness. Neither; usually, accept the apology. This is a huge problem in relationships... yes, you have a relationship with self!!!

And if you are like me, self is the cruelest relationship.

Yep, I'm mean to me!!! I'm hard on me!! I carry deep regret!! I expect myself to be perfect, but I often fail. Sometimes, moment by moment. Sometimes little things, like being late!!! And sometime, huge things like getting so angry that I say hurtful things.

I'm currently in a deep despair cycle. I'm carrying completely depressed feelings of sadness. It's ok!!! Yes, it is OK!!! In one year, I've made drastic changes that have been draining my energy. The death of my husband has set me back. Cold weather and huge heat bills, building a house, a business, and failing to get it put together.

No, I'm not a failure, but I'm far from being organized. I don't know many who would go thru this year of my life and not feel depressed, pushed down, or squashed!!! The amazing thing about me is 1. I recognize when I'm down...2. I know it is temporary. I'm not unhappy with my life... I have a great life, good friends, and a promising future Jesus put these trials in my life. Sunday was well planned, yet it turned into a horrible day. All the good was destroyed by screaming and hard feelings. As 2 of my kids got to fighting, as mom, I stepped in, taking a side. Forgiveness will never come. 2 people can't hear the apology, and I will keep kicking myself. The fact is all 3 of us were right in our words and wrong in how they were said. That is a tough place to be.

3 or 10 apologies and justified never go together. A sincere apology will do no good till the receiver can "hear". Guarded and trust issues very rarely get fixed. Trust in self is the worst!!! Hardest.

I'm Gonna Tell God Everything

Thoughts;______________________________________

____

____

Family
Pain
Motherhood

3 or 10 A beautiful well, planned day. Food, cloth napkins, 2 days of cooking, a month of planning, lovely dishes, and church clothes. Completely destroyed by hard feelings and resentment. It's funny how that happens. Not!!! Harsh words and tears. 100% Drained, angry, and trying to sort the bad into categories of justified. Embarrassed and ashamed. But that doesn't really matter. The one causing all of this will never admit it. What creates these moments in our lives? Not hearing!!! I'm a communicator, so I know I've spoken about the pain. Explained it. I have asked to have it stop.

I know others have done the same. The core issue at this holiday is held by 3 or the 4 involved. And then another got involved that was not involved. A side was picked with no knowledge of the issue. So that was ignorant. But it has created more hard feelings from all 3 of the original 3 hurting. Once it all got rolling, 3 people are in tears, 3 dismayed, and one was angry and hostile. The angry one tossed a chair in a display of superiority!! Well, that was absolutely stupid. Making everyone realize how "small" the biggest person in the room really is. The statement "defending" followed by "never do it again,"

3 or 10 4 hours on the phone yesterday but not with the one that created the pain. Because other people are the problem. Funny how that works. But I will surely be scolded for not participating in my grandson's party. I was scolded in July for not participating with a liar, cheat, or abuser. Yep, I was scolded for not showing to be abused. 2 of 3 of my children yesterday stood loyal and loving. It is impossible for a person to be loyal to another person that can't even spell "loyalty." I didn't start the fight. 3 siblings were fighting it. I didn't finish the fight because I didn't need to apologize for the behaviors of others. And the center of the fight wasn't even there to participate.

3 or 10 Pain is a driving force. That is a fact. Yesterday, I spent 4 hours on the phone in tears. Lots of healing, we hope. Festering bs took over Easter. But yesterday, I wasn't on the phone with the one creating the pain. That is sad because this mess will fester again because the behavior won't change. 3 or 10 pain is a reality, but both sides need to value each other to heal it. Because healing isn't the goal of both people, there is only one thing happening. One person has their fee-

stubbornly set, and the others are on the phone bawling. I bawled but realized this would continue. It will fester, bubble up, and be pain until someone else is ready to face it. My options are few. I recognize it is not mine to carry. That is a fact.

Pain will leave, once it has finished teaching you

Thoughts;____

____

____

Narcissist
Apologizing
Dogs Unconditionally Love

3 or 10

Severe Narcissist are a horrible thing to deal with. They have the ability to twist anything into an attack on them. I was invited to be on the Dr Phil show because of a narcissist. But the funny thing was I received a 4 day 5 star flight and paid for vacation to LA. That was in 2014. People in Emida got wind of it in 2021 and chatted about it. HaHa jokes on them. While they are scouring the internet for dirt on me, I'm happily living my life and, for the most part, don't even know their names. Priorities are a funny thing. Doing my research, narcissism has no diagnosis or treatment unless others come forward to tell the therapist about the behaviors. So, the abuse from the abuser goes unchecked. Narcissistic behaviors come from a protective reaction to severe abuse at a young age. This fact leaves me to pity them. I feel empathy toward them. Frustration, but also I hurt for them.

3 or 10 because I feel guilt and empathy, I know I'm not an abusive, narcissistic person. BOOYAH, that is all 10 grateful things to count. Narcissistic people can't apologize; I often apologize. It's a blessing every time. Narcissists suck the happy right out of the people around them. Another blessing is that I can avoid them. Dogs are never narcissistic, which might be why I enjoy them more than people!!!
Haha

"I don't know who needs to hear this but accusations from a narcissist are actually confessions". – Stephen Szczerba

Thoughts;____

____

____

Foul Words
Low Self Worth
Sadness

3 or 10

"You're a bitch" 3X

"That's why no one likes you."

"Your problem is you're too friendly, that's why EVERYONE hates you."

"The customer ISN'T always right."

"You don't tip enough."

"$37 in tips for lunch is not enough."

"Customers should just tip $5 to make it easy."

"I can't do this; she doesn't know how to cook."

This was all said to me by a waitress in one day. In public, so degrading me, the customers, and the cook. So the question is, "who has the issue?" Well, by the time it was rolling, I was fighting back. So it is surely my fault. Haha!! I feel bad for the owner; this crap coming from her staff has been going on for a year (this was the first time I fought back); normally, I just let the vial words roll off me and ignore her. I'm not a bitch, and not everyone hates me. She talks badly about all kinds of people in the community. She puts f-bombs in about 1/2 of her statements. The boss is looking for new staff, and I believe it is because of this person being rude. (She parks in front of the door, leaving the customers and elderly to walk thru the snow and mud) (tie-dye muscle shirts where the bra is the actual shirt is a horrible look for a 60-year-old woman) But: 25 miles from nowhere the boss is kind of stuck. This behavior would never be tolerated in an actual town. But we don't live in a town. We are a pee stop on a rural highway.

3 or 10. I am very friendly and bring a lot of inclusion to the people around me. I tip really well when the service is good. Lots of people get $5 bills from me. I'm not normally a bitch, but when pushed (for a year now), I do fight back. I feel terrible for cooks being degraded openly in front of customers. That is sad to me. I feel sad for the locals being

degraded. That is sad to me. Funny, I feel sad for the waitress to walk
thru life, so the vial must feel horrible. While she boldly thinks she has
good self-esteem she really doesn't. That is sad to me, too. Her cutting
words had me in tears last night. I feel sad about that, too.

Well, well, well, if it isn't the consequences of my own actions.

Thoughts;____

____

____

Heaven
Family
Intuition

3 or 10

For a couple of months, I've been looking for a psychic. This has caused people to pray for me, worry about me, and send me strange messages. But Lott, Moses, Mother Mary, and Sarah spoke of communication with the other side, so I think I'm safe to follow the lead of the Greats that made it into The Bible. My family is filled with "knowing," so wisdom and knowledge have always been a part of my world. My search lately is because I've been blocked from my gift of "knowing" since Indy died. A lady messaged me and told me she wasn't psychic, but was "knowing". Her gift was to help with trauma. And then she started typing. She knew of Indy and his reddish hair. She talked of my mother smiling, and then mom scolded me, "you were raised better." "Jump in feet first without thinking, just get it done." she told me I was wearing mom's rings. She then said your mom wants you to go garden, but she is laughing. It must be an inside joke. I was giggling and crying at the same time. Mom loved her garden. I did not, but I loved mom, so I spent a lot of time weeding. Then I asked the looming question. Were the twins boys or girls? Boys, and your mom calls them Adam and Jack. One has fiery red hair. Your mom sings to them. Then the lady said 3, not 2. I said "yes, I have 3 grandchildren in heaven". She said "2 are in a lot of pain". I said "yes, they were murdered". Then she said, "your mom has them; she is teaching them silly stuff." sometimes comfort comes from strangers.

3 or 10; my twins are boys, and their names are Adam and Jack, and one of them has the family red hair. My mom has them, and she sings to them. And I feel comforted.

Always trust your first instincts.

If you genuinely feel in your heart and soul that something is wrong, it usually is.

Thoughts;____
____
____

Happiness
Thanking God

3 or 10 Happiness is a choice... unless there are scientific things creating unhappiness. People can NOT will away illness any more than they can will away evil.

Adrenaline makes me very unhappy; it causes my stomach to want to throw up. I can not choose when a deer will bounce out from the side of the road or an idiot will pull out in front of me. But the choice does come. I pull over and breathe deeply till the throw-up feeling goes away. And I always thank God for my body's scientific reaction to jump into action when I need my fast instincts to save me.

I still hate adrenaline, and that is why I don't jump from airplanes. But my hate for adrenaline is a perfect way for others to look at their science. Happiness is a choice; to feel it, I must avoid adrenaline. Even though it is a God-given, a gift.

3 or 10 last night on the drive home, I had seen probably 50 deer; only one jumped out in front of me. My fast reaction saved her life. And the front of my pickup is CREATING HAPPINESS. The adrenaline needed was there just like science said it should be.

Happiness is a choice, not a result. Nothing will make you happy until you choose to be happy. No person will make you happy unless you decide to be happy. Your happiness will not come to you. It can only come from you.

Thoughts;____
____
____

Prayer
Overwhelming

3 or 10 I'm in my pajamas playing solitaire today because I'm absolutely overwhelmed. Bought a house, a business, a new horizon. I got the keys yesterday. Oh my!!! I sold my house in Lind... glad it's in my rear view mirror and I am terrified. Owning outright vs payments. Such a blessing to a new family that is excited to have goats and chickens. I worked on the contract yesterday and today. I'm beat up. Snow, rain, sunshine, snow again, big black clouds. Idaho is not cooperating with me moving. So, I did 8 hours today and went for a nap that I did not get.

3 or 10 overwhelmed is ok.... when it is with a goal of making life better. Please say a little prayer. My dogs and I need it.

The only person you should strive to be better than, is the person you were yesterday. – Matty Mullins

Thoughts;____
____
____

Overwhelmed
Mom's Wisdom

3 or 10

Fuel for depression has signs. I am currently completely overwhelmed and this will lead to depression. How do I know it's on its way? As I look around… I can see what is "not" done. Stinkin Thinkin!! It is called an ugly storm. One self-care at a time to get out of it. I feel completely negative at this point. The vacuum belt broke, there has been no power or heat for 23 hours, the store is cluttered and chaos, I need 40 hours a day and am only motivated for about 3, and it is so overwhelming! Overwhelmed! And no releif in sight. I need my mom to call and tell me, "grab your bootstraps," as only she could. So it's up to me to mantra such things. So, then self-esteem fails cuz it is more failure, not less. Mom used to say, "pick one thing, get it done, and feel good about it." this is called "Mindfulness," and it works really well.

3 or 10, I'm in a bad way. Life has pushed me to a breaking point; I can let it win or fight back. So, I need to do deep, slow breathing, focus, and be mindful of my world. I might still be depressed later today. That's ok. I'm not letting her move in; she is just here for a visit. I called peace, self-esteem, hope and invited them to come sit with me, I trust they are on their way.

My brain has too many tabs open!

Thoughts;____

____

____

Motherhood
Self Esteem
List of Good

3 or 10 I raised two extremely headstrong BRATS. Amen, THANK GOD!!! Some of it was from mutual respect. As little as age five, they had to cook dinner one night a week. At 5 their menu required no cooking. PB&J or lunch meat and chips. Boosting self was my goal. And yes, I ate a mustard sandwich (Whisper) cuz that's how it came on my plate.

Some of the headstrong came from competition; 4H, and FFA was the tool I used. Saige excelled, and Whisper didn't care about the ribbons.

Some of this came from conversations. The constitution applied to them, and yes, liberal schools denying them those rights created me to fight the school. So they witnessed a "woman" standing her ground. So they learned they could "stand their ground."

Sometimes, this backfired, and the fight would come. My girls would stomp their feet... BOOYAH, yes BOOYAH!!! Yes, I like it better when chatter is the solution, but I indeed taught my kids THEY COULD DO IT. The girls and I put in a septic system one summer. We failed 2 inspections, but on the third, we passed... and we celebrated success by going out to a nice dinner. At 13, they got a cell phone... with a bill, so they went to work. $10 a month, so babysitting on a Saturday night or sweeping a sidewalk paid the bill.

And look what I created... homeownership, promotions at work, voters, calls to return to past jobs, a work ethic, and lots of volunteer hours. Law-abiding, moral, and independent woman that will show/teach by example.

3 or 10. I made a lot of mistakes in my life. That is a fact... but I have also been completely successful. Celebrate the good me!!! Because even when others can't see it... I have a running list.

Believe in yourself, especially when no one else will. – Sasquatch

Thoughts;____
____
____

Change
Peace

3 or 10

Oh My, Today I Need My 3 or 10. I need my friends and family to give me a boost of mental health. God showed up and provided me with a home in Idaho. Yep, with prayer and dedication to his path, I'm not being forced to return to Lind. Oh my... every penny will need to be counted, sorted, and placed in the HOME account. But, oh my moving. One more trip to Lind, load up the semi... I already paid the driver, so that is a blessing. Then a trip for the 5th wheel, and I'm done with the move. But then there was the move here inside Benewah County. Normally, I would have money to pay for help. But I bought a house this month, so the money is all gone. It's 3 or 10. Oh my, I bought a house, so PEACE is coming. 3. Peace... peace... peace. 10. Blessings... if I work really hard in 10 days, I will wake up in a different space.

Photo; A team of draft mules, massive, with their shoulders 7 plus foot, Men in work clothes the photo is from around 1900

Thoughts;____

____

____

Motherhood
Self Esteem
Pain
Prayers Answered

3 or 10 Last night after a rough work day, Whisper called, and we chatted for 53 minutes. The topics were life, Easter dinner, a car, etc, just mamma and daughter chatting about nothing. Then Saige called for an hour and 13 minutes. We, too chatted about her career, the boys, a new cat named spooky, being tired because of being busy. But I received 2 hours of attention from two people who love me. I gave birth four times. Yet, I only have two kids. The pains of divorcing a control freak and his need for control have always outweighed what was best for the kids. And as adults, the pain and lifestyle have created distance, sadness, and resentment, not one-sided at all. I love them but don't like them. And I believe the reverse is also true. The pain created runs deep. The resentment is clear. And the future is bleak. I prayed for all four of my babies; Satan only wanted me to raise two. Satan got his way because his hold is stronger than my moral code of right. I look at my kids' lifestyle and am basically proud of the two I raised. Not so much of the other two.... choices. I know "free will" is a God-given gift or a curse... I used to spend a lot of time sad over the relationships. Not so much anymore. Past 30, their dad isn't making their decisions anymore. They now choose to see good, sort the truth, and behave well. Good is relative!!! And because of their father, they seem to believe they are good.

3 or 10 relationships are always evolving. They are in motion. Sometimes, that motion is "waiting at a stop light," and sometimes it is hours on the phone. Sometimes, it is waiting for behaviors to change; sometimes, it is celebrating the relationships. Sometimes it is a living pause... could be loving self!!! I believe two of my kids are waiting for me to change. To become what Satan seeks. But I'm praying they become what God seeks. I will keep praying... they don't know how often I pray for them, but God promises ALL PRAYERS are answered. So I wait.

I still remember when I prayed for the things I have now.

Thoughts;____

____

____

Choices
The Book of Job
Positive Thinking

3 or 10

Job and Norman Vincent Peale saved parts of my soul. I'm a reader and love to ponder the thoughts of the author. I've read more books than I can remember the names of, but one thing is for sure: I have enjoyed every book I've finished. People assume I'm lazy because my priorities are not a spotless house or laundry folded and put away. But I'm busy 12 hours a day. Playing with my dogs is far more important than the dishes in the sink. READING... is my most important daily THING... yep, I would rather read than clean out the junk drawer. 

Advice to anyone who needs 3 or 10 in their lives is to find the author who inspires you to think better. Job and Norman came into my life during the last 3 months of my pregnancy with Saige. A particularly tough time for me. I was thrilled that she was on her way, a planned celebration. But, life happens, and at 6 months pregnant, her dad left. Terror of having a baby alone, money was really tight, but I went to task, found a coach, saved money, and got to reading. Job showed me everyday that FAITH was and is the key to happiness. And Norman showed me choices. His book has lived on my nightstand for 29 years. A treasure I return to often.

3 or 10 look for the good in people. My dirty house is not because I'm lazy... dusting or writing my 3 or 10? Dishes or reading a book? Vacuuming or helping a friend? Making my bed or playing with a dog? Choices... happy choices....

Change your thoughts and you change your world. – Norman Vincent Peale

Thoughts;____

____

____

False Witness
Knowledge

3 or 10

Yesterday, I sat to write my 3 or 10; backspace, erase, re-type, delete... so I didn't finish it. Some days are like that. And that's OK. Life gets filled with stress. Other people's BS drains the mind of good will. A sheriff showed up. An "animal rights" group called them. First, he had the number of dogs wrong, then he stated I was keeping dogs in my shop; he was unaware this "shop" is my home, so who ever called has obviously never been here. I assume it's a FB troll because someone also called the restaurant asking if it was illegal to raise dogs here. I told the sheriff he could see the dogs in the yard 3 times a day, and with a surprised look, he said, "you let them out 3 times a day" I responded, "of course" "they have a 1/4 acre play yard with their own swimming pool" PEOPLE CAUSING PROBLEMS suck!!! Why do people be creeps? Because their moral code says, "sticking their nose in other people's business is ok." IT IS NOT OK!!!

3 or 10, not knowing how many dogs I have or that they live IN my home means there is a TROUBLEMAKER!!! THAT HAS NEVER WITNESSED WHAT GOES ON HERE!!! Oh, I just hate those kinds of people. We were told in kindergarten being a troublemaker isn't good. Jesus talks about "bearing false witness." And today, I am sort of trying to find positive things in life. I'm not a troublemaker, I don't chatter to people about things I don't know, I don't bear false witness, and the dogs are sleeping on the couch...

We can talk facts or we can talk feelings. The first step is separating the two.

Thoughts;____

____

____

Happiness
Soothing The Soul

3 or 10.

Me and birds. All my life, I've loved birds. It might come from my dad loving airplanes, explains wing flight. Might be going to the dump and seeing the crows eating the leftover food scrapes. Might be having chickens as a child. It could be "Lil" Grama raising canaries. Maybe it was camp robbers on camping trips. The blue jay that would scream when we got close to his tree. Or my Grama watching the robins pull worms out of the yard with morning coffee and homemade cookies.

The mighty bald eagle as the American bird. Or in the 4th grade, learning about "the blue bird" as the Idaho state bird (they are perfect). Not sure why I love birds. But what I do know is they make me feel happy in a society that puts therapy as important. Talk it out. Find the trauma, change the behavior or prevent the stress. It is also important to focus on "happiness." 1/2 of therapy is putting things into our life that make us "feel" better. Well, if we "think," we can find the happy stuff.

3 or 10. I am not sure why I love birds. But it is a fact of who Annette is. I love big birds, little birds, red, yellow, gray, chirping, screaming, and the woodpecker hammering a tree. I love the fluttering around, the ducks chasing bread thrown in the water, or the eagle souring over head. I love birds. They make my soul feel rest. They soothe the day. They remove junk in mind and replace it with "God is amazing."

Photo; Two ducks heads down in water tails pointed straight up, feet perfectly balancing them

Thoughts;____

____

____

Time
Priority
Happiness

3 or 10. "I don't have time" maybe one of the biggest lies we repeat over and over that drains the soul. I continually stress myself out being pulled in 35 directions at once. When the self talk is a lie, the mind knows you are lying and responds with turmoil. Fact is!!! If I had no "pull," I would be board and unhappy. My volunteer work feeds my being and makes me feel productive. My store is a complete disaster at times, but I work on it daily. When friends stop in, I take time for them. When people call, I answer the phone.

When research is needed, I go to task. When kids need mom, I'm always there. To look around my life, all that people see is clutter; in fact, I'm not high maintenance... nor am I OCD. Happy note: Dust Bunnies live here. I read and write far more than I have time for... filled with and sharing knowledge. I scold myself that I need to learn to say "no." The fact is I don't like to hear no!! When I ask a friend for help (which isn't very often), I always want them to say yes!! So I say "yes".

3 or 10. What negative can't be seen as a positive? The lie it's self!!! So, just after the lie, I remind myself of the truth.... I could take time to clean, be organized, and have life look perfect... I do have time!!! I used to say "yes" and talk with friends, and help my brain gain knowledge. And I'm not trading my good…

The way you speak to yourself matters.

Thoughts;____________________________________

____

____

Angels
Prayers

3 or 10

"My angels!" Where are they? And why do I pray to them? It started when I was 15. On the school bus, a girlfriend that we did Bible study most days in the hour it took to get to school. One day, we read about Mother Mary being told by an angel that God had found favor with her in the hills of Bethany. I'm not sure why that day impacted my entire life. But it certainly changed me as a person. I knew that day that my first baby girl would be named Bethanie. I knew if God sent Mary an Angel, he would also send them to me. Then, to cement this knowledge, Alabama had a number 1 hit that rattles me… "Angels Among Us"… if ya take time to understand the story, we (mostly) have all had Angels show up.

3 or 10 Why pray to angels? Well, they are 100% comfort! Some prayers don't need God, and he is very busy with many prayers from many believers. Sometimes, my prayers for me or others are for presence or comfort. Of course, I have big prayers for healing, change, or knowledge that go directly to God. But sometimes, it's a flat tire, getting things done, or needing to focus. Those prayers go to my angels. And they have never failed me. Someone calls, compliments, or sees me having a problem and offers help. My Angels always show up with comfort every single time I ask. They always show me I'm loved. Mother Mary was one of us and was picked for great things. Why not me? Why don't I receive an Angel? You have Angels at work in your life. They are everywhere all the time. Look! You will see them, feel them, know them. Beautiful!

Thoughts;____
____
____

Heaven
Forgiveness
Worthy

3 or 10 Heaven has been on my mind a lot lately. My end-of-times friends, Jake passing so young, my surgery, are my papers in order? What does Heaven look like? So, I did a search asking that question. When ya ponder, open the book with the answers!!! One thing I know for sure is I'm not worthy of complete forgiveness... so why did Jesus offer it? Does he love me as much as that book says? The "Father" calls me his child? Why would he let a sinner like me into

Heaven? My harsh words, my white lies... to myself, my unforgettable resentment of those that have wronged me, and of course, keeping track of sins against me (a judgement that I'm warned about). How can we "know" we get to go to Heaven?

Through The Son!!! God said. And he wrote it in a book... the Bible has all the answers when we doubt. The problem is the Bible is hard to understand. Contradicting itself. My personal favorite is "an eye for an eye" versus "turn the other cheek." how do we walk those tight ropes? An LDS elder asked me why I didn't believe in The Book of Mormon. My answer was simple: The Bible has all the answers; I don't need to look anywhere else.

3 or 10, my mind will always look for answers... and I'm blessed they were written down!!!

1 Cross
+ 3 Nails
----
4 Given

Thoughts;____

____

____

Grief
Hurt
Pain
Survivor

3 or 10 "What hurt you?" let that wash over the soul. Getting a big bloody wound, stitches, a broken bone in a cast... the visual is clear, and we take time TO HEAL!!! The wounds of the heart or soul are not external, but can be seen if we chat with the person. My tattoo

was/is the most healing thing I've ever done. My plan was to hide it (women and visible tattoos are a generational thing), but I put it on the inside of my "right" forearm. My plan when Garrison died was to be strong, push thru, and "get over it." Well, that was a stupid thought. A complete failure to think I could "hide my wound." So, in typical Annette fashion I tried to appear "the strong one" by placing this tattoo in bright colors; people asked about my "Garrison," and what I had to learn was to let the tears come AT ANY MOMENT tears wanted to come. NO GUILT!!! Oh my? What? Yes, I permitted myself to feel sad, angry, loss!!! To smile, feel love, and celebrate Garrison!!! The little man who took my heart to Heaven. Yep!!! Broken wounded!!! I have one!!!

We can't tattoo rape, incest, beatings, car wrecks, things we witness, or guilts we keep private. But the longer we rub salt (hiding) in the wound, the longer it takes to heal.

3 or 10, place the wound in the sunshine, talk it out, cry, kick, scream, and let yourself celebrate it... I am a rape survivor... beaten and violated... but the truth is, when I close that off... it festers... gets infected... bleeds... how can I celebrate it??? I AM A SURVIVOR!!! I have compassion for others that have been violated... I preach personal protection... and yes, I have a pistol to make sure it never happens again... my tattoo was the most healing thing I've ever done for myself... find your tattoo!!! Write the book, council others, educate teens, give testimony in church.... ETC...

If you don't heal what hurt you, you'll bleed on people who didn't cut you.

Thoughts;____

____

____

Choices
Happiness
Content

3 or 10 When the soul gets negative comments, it feels drained. I know I must stay clear of other people's doom and gloom. Life hands us doom minute by minute... this week I broke the handle off the refrigerator door, and now, every time I reach to do a simple task I'm forced to learn a new trick. Some days, we get to the end of the day with nothing. Feeling tired and drained. A fact of life, Murphy Law, or karma, yang; no YIN!!! As people who suffer from the brain chemistry of depression, it is our job to find happy! Sometimes, that job is so hard. Sometimes, I completely fail the task. Sometimes I sit and list the crap in my life. This is broken, that costs too much, if only there were more hours in the day. My first husband beat me; the second was so drunk he had no money and didn't remember any conversation after 4 pm; and the third stood at the kitchen sink blowing air; a want, a dream, a plan was always met with his disgust at any words I spoke. That long blow that normally had an eye roll with it... of the 3 husbands, that was the worst. No value in me as a person. Just like the beating and the drunk, that disgust at everything was actually not my problem. How to think positively when the "other half" is negative is impossible. But putting my happiness in their charge was stupid, to say the least. WE MUST CREATE OUR OWN HAPPY!!

3 or 10. happy or sad, is a personal choice. Oh my, isn't that freeing!!! I am in charge of my happy!!! What??? Yep, I can choose to avoid negative; I can work on "seek and ye shall find." God gave me "free will," in other words, choice. So, at this very moment, I can look at my dirty house and thank God for the house. I can check my bank balance and know "I paid most of my bills." I can see the unmade bed as a "to-do" list or a soft, comfy, safe place. I can see the to-do list as overwhelming or a map to feeling accomplished. Choices!!! Oh my, I get CHOICES!!!

I used to think communication was the key until I realized comprehension is. You can communicate all you want with someone but if they don't understand you, it's silent chaos.

Thoughts;____

____

____

Grief
Gratitude

3 or 10 Today, Jake turns 57 in Heaven. It was the first of his birthdays without him. Fifty-three years of remembering or celebrating him on this day. Whisper called first thing to check on me. What a good daughter. She misses him, so her own torment is going on. They were very close; despite the family forgetting her, she grieves.

Young death (56) is so unfair... yet Jake decided to pass away so young. Negative people always have poor health. Jake was indeed a "catastrophe" waiting. He was also tender. Sometimes, with all his doom comments, a "thank you" would come. He thanked me for my love!! He thanked me for Connie!! He thanked me for taking on his sister for his mom!! He thanked me for the air conditioning (yes, he did). He thanked me for both attorneys. He thanked me for getting him sober. He thanked me for his care after his back surgery. It is those thank you's I hold dear!

3 or 10 All people have good in them. Day-to-day personality is not what lives deep inside. Knowing the trauma and pains inside a person helps us to love their soul. The intimate conversations we have with people, guard down and vulnerable, we need to see as a gift. Honor them, hold them dear. If someone has shared those inside things, it is an amazing thing. I know why Jake was a catastrophe in waiting; I know why he was so negative; I also know this: his first birthday in Heaven is the first celebration of him being born. We all need to celebrate being born cuz inside, where we keep our secrets, there is goodness.

Behind every strong person is a story that gave them no other choice.

Thoughts;____

____

____

Forgiveness
Free Will
Nurturing Self

3 or 10 My morning moments to ponder life, with a cup of hot coffee, and quiet. Every day, I try to have my favorite part of my life, but not every morning is possible. Today was a good day!!! Forgiveness is what I have on my mind. Death always comes with anger, for both the dead and the self. I'm angry at Jake for at 56 and choosing to die rather than taking care of the 5 years he was sick. On the sick days, our relationship suffered because he felt like crap, was in severe pain, or I was mad that he refused to go to the dr. During the last 6 months, when the pain was bad, my frustration led me to say, "you like being in pain, or you would solve it" (5 years of begging him to get a diagnosis) that led me to anger at self. Did I do enough to be a good wife? When ever someone dies (not of old age), there are always words unsaid, guilt, and regret. Today's topic is "forgiveness." Self forgiveness is as important as "forgiving others." I know I was loving, kind, and supportive. That is a fact!!! But is that enough, or should I have forced him to the doctor. Free Will... oh the dreaded "free will" God's gift or punishment??? When my mom, dad, and Garrison died, the guilt was there too. Did I do enough? The 5 stages of grief are documented psychological facts.

Forgiving self is so important. Knowledge about how is a secret. "Give it to God" is common advice. "Let it Go" is a big one told off the cuff. The 5 stages of grief, has "Acceptance." oh my, when in the cycle, how do ya get from guilt to acceptance?

3 or 10 It is simple reminders, yep, the moment-to-moment self conversations we have. For Jake, I remind my self "he" made the choices. For mom, I remind myself "I made ever dr appointment, cooked good food, and cleaned her house." For baby Garrison, I remember it is ok to feel robbed because I was. Forgiving the Self is important in every part of regret, guilt, and mistakes, even the ones unintended. Nurture the self!!! "Forgiveness is a gift you give yourself." that is a fact!

STRESS comes from trying to do it all on our own. PEACE comes from putting it all in God's hands. Amen

Thoughts;______________________________

____

____

Fairness
Right or Wrong

3 or 10 Right or Wrong... the problem with the American Justice System is the scales don't balance no matter what. Motion to Compel... one side looking for information... from the other party... Denied!!! What kind of a judge would deny questions asked being answered? St Maries, ID!!! Lawyers are as crooked as can be... they are paid to win a fight... no concern about Right or Wrong... just WIN... and there is no moral code involved. Jake and I were married 5 years... his selfish, narcissistic behavior forced me to leave... his refusal to play 50/50 forced me to file a lawsuit politely... the law says I'm entitled to 1/2 of what we did together.

Backhoes, property, tractors, guns, culverts, property taxes 3 years behind that I paid, fraud filing state title documents. Oh yes, THIEF, but a trait of the narcissist!!! I call it divorcing a cult!! Because of the lies and hoarding behavior. Mine, mine, me, me!!! It's a sad way to live. So, Jake's dead, it doesn't change the fact he was a thief. So again, "polite," I filed the same lawsuit against the estate. No one is in charge!!! Yep, CULT behavior!! One family member said they were in charge and even asked I serve them, then days after service claiming to not be in charge!!! Cult behavior is a group exercise that is how a Cult survives. I've served the estate, the person claiming to be in charge, a son, and a brother... yep, no one has the backbone to do what's Right!! Protect the cult!!! Counting my 10 things I'm grateful for...

I know how to behave Right!!!

Emma is sure to be reading this... cuz he married me, not her...(40 years of history with that love triangle)

My book "Divorcing a Cult" is gaining ground. The pages and pages were created by this fight for Right or Wrong!!!

3 or 10 The judge will be getting more papers from me. The scales of justice are going to work. The law is clear: 50/50. Even a high school dropout can figure out that 4 quarters means 2 for each person. Jake asked me to marry him, then he scheduled the wedding, took his vows, and entered a contract for 50/50... his death doesn't change the facts of his life.

Hi CULT... good morning, Emma!!!

Visualize the beautiful Scales of Justice

Thoughts;____
____
____

Parenting
Daddy's Girl

3 or 10 A good daddy! Keith and I were driving a dirt road, and my dad popped into the conversation. "My "daddy" never left us kids!!!" As it came out of my mouth, I was then to explain. Mom and Dad divorced, but dad never left the house. He lived in a camp trailer by the shop or 1/8 a mile away. He got my brother and me up on Saturday morning, and off on adventures we went. Not every other weekend but every Saturday. Dad wasn't a big "is your homework done?" dad, but he was very much "is the job finished?" he wasn't a big church goer but always made sure I had the most beautiful dress and was ready for church on time. He never took me school shopping but made sure there was money in my pocket, warm boots on my feet, motorcycles to ride, camping trips to go on, fireworks to shoot off, and sweets to eat. My bicycle had a steering wheel. Yea kinda funny! We played a million hands of Rummy 500. He tried his best to teach me the origami box folds. My eyes always lit up when he would blow, and the box would go from flat paper to a box. We not only flew paper airplanes, but he also knew the folds of jets and planes. Yep, there are several kinds of paper planes. He didn't show us a work ethic; he pushed us to have one. He only took me to a sitter on Friday night to take mom out to dinner. For my mom's big surgery, he took vacation, so we kids had supervision. He didn't take me to the gun range; he taught me to shoot. While in Germany, 1 or 2 times a week, I got a letter or post card. Short and sweet, signed "love dad"

3 or 10. I hope Keith came off the dirt road knowing, "I was daddy's little girl, and he loved us kids." Even divorced, he never left us... my dad didn't divorce his kids. I am so blessed to have a dad who wanted me!

Norwegian Blessing

May da ruts always fit da wheels in your pickup.
May yur ear mufs always keep out da nort wind.
May da sun shine varm on yur lefse.
May da rain fall soft on yur lutefisk.
And until ve meet again,
May da Good Lord protect ya from any and all unnecessary Uff Das.
JAN HOLER

Thoughts;____

____

____

Narcissist
Self Preserving

3 or 10 Here we go again. Our mental health treatment in the US so saddens me. What to do when another person can't stop bad behavior? They shatter relationships, self-worth, and energy. I'm absolutely exhausted by narcissism. Most people are at some point abused, manipulated, or harassed by another person needing to be the center of attention. Yet, the ones in therapy are not the narcissist... the one begging God for relief is not Satan... Today's challenge is my phone. He has books, magazines, newspapers, calendars, a clock, an alarm, and talks on his phone for hours. But my phone is the problem in the relationship??? No!! His ME ME ME is the problem!!! But I'm the one looking for solutions, support, and changed behavior. Am I an idiot? I can't change another person... I'm not jealous of his books, magazines, newspapers, calendar, clock, alarm, or talking to his family FOR HOURS. This is not my problem... I'm not a narcissist!!! All these overwhelming feelings come as another narcissist turns up again. Yea, I had hoped it was over... oh hell no!! Of course not, Dec will be 10 years. Oh My!!!

3 or 10 if you are selfish... I'm exhausted. If you want to harass me, I'm numb. If hurtful makes you feel powerful, I know a therapist who can help you. 3 or 10.

EAR PLUGS are in my future, so I can read a book (on my phone) and not be irritated by babbling, ME ME ME!!!

Before you fake your lifestyle on Facebook, at least block the people that know you in person!

Thoughts;____

____

____

Thankfulness

3 or 10 I hate adrenaline! It makes my stomachache and gives me diarrhea! Yesterday, I got crossways and ended up in a ditch. The pickup was so slanted that I could not open the passenger door as I tried to climb out. And when Jake got to me, he couldn't drive it out either. Two wheels were digging in, and two were not touching the ground. So, a chain and a one ton on a slant with out an inch to make a mistake. It is not a slope but a 7-10% grade with fences and a house. Jake stood firm, knowing what needed to be done, and I stood clear, praying for it to work. Well, as always, "It Worked," and my "little girl" (my pickup's name) was safely on all four wheels with no extra damage. I drove her home shaken but not stirred. I walked into the house, and then here came the adrenaline. Oh My, I HATE ADRENALINE! My dad was an adrenaline junkie, faster, more dangerous, testing gravity just a little more. I don't get it! I believe my hate of adrenaline came from my dad's love of it. As a tiny little girl dad should put me on the gas tank of his motorcycle and drive around the yard. I know I was safe, yet, learning your feelings, the balance, the speed, was scary.

3 or 10 I ripped up my pickup, but I am not hurt. I can fix what I broke, and Jake will tease, taunt, and poke fun at me. But "little girl" is on all four wheels, with a few new scars.

Amazing

High Score

791

Thoughts;____

____

____

Family Bonds
Thankfulness
Greed is Ugly

3 or 10 I took time this morning to thank my brother for his love and support during the aging, cancer, and death of our parents. Why did I feel I needed to say Thank You? Yep, a family being destroyed by greed! Bitter, ugly, greed that needs attorneys, police, nursing homes, horrid nasty words, and headaches. I'm in pain for the mother at the heart of the fight... but she created the greed.

My brother has no greed in his soul! Thank You! In my world, while I was hurting for and missing mom and dad, grieving their failing bodies and holding their hand for their last breath... my brother had my back! He supported my process, but I, too, never stepped over the nasty greedy line because I have no greed in my soul.

3 or 10 Life is a list of lessons, some are learned as children, some with gray hair, but they all have value. I'm glad my brother and I were taught to share, respect, and value. Thank You Mom And Dad, for teaching us good stuff. So, as the hardest days of our lives would come, we still stood together.

Don't be afraid to start over. This time you are not starting from scratch, you're starting from experience.

Thoughts;____
____
____

Personal Responsibility
Self Worth
Excuses

3 or 10 "IF" is the most dangerous word in the dictionary. It is an ultimatum... "if" you do this... I will do that. It is also "facts" not in evidence... "if" he did this, "if" she does that... "if" you loved me... and that is in all relationships from God, kids, bosses, husbands, wives, even the bank, the news, and school. So how do we stop at the "IFs"? Sometimes, it is with tears that we choose to get rid of "if," and we are then forced to say things we didn't want to say. "If" you loved me!!! Turns to "name calling," which means you don't love me. "If" you respected me, it turns to "cheating" is disrespectful. As we can throw away "if" we are free to take personal responsibility or place "facts" where they truly belong.

3 or 10 "If" painfully looks backward, "if" doesn't accept responsibility, "if" places blame on false fact-finding; today, I will try not to. "If" myself, my life, my people! "If" I love me!!! Nope!!! Facts in evidence... I do love me!!

Thoughts;____

____

____

Self Worth

3 or 10 People like to put other people as #2. boss/employee, corporate Profit/Medical Insurance, God/gossiping, children/Dating, and even simple things like Hobby/BackRubs. The fact is the tender moments, the life snap shots, the tickled giggles of a child, or the stories grampa tells.... are the most important parts of life. Every relationship we are in has a choice of being #1 or being #2. Mainly we like both, a friend's wedding day, becoming an aunt, or second place in a competition, are all #2 without feeling second class. Sometime we need to be #1 for our own self worth. Sometimes we become the bride, we give birth, or we work really hard to take 1st place.

3 or 10, I wish everyone would think about the ways they can make the people around you #1.

Rule #1: Never be #2

Thoughts;____

____

____

Count Blessings

3 or 10 Oh, My, sometimes a little reminder just hits ya in the face. A million things to do, no one is cooperating, and I have miles and miles to go!!!!

STOP to count blessings, not problems!!!!

Oh My!!! Look at that... my kids and grandkids are healthy, I'm having dinner with family, the sun is rising, the crisp cold air of fall is laying on my face, I am loved, my work is paying off, paying bills, making a more comfortable life, food is good and I have choices, there have been times beans were the option, but today I can choose steak. 3 or 10 Life is good!!!

Stress comes from tying to do it all on our own. Peace comes from putting it all in God's hands. Amen.

Thoughts;____

____

____

Angels
Answered Prayers
Greediness

3 or 10 God is amazing if you let him work miracles in life... he waits to hear Thank You, and every time you say it, he shows one more miracle to say thank you for. If ya watch, you see him teaching his kids. I was married to a man so greedy and selfish that happiness would never be found. He wouldn't let me take my stuff; I refused to fight, and driving down Shay Hill, I said to God... "help his heart". So, how do I get my stuff? Well, I'm civilized, so prepping for court. Today I go check the mail... LAND VALUATION forms were mailed to me. They do that once a year, and there we go. My name is on Shay Hill Land. I guess Jake can't really fight the state over my ownership. I looked up to the heavens and said, "Thank You," so as God blessed me, he is teaching another child... Jake brags all the time that he hates greedy people... BOOYAH, open your eyes, young man; God said greed is Satan's tool. Your greed will be punished.

3 or 10 My Angels always come through for me... they always help me with God answering prayers.

I believe in Angels.

Thoughts;____
____
____

Trust
Liar
Respect

3 or 10 Been a busy week with lots of projects, yet nothing has been done. Normal life.

I'm sorry you chose to LIE to me. What reaction did that create? It caused me to no longer trust, have faith in, or respect you. And I'm sure when you need a friend I'll be busy. When you need understanding I will have resentment. When you need forgiveness, I'm sure to feel the hurt. What did you lie about? Big or little, it doesn't matter. Lies distort friendships, families, government, and community. This lie was business, but the same thing happens. Trust and goodwill shatter.

3 or 10 relationships are hard work. Sometimes, it's as simple as the hard work of telling the truth. My advice to the world, even when hard, is to tell the truth so you are not labeled a liar.

Pray for our Nation

Thoughts;____
____
____

Patriotism
Thank You

3 or 10 Is it passion, is it humbled, is it friends become family, is it to honor the past or teach the future? RED, WHITE, & BLUE. 2 years of fussing, and today was the day...THEY ARE HERE!!! In the St Maries Federal Building conference room, there were no flags. So I made it a mission to have my beautiful America stand tall and inspiring. I went to a American Legion meeting and asked for help. Some raffles, some chatter, and these men helped me change the landscape of a room. The American Legion men are dedicated to making a difference in this little town.

3 or 10 With a GRATEFUL HEART... and tears... THANK YOU SO MUCH.

Thoughts;____

____

____

Wisdom
Family

3 or 10 I went out of my "normal" and bought a coat for myself. 15+ years ago, I was given an Alaska parka; it was wonderful… green, my favorite color; it was a windbreaker, had a warm removable liner, and huge pockets for me to not need to carry a purse. It got rips, the zippers gave out, and I continued to wear it for two more years. It became clear it either needed to go to a seamstress or retire. I went with a Carhartt, the #3 of 4 for warmth, green (but olive, not emerald). I picked one size too big so I could layer it, and I picked one that was "tall," so it covered my bottom instead of letting the wind blow in my waist.

It is a wonderful coat with pockets large enough to put my gloves safely and securely. The reason this is "important" is a little thing my aunt has commented on twice this month. I am amazing with money… my aunt said, "We know you are like your mom and have money hidden in your mattress," and then, "You can squeeze a nickel; I didn't get that gene." I am indeed very good with money. But I don't worship it. It is only a tool I use well. We all pick the tools of life in our world. Paper towels and garbage bags irritate me, and buying a hand towel and garbage can is far cheaper. Yes, it irritates me to buy paper towels and garbage bags.

3 or 10 I take what my aunt said as a compliment. Not sure if that was her intention, but it screamed to me "a true quality." At a minimum-wage job, I bought my first home. It was a mobile in a park, but it was mine. It bettered my future. It gave my kids stability, a "HOME" that no one could take away. Then I bought another, and my "dream" home was a farmhouse built in the 1880s. Then, coming back to Idaho, I bought again, then with Jake, I took his 40 ft to become an 80 ft with a 40x80 pole barn to build another dream home (his kids should thank me), and now a 40x80 building again. I spent $179 on a coat worthy of Idaho winters…. $179 divided by 15 years is $11.93 a year…. Yep, I'm good at managing my money.

My dark days made me strong. Or maybe I already was strong, and they made me prove it.

Thoughts;____

____

____

Knowing
Truth
I am

3 or 10 Lack of Knowledge is always a problem. I'm a dog breeder, history buff, true reader, college goer, accountant specialist in trucking, a woman, mother, grandmother, divorced, widowed, Christian, God Fearing, political activist, militia supporter, international traveler, business owner, I have been very poor and pretty wealthy, stood alone or surrounded by support, and today, 9mm socket has me beside myself. I need to replace an exhaust blower motor on my pellet stove. Jake did it about five years ago, and it took him about 15 minutes. UGGG, I've watched 3 YouTube videos (so 45 minutes invested), and this is an "easy" swap out. Ha, I pray that is true!

3 or 10 Trying new things is always exciting and scary. The 9mm problem is I've never bought the ratchet set, so I have a box of miscellaneous "stuff" to look through. I hope it has a 9mm in the mix. Driving to town for a socket is sure to irritate me. I need… a shop… the problem is that it requires a man… ug, maybe I'd rather be cold… or not. So far, I've built or helped build three shops. Ugh, do I have… a socket that I need? Maybe for my birthday, I should ask for a toolbox. Ya know, the big one with wheels on it… like a starter (restarting) to buy tools. Points to ponder!

them; are you afraid of losing friends over your post about controversial topics

? No, I am afraid of remaining silent and seeing friends and their loved ones suffer due to lack of knowledge.

Thoughts;____

____

____

Wisdom
Blessings
Grateful

3 or 10 When life's pressure is so dark, writing positive or grateful things becomes hard. They are truly a part of the day, but it's hard tc just see or feel them.

Psychology has tips and tricks, strategies, and meditations to help us pull through the dark moments in time. A Fake Smile is always recommended. As we "fake" happiness, soon we feel happy. It can be a good strategy that does indeed work sometimes.

As time passes, we all have changes we don't see coming, but as we look back, we see that life has changes we didn't plan.

One drastic change in my age is funerals. It drains me as I get death notices or obituaries of people in my generation. 2-3 years ago, I lost all of one aunt's children. Yes, in 18 months, I lost all four cousins from one aunt. And one other cousin from another aunt. All five were 20+ years older than me, leaving a hole in my life.

Another drastic change we can't prepare for is wisdom. Seeing truths that are not in our 20s and 30s in our late 50s, we acknowledge. One that haunts me is "multitasking" In my 20's, I was amazing at it; today, I suck at the to-do list.

3 or 10 Wisdom is a painful thing we learn. Today I know "days" are important. At this age (57) I may not see decades. So this day I have been given. It is painful to think I'm absolutely heart attack age. So on this day… I have been given the blessing of this day. My heart is good, my health is stable, but today is a gift.

Thoughts;____

____

____

End of Life
Inheritance

3 or 10 I called on a house for sale… it's in bad shape. There is no kitchen, no bathroom, subfloors are exposed, electrical wires are exposed, and heat is only in the living room—$ 115,000. No bank will touch it. And the sellers refuse owner financing because they are in probate. (Probate allows persons to accept a contract as long as the money goes to bills) So, I shake my head. This is crazy and not realistic at all. Probate is one of the American issues that very few people understand or care to learn about, yet it will come to every one of us. Because I understand probate, I have already taken steps to prevent 33% of my hard work from going to the state or feds. A dear friend told me of his issue with probate, where he was forced to write a $400,000 check to pay for his dad's 70-year career and wealth. Part of the probate issue is it only affects law-abiding people. By law, Jake's estate was required to file probate… but they did not. I requested it, and the judge dismissed me… but didn't require it to be filed.

3 or 10 I'm proud to say I've given "my stuff" away while living. Value: $16.71, so it didn't take me long…. Casady wears the engagement ring from her dad, and Saige has a diamond from her father. And my bank account has $56.20 for them to split. Ha! Probate, inheritance tax, a will, a power of attorney that continues after death, last wishes, and a living will are all things everyone should have in place. And, of course, a final expense plan, whether insurance or cash, in a safety deposit box. And a pet plan… I preach this to everyone, and I'm sad to say that very few listen to me. By the way… the government doesn't care about you other than your value ($$$) to them… why be lazy and let them take your worth? Your hard work, your assets, even your headstone? I wish the house seller good luck in selling a box with a roof for a cash out of $115,000. I'm sad that "death" wasn't planned for cuz, like it or not, we all get to go there.

Thoughts;____
____
____

Relationships
Morals
Perspective

3 or 10 I've loved and have been loved by many men. Some lovers, some buddies, some best friends. In 7th and 8th grade, Delbert was my bestie. 9th to 11th, Louis was my go-to guy. (Neither lovers just great friends).

I only have one past lover relationship that turned my love into hate.

This last week, one of those dear men said something that took me back. His memory seems far different than mine. Which would seem normal as the lens through which we look is full of different perspectives. He doesn't seem to remember his cheating, verbal abuse, and hitting me.

Years ago, on a typical day and time, 2 of the men from my past made the irrational decision to fistfight. As this bubbled up over the weeks, I told them to knock it off. One was fighting over ownership of me (which he did not have), and one was fighting over a moral value. Moments before the fight started, I told them to stop arguing and leave my house. They went out the doors to create a bloody, broken-bone battle that ended with the one fighting for a moral cause, standing and the one for ownership, hiding under a pickup. I was in the house watching with a 3-year-old behind a sliding glass door. The fight didn't last very long, but the effects still hold a place in my mind.

A moral position, it would seem, comes with more strength than property ownership. Neither man is currently a part of my life, but if I saw them today, I would hug them and catch up about their life. The blood was washed away, the broken bones healed, and the moment in time and the relationships are history. Yet, my valuing them both remains.

3 or 10 I've had a lot of male friends, far more than females, and I believe the reason is Yin and Yang. Opposites (created opposite by God) complement each other. And working in a male-dominated world exposes me to more men than women. The underlying friendship is my motivation. And is of deep value to my self-worth. Mostly, the relationships have blessed my life and given me perspective and balance.

I've been a drug counselor, marriage therapist, designated driver, parts runner, little sister, and secret holder; I miss Louis and Delbert and the hours of just hanging out.

Some lovers broke my heart as they or I made changes I did or didn't want. But one fact remains: "If I loved them, I still love them today." I hope they all know that. I hope that through their lens of perspective, they value our history. And from time to time, they smile when they think of me. Because I smile when they come to mind.

Thoughts;____

____

____

Family Lore

3 or 10 Family Lore! When I was very young, I had a black lab named Hubbard. I don't remember getting him because I was too young. I also remember a man named Faye Hubbard who visited my Grampa; he always had some animal with him. His visit once included a Cadillac with the back seat removed and a horse in its place. I came to find out it was Faye who gave me the black lab. As lore goes, Faye

trained horses to be in movies. He trained for names like John Wayne and films like Bonanza, etc.

I read a book about Hooper, WA, called "Cowboy in the Classroom," by C.C.Coe, about a school teacher who went to DC to "standardize" the 8-second ride in the rodeo for bulls and broncs. Faye was in the book by name, and I don't know, but I'm sure my Grampa was in the very rodeos glorified by the author.

So, "the lore" yesterday, I went to task to find film credits of Faye and Kay's horses in the films. Well, it took about 1 minute because Kay, a world-renowned musician, wrote a book about her time as Faye's wife in OR, training the horses for Hollywood, which was then turned into a movie for which she wrote the music.

3 or 10 I need to find the movie so I can watch it. I need to find a copy of a book written in the 1950's. (Which means searching antique bookstores). I read Kay's bio from Yale Library; she was an amazing talent and was also with Gershwin… Radio City, and in New York. Family Lore feeds my "history bug," and I love being bitten by the "bug." I had a black lab named Hubbard, and when I watched my treasured westerns of the 50s, I knew the trainer of the horses. Some were trained to fall dead, some to rear up and throw the rider, and some trained to run. I knew the man, he drove a Cadillac and his name was Faye, he was friends with Grampa, and would visit often.

"Never a dull moment": To Oregon and back again (1939-1952)

Kay Swift, who could ask for anything more? (New York: Simon and Schuster, 1943)

After 18 months at Radio City, Swift left in 1936 to become the Director of Light Music for the 1939 New York World's Fair. Here, she met her second husband, the rodeo star Faye Hubbard, with whom she eloped in 1939 to a ranch in Bend, Oregon, lovingly

named "The Faye and Kay." In 1943, Swift published her account
as a city girl.

Thoughts;____
____
____

Technology
Back to Basics

3 or 10 Clip Board… becoming an adult comes with good and bad habits. We get some from our childhood and learn some along the way. For most of my life, I've had a clipboard, notes, to-do lists, doodles, and THINKING about goals and solutions to "life" stuff. Before email we wrote letters to family and friends. Then, the great computer, internet, and email technology changed how we handle tasks.

I remember the moment I started participating in my downfall. I changed from a landline to a cell phone; then, I made the biggest mistake in goals, reaching dreams. I got an iPhone and started playing FarmVille. This plan was to free up my time, making life more productive. Well, it didn't free up time, it didn't make life easier, and it certainly doesn't help "dreams come true. 'Three days ago, I received a book I wanted to read, and I searched for and found my clipboard. Where is a pen I love? Where is my highlighter? Why is this shift significant? Because my iPhone has far too many downloaded games, it's far too easy to waste away time clicking on too many posts, to witness many memes, jokes, and pictures of things that are not a part of my day. And I find the videos that pop up one after another are ineffective in reaching goals.

So…. I've been deleting groups and unfollowing things that don't help my day, and I will delete all the downloads of games that waste my time.

Within reach of my morning coffee currently are three iPhones, my old, Jakes, and my current one, one tablet, two laptops, and four desktops that go back to Yakima (1998), which I moved from in 2002, moms computer, that I need to download all her pictures, two external hard drives, that hold a T, (which one is big enough to hold all my files), and a programmable coffee pot that I have no idea how to make it stop beeping, and of course a 55-inch flat screen with probably 50 apps. Hence, it's possible to watch every TV show from the 1950s. My therapist and I meet on Zoom, and my banking is a mobile app that allows me to deposit checks with a couple of clicks and an iPhone picture. Because of all this, I've lost some important stuff: my watch, thermometer, handwritten letters, books, people, and MY CLIPBOARD!

3 or 10 It's time to get back to what works. This crazy mess has indeed changed me for "the worse." Time management, connecting with loved ones, leaving the house (pajamas), and doing my hair and makeup (Amazon and Walmart orders) don't build relationships and leave us lonely because we have zero human interactions. So... MY CLIPBOARD is to reach goals, lift depression, become more productive, and connect with people face to face. I need to get rid of a $1,500 "life management box" in my hand. Just that $1,500 could have given me a 3-day weekend with the grands, room service, and a pool, building memories made and treasured.

Shifting back to what I know works. Purging the "stuff" that got my clipboard lost, thank goodness I didn't throw it away. It was right where I left it.... But it was covered in dust. Ha Ha...

Don't Forget, while you're busy doubting yourself, someone else is admiring your strength.

Thoughts;____
____
____

Mother's Love
Family
Healing

3 or 10 I think of my oldest whenever I see hippie pics, especially with tie-die or rainbow colors. We haven't spoken since 2014. I've tried unsuccessfully, leading me to know it's not solely my issue. Some parts are mine. That is all I can fix, change, or adjust. But until she wants to make way for a relationship, I can do nothing. Leaving me broken inside. The problems started in 1991 when she was 4; NONE OF THAT WAS HER FAULT OR DOING. But the trauma or resentment was put in motion. Now she's 36, so for 18 years, it is hers to carry, heal from, fix, change, adjust. The last time we texted, in 2022, that 4-year-old was screaming pure pain. Fixing and Changing is impossible as history is just that HISTORY!!! Adjusting is the only power she or I have. She has demanded I not be in her life. I've, with a lot of pain, respected her request. I have pain for so many involved. Her, of course, me; certainly, and two grands that will never have wonderful memories made with Granny. Three other kids and three othe grands that won't have "family bonds." There is absolutely no way to look at this mess as positive, but there is possibly some positive to come from it.

3 or 10 Hippie, rainbow, tie die…. It is cute, for sure. I've respectfully honored her request. The two grands will come searching for the truth about me. At one point in time, Saige will call to let her know I've passed away. She will choose to cry or celebrate. And on that day, my hope to ADJUST… will become history, and fewer choices will be available. I pray daily this mess gets healed, fixed, and adjusted long before that day. Yet, recognize I'm only 1/2 of it all. And as I age and watch people my age pass, I know the days are numbered. I wonder if she realizes that unchanging fact. Or, on that day, will she be filled with things unsaid? I pray to fix, change, or adjust! And I know prayer is always answered; sometimes the answer is "no."

Thoughts;____

____

____

Life Happens

3 or 10 What makes or breaks a perfect day, week, or year? Not talking about trauma, death, illness, or grief. For the big things, LIFE IS HARD! But just get out of bed and have a great day. I have a list of crap in my life right now; the blower motor went out of the pellet stove (thank God I installed electric heaters also), the tank heaters are not keeping up, I shoveled snow for an hour, need another hour to get pickup dug out, STUFF! But power was out yesterday, and I've lived through 3 and 5-day power outages. I forced the dogs to wait to go out for an hour to see if the lights would come on. Holding a flashlight to do chores is hard. It is not fun 10 minutes after getting the dogs done, poof, power came on. I thanked God! I have a huge generator. It's not hooked up cuz I don't know how, but it's part of my plans.

I'm normally prepared for "stuff" and always have "life plans," but sometimes things don't work out. My world is currently "hopeful" but slow going. I paid for my Ford to be fixed for winter. The mechanic stood me up. 4x4 isn't working on Tahoe, so that's a challenge, and bald tires scare me in winter. Walmart delivers groceries (which I don't want to eat, but a person can't live on chili and coffee). The 12+ inches of snow is a problem, but today, there is no new snow, it comes again tomorrow; I can't complain cuz the more snow, the fewer forest fires. Forest fires are ugly! Water, wood stove, pellet stove for downstairs, another 300-gallon tank, tire on the trailer, web site, I got stuff going on… feeling overwhelmed and won't get it all done. After the -27*, I was worried that the Tahoe wouldn't start, but Thank God it did. It is supposed to be 40* on Saturday, which, for those not from north Idaho, means a thick layer of ice will be under the snow. Ugg but -27* or 40*, well, duhhh.

3 or 10 It's a good day! Happiness! Or just Okay! I ordered stove parts and the bigger tank heater. My electric blanket keeps my chair warm. 40* makes the dogs happy. So, is it a good or bad day? It's all relative, and today, I want to feel happy, so I am.

Don't worry about the haters…. They are just angry because the truth you speak contradicts the lie they live.

Thoughts;____

____

____

Giving
Kindness
Blessings

3 or 10 This t-shirt made me giggle. Giggles are good.

Giggles feel good.

Giggling benefits last long after the giggle stops.

The best way to stop a child's bad mood or behavior is to make them giggle.

But, as adulting goes, we forget to giggle. We forget to make others giggle.

Flowers delivered at work make us smile and feel good.

Sending and receiving a thank you card gives us a feeling of appreciation and happiness.

A single rose from a lover makes us feel special.

A rock or dandelion from a child gives us warmth but gives us happiness.

The box of candy is heartwarming, and we share it with others.

That unexpected phone call warms us. When it's from the person you've missed for 20 years, amazingly, you were thought about.

3 or 10 A life filled with stress, fatigue, grief, and unhappy moments— yet all can be lifted up. People want to be seen as quality, respectful, and dedicated. All are great things, but love is a gift to others. Jesus talks a lot about service to others, giving without keeping notes, tithing, and knowing God will return it 100-fold.

I can honestly say I have never been without. It amazes me that no matter what I "need," it always shows up. No, not the Corvette that I dream of, but things I truly need. What do you "want" or "need"? Give it away! Have a box of thank you notes on your desk. Know the phone number of the florist. Make candy and mail it out. Have time to make a casserole when a friend has a family death. Sit with the one going through a divorce. Visit a nursing home or hospital. Jesus gave two of his disciples the nickname Thunder… give the nickname. If I call you honey or sweetheart, it's because I adore you, OR I FORGET YOUR NAME! (Ha Ha) Give a 5-star review. Pay for the cop's lunch. Shake hands, give a hug, and make eye contact. Tell the child "thank you" and keep the dandelions where people can see them. How do we fix society and America? One act of kindness at a time. GET BUSY WITH MAKING THE WORLD A BETTER PLACE.... And never forget to giggle! Turn off the news, and turn up the music. Tell the joke, watch the comedy show. Turn on a tear-jerking movie. Celebrate you and others. Make the world remember you!

I'm not mean; I'm honest. The truth hurts; here's a band-aid.

Thoughts;____

____

____

Rights
Victimhood
Narcissist

3 or 10 I had an interesting conversation this week about Queer Rights. The person I was talking with is very liberal and a "victim".

I don't know her gender identity or pronouns because, frankly, I don't care. But I was intrigued that this "victim" could not identify what "queer rights" were denied above human rights.

The conversation started over a very well-known, nationally known shelter turning "queer" people away. At her request, I googled "queer rights," and I found the problem. Discrimination! So, I assume the shelter was trying to keep people safe from rape and violence. Gender Identity vs. bio genitalia. I know hundreds of members of the LGBTQ group. Mostly, they all just live, work, socialize, have families, and want the same thing as almost everyone else.

LGBTQ that are flaming, extreme pro-choice, BLM, gangs, protests that become riots, and The Squad, all have a common thread. They demand that I abandon my beliefs to give them recognition. Because they are "victims" of their or my beliefs, this "victimhood" clouds reality.

3 or 10 As The Squad screams for the death of America and Jews, as the LGBTQ demand males allowed in women's spaces, as BLM demands, I see the burning down of property as "a right," as extreme Pro-Choice demand abortions to birth, I see extreme discrimination against others. As victims, they can't see themselves as doing EXACTLY what they see as my problem. They, the victims, want to remove the rights of others.

How dare someone build in Portland because BLM will burn it down.

How dare someone own a home in San Francisco because drug-addicted homeless will pitch a tent and poop in their yard.

How dare a homeless women want not to be raped in a shelter.

How dare a viable baby be born.

How dare a riot be brought under control. How dare we pray on a sidewalk for an unborn baby.

How dare we not want children under the age of 12 not to know sexual things?

How dare we "carry" to protect ourselves from violence?

How dare a store owner not want to be robbed?

How dare we, as parents, want our children to know our values?

How dare we not embrace "drag queens" sexualized dancing for children?

And finally, how dare we have a conversation about "you are not a victim" when we are dismissed?

How dare I ask, "What "rights" have you been denied?" Because the answer is none, to face that, they are forced to see they are not victims.

No one gets to decide your worth or value except for you!

Thoughts;____

____

____

Justice
Fairness
Rights

3 or 10 The beautiful Constitution is our founding document. It is a beautiful collection of a population's rights.

Judges are out of control, which is one of our society's fractures. The Bundy Ranch posted today a shocking post, property, and entire farm taken by a corrupt judge. And I read a blog post that took me back to a southern Idaho judge who took away my constitutional rights. First Venue, then Jury Trial, then my 1st Amendment. I went to help aid the Bundy case, but no one came to help me. My case was a Mormon judge, attorney, plaintiff, vs. me. I believe the Mormon part was the driving force. I even filed court papers requesting the judge recuse himself. I received a 10-minute speech on the record about the Mormon church structure, which was assuring me I was correct.

My Grampa, in the '50s, entered into a contract with the Mormons to grow sugar beets. U & I Sugar. His contract wasn't honored at harvest because the Mormons harvested, and his beets weren't needed. U & I moved from WA to southern Idaho and eventually Brazil.

When plaintiffs asked for a permanent injunction to remove my 1st Amendment, I responded with a motion. I was denied. And the chatter, lies, and abuse continue. Being raised here in Idaho, but Grampa continued to live in a Mormon community, I've seen great Mormons and horrible Mormons. Today, watching Ammon Bundy have his farm stolen because of a corrupt liberal judge and corrupt attorneys; I must note that I've had some very fair judges.

3 or 10 Mental illness untreated is a terrible thing. Richard and Randy are not the same thing. Annette and Abby are not the same thing. God says I should pray for my enemies, forgive my trespassers, and give him my problems. Boy, that is tough when the abuse continues, and mental illness is so bad that logic isn't possible.

Judges out of control are a horrible fact in this Constitutional Republic. That makes me sad, Not the same thing as mad.

We The People

Thoughts;

Blessings
Multifaceted

3 or 10 As I prepare for the publication of my book, I need to write an acknowledgment, preface, and bio. Stop laughing! It feels like I'm writing my obituary. A paragraph explaining who I am, and a couple paragraphs explaining the book.

Born as a first child and raised in the PNW, my childhood was filled with outdoor sports, four clear seasons, and shenanigans. A baby brother blessed my life; only 18 months apart, we are very close, and he is my family rock. Mother of 4 children as different from each other as can be. Granny to the most perfect grands in the world. A life riddled with the struggles of bad choices and depression. I was a high school dropout who, in my 20's and 40's, became college-educated. Married and divorced 3 times. Blessed by the US Army to live in Europe for 3 years. I'm a dog lover and history buff who spends more hours reading and playing with dogs than housework. I live biblical conservative values, my moral fiber runs my life, and heaven is my final destination.

3 or 10 Annette Kaye is a multi-faceted person who really has a wide variety of experiences from which to draw. Tho I appear scattered; my soul is very set in her ways. Depression is evil, and 3 or 10 is one of the antidepressants (prescribed by a Dr) that keeps me centered. Positive Thoughts and Blessings are easy to find if I "seek" them. Thank God, above all, for helping ghostwriters write and edit my story.

Thoughts;____

____

____

Human Needs
Personal Responsibility

3 or 10 We all need LOVE. Years ago, that was a phone call (that was expensive), a birthday, thank you, or sympathy card (not many mail cards anymore); we used to gather together for church, a picnic, or family gathering (everyone is now too busy for that nonsense). Everyone needs to feel RESPECTED. We used to shake hands firmly (that is old fashioned), we made eye contact as we talked (no one is talking), and we used to debate our differences without hating the other person (debate is impossible when safe spaces are available). We used to Peacefully protest (loved sit-ins of the '60s and '70s). Now, cities are burnt down, and cops are the enemy.

I'm beside myself that praying on a sidewalk in front of an abortion clinic causes the one praying to be arrested, and the staff is protected.

I shut down when someone says, "This is my truth," because Truth is a fact, not a feeling. Judges refuse to punish PERJURY, so the foundation of our system is gone.

3 or 10 I love… I respect… I peacefully protest… I tell judges the truth… I shake hands… I call for no reason… I send mail… I pray for babies dying… I plan family parties… mainly I tell the truth… I make eye contact… I mostly mind my own business, so my circle is small… I'm me… I'm okay… I'm solid… I'm old-fashioned and raised kids with old values… my kids know both The Bible and the Constitution… I'm good. Yep, it's true, I'm Good!

"Healing Also means taking an honest look at the role you play in your own suffering."

Thoughts;____

____

____

Manifesting
Recognition
Healing

3 or 10 "Mom, can you manifest….?" Well of course I can. Today, I was asked what "centers" me—prayer and meditation on any topic. I personally believe all three are the same thing…goals. I have a horrible habit of self-talk: "I'm never going to get caught up," and I am 100% correct, not because I'm lazy; it has more to do with my goal list and not saying "no" to adding to my to-do list. So, at times, I need to list things that I did accomplish or hurdles I overcame. In 2021, I almost died; the critical care unit had me for 5 days after 4 days of being really sick. Coming home from the hospital, I had supervision (Saige) for another five days. Was it over after 14 days? Oh, hell no! It took me 6 weeks to not need a nap and 6 months to lift 25 lbs. So, how far behind was I? Well, a long way because even at six months, I wasn't strong; I was just better. My incision was from breast bone to pelvic bone, so lifting was a challenge, but so was coughing, sitting up, and even rolling over in bed. Lots of cut muscles are needed to work on healing.

3 or 10 Just like an AA Chip; 30-day, 3 months, 1 year… 10 years… we should all get "celebrated" for overcoming junk in our lives. With the passing of Indy, of course, the milestones and anniversaries were noted. But no one came to notice the days I took a shower. Jake noted that all I didn't get done was make me feel worse. I needed a 30-day chip of making it through the work week without bawling. Just as near death was a milestone for the better. The day I carried groceries upstairs and wasn't pooped was a big day, and I remember calling Whisper and patting myself on the back. Yep, it was a big deal. Milestones need to be noted to keep positive momentum. We do it with our kids, yet forget it for ourselves or adult peeps. Maybe we need "goal" meetings! Cigarettes, clean house, and clutter busting. I need to work for my 30-day chip! Fact: I can't dust 5000 sq ft in a day, but maybe I could get three rooms done in a day. Self-talk… I got this or that done! BOOYAH, that would be better self-talk!

Every experience, no matter how horrid or joyful, is something to write about.

Thoughts;____

____

____

Empathy
Respect

3 or 10 Editing has been a nightmare, as I had to wake up to know I was fine. I need copyright permission slips or just change all the names. I believe in resolving the conflict of hurting people I love and knowing.

3 or 10 Is still my path, and it is a conflict only inside me. Very few people pay much attention to the people around them. Very few people listen to hear. And very few people stop in to check on others. But publishing my reality might bug some people in my world. I have one child who looks for things that cause her to be a victim, and "you have the right to remain silent" escapes her. Her core anger at me is not only justified but I agree with her. She can't hear the "agree" part cuz being a victim fuels her life. Then I have another child, and her approach is silently quiet. I had no idea how she felt until the explosion. And then it's just a game of "Oh my god, I didn't know." These humans mean the world to me, but how will these "published," "public" memoirs improve or impact our relationship? I'm frozen in fear. It's not like using a pseudonym is going to "fool" my peeps.

3 or 10 I won't completely impact readers if I delete (edit) every emotion I have because of or including peeps. I've worked hard to use 3 or 10 to improve my life. And it has touched many already. To publish it can reach even more people. But let's face it: the negative has to be faced, accepted, and embraced to become stepping stones to change and positivity. I wasn't blessed with a positive, happy outlook all the time. And to get out of "that" 3 or 10 always shifts my mind.

I'm not in a traffic jam, and I'm part of a traffic jam.

I'm not poor, yet I spent all my money.

I'm not the "family problem," I'm in a family with problems.

"I am what I am…. I don't need your approval."

Thoughts;_______________________________________
____
____

Listening
Communication

3 or 10 I try really hard to be precise. I do like to communicate clearly. I re-read many times to understand, which is uncommon.

I currently have an ad about tearing down and removing a trailer and two buildings. I received the question, "How much for the land? I only need 1 acre." I shook my head. What is wrong with people?

I posted about being lonely and wanting a relationship in a group; I got 50 comments, including "love yourself" and "get a dog." What is wrong with people? I have many dogs and am a good trainer, but none rub my back, take out trash, or cook breakfast on Saturday morning.

I watched TV, and I'm angry. Carl's Jr. has made a decision that is woke. El Deoblo (Satan) burger is $6.66. This is truly a WTHECK moment. What is wrong with people? So, I'm boycotting Carl's Jr.

3 or 10 It is not complicated to read, re-read, or think through. I was at military honors this week. Tapps was played, and it upset me (as if it were supposed to). The military prayer of The Marines shook me so hard that I only heard part of it. So, I asked the commander for a copy of it. He was so loving that he gave me a copy. It again moved me to tears. Sometimes, we must re-read or ask for a copy. Those of us who are "communicators" just instinctively do this. Then there is "WTHeck is wrong with people" kind of people. The WTHeck people are exhausting! They waste so much precious time. WTHeck!!! I try hard to communicate well, with knowledge and understanding. I'm really good at communicating, and I wish people could hear me. The saying "some people listen to respond, some to understand" I'm the one that wants to understand. BOOYAH

Understanding a question is half an answer

Thoughts;____

____

____

Self Love
Boundaries

3 or 10 I am a friend worth having. At times, I see others' value, lift them in times of trouble, and help them with their needs and goals. Yet, I forget to give myself the same thoughts and energy. As a Type A Personality, I put challenges on myself that I would never expect of others... WTHeck! Why would I kick myself harder than ever on someone else? This pops up because of a boundary issue that happened this week. I sidestepped a boundary to gain some help. I felt guilty letting myself down. About two hours later, I put the boundary back in place. Are my beliefs wrong? Nope! Are my boundaries outrageously ridiculous? Nope. Are my boundaries moral? Yep! Are my boundaries legal? Yep! I am a worthy friend! I forget that sometimes.

I was in three different situations this week. Three men I adore, three opinions I value. Three times a line in the sand... I had to make choices.

3 or 10 I define my value.... For those who don't see it, I feel bad for them. I am worthy of love, respect for boundaries, and an opinion. My mantra this week is "I am a worthy friend... PERIOD," and as I pencil on my to-do list, I will make the period a dark circle, not just a dot. "I am...PERIOD" That feels good already... PERIOD!

Happiest of birthdays to the one who gave me life! She deserves the world! She is strong and beautiful! She is outgoing and carefree. She is creative and supportive! She is MOM! She would go to the ends of the earth to help anyone who needed it. She is my superhero! I love you, momma, and I hope your day is all you wish it to be. Because today is YOUR day! (Whisper)

Thoughts;____

____

____

Faith
The Holy Spirit
Listening

3 or 10 Have ya ever noticed that sometimes there is meaning in nothing? I'm very much a "hidden message" person. Some say we repeat the lesson till it's learned. Or "messages come if we pay attention" or "the Holy Spirit lives in you." It seems at times that when I see a post with a message, it's so weird; it pops in, posted over and over, or with a new background. God speaks if we notice. And then I ponder the message. I've noticed I can block the messages and push them down. It never works out well. The last big one is the Rascal Flats song, "I Won't Let Go"

which is all Bible verses. I saw 10+ versions in about three days. What? Ok, so I paid attention. It is absolutely beautiful. God's words of loving me. What?

3 or 10 Pay attention! God, Jesus, and The Holy Spirit are talking

"I won't let go

… It's like a storm

That cuts a path

It breaks your will

It feels like that

… You think you're lost

But you're not lost on your own

You're not alone

… I will stand by you

I will help you through

When you've done all, you can do

If you can't cope

I will dry your eyes

I will fight your fight

I will hold you tight

And I won't let go

… It hurts my heart

To see you cry

I know it's dark

This part of life

Oh, it finds us all (finds us all)

And we're too small

To stop the rain

Oh, but when it rains

… I will stand by you

I will help you through

When you've done all you can do

And you can't cope

I will dry your eyes

I will fight your fight

I will hold you tight

And I won't let you fall

… Don't be afraid to fall

I'm right here to catch you

I won't let you down

It won't get you down

You're gonna make it

Yeah, I know you can make it

… Cause I will stand by you

I will help you through

When you've done all, you can do

And you can't cope

And I will dry your eyes

I will fight your fight

I will hold you tight

And I won't let go

Oh, I'm gonna hold you

And I won't let go

Won't let you go

No, I won't"

A beautiful song, written by God, sang by Rascal Flatts

Thoughts;____

____

____

Self Love
Loyalty

3 or 10 At times, when we want to cry, fight, or even "get even," we must laugh! We all run into people and think, "How can you be so stupid"? As everyone knows, I have a stalker, and it's been years and years of crazy. But the amazing part is that some people on this page keep feeding her the little tidbits of my life. That is HILARIOUS! Who on my profile is so disloyal? I don't care! It took me years to reach the "I don't care" stage. I got all puffy about the lies and fought back for a long time. Now, it just is a part of life. It doesn't affect me much. As I said from the beginning, IT IS PATHETIC, but whoever is feeding him/her is also pathetic.

3 or 10 I'm very aware of who is loyal. And they are the treasures of life. Ridiculous people make me laugh. This 3 or 10 isn't about my stalker; it's about hilarious! The stories told about me are so far-fetched that they seem like stand-up comedy—comic relief. The fact is my peeps, the ones close to me, know better. That is truly a blessing! Yes, my stalker still tells outrageous stories, yet she knows "not much."

Thoughts;____

____

____

Loyalty
Dedicated

3 or 10 We always hear "buy local," and it makes perfect sense to support local businesses. I always check prices, and if the fuel to drive to the big town is saved, then I assume "local" wants me to eat Taco Bell. This week, I had a weird thing happen; a month ago, I checked prices and would save $21 to order online—$ 21X12 months…$252 a year. But decided to "buy local". But I drove 20 miles, and they didn't have what I needed. So, I asked if there was a substitute. There was, but it boosted my price from $30 a week to $45 a week. So, I said OK, when will my normal one be here? Oh, a week! (Common medication, so them not having it was just a lack of organization) So, how much is shipping? $15. Being a retailer, I know that was stealing! So, I pulled up my postage account, and shipping is $3.99. Ok… local… now I'm mad!

3 or 10 Customer Service is the heartbeat of every business, right alongside Prices. My checking account makes life decisions, saving $252 plus free shipping, no gas, and has what I need. And even auto-ship, so my time is valued. I'm sure the owner of "local" wants me to be dedicated, but the $15 shipping felt like "local was a thief". I think I'm a little dismissed. It's a little unwanted. It's a bit taken advantage of. I don't like those feelings! I understand profit margins, but I also understand a budget.

I'm grateful that thoughts don't appear in bubbles over our heads.

Thoughts;____

____

____

Relationships
Friends
Family

3 or 10 Late today because I woke up late, feeling drunk (a side effect of 1 medicine I'm on) and the start of a migraine. I'm refusing to do migraine today, telling my head to straighten up. Usually, it is a tension headache that I can solve. So, the dogs were all patient with me this morning. Now they snore in their napping spots… job well done on my part. Today, I've been blessed with two dear friends, and I'm checking in for a little problem-solving chat. Sometimes, support is in the question, sometimes in the answers. Sometimes, most times, it's in not feeling alone. It's always funny how the chit-chat is the best part of life. I do love my peeps! Whether professional or friend, PEEPS are very important and dear to me. I hope they know that.

3 or 10 I have peeps. I try to keep them all, knowing they are valuable to me. It is that value that adds to life. There are smiles, giggles, tears, and the occasional WTHECK. But they are always in my heart, snuggled in with A PLACE. And sometimes, from their actions, I know I have A PLACE! In their hearts as well. That feels great! And I love it.

Knowledge is of no value unless you put it into practice.

Thoughts;____

____

____

Siblings
Laughter

3 or 10 This shirt is hilarious! I love laughter so far down in the gut that my eyes water. My kids take me there often; yes, my kids are silly and absolutely roll on the floor funny. It's weird how sometimes you do something with solid reasons (I didn't want Saige to be an only child, so I had Whisper), but it worked out; they are so close, fight like crazy, and would fight for the other to death. They "know" the other as well as they know their skin. My "baby brother" and I are that close in a different way. But indeed, he stood beside me through some great stuff and some devastating stuff, too. I'm so very blessed. Lucky mom and sister. Even in bad moments of life, there are things we hold onto as good.

3 or 10 It's hard to schedule gut-rolling laughter, but it is a great part of life. I love it when the girls are hilarious. I love my brother, knowing all my life's secrets and saying a word or two to make me laugh. I was talking with Jerry, "My brother calls me "Fathead" it's adorable. Please don't be offended." I got a bit of an aww look, but I've been Fathead since I was 5…, and it still makes me smile. The girls and I share a Hulu log-in… the other day, a new user was added, "SHRIMP," which cracks me up. Saige has called Whisper "shrimp" for as long as I can remember. That is just too funny. Laughter is GOOD medicine.

I have selective hearing. I'm sorry you are not selected

Thoughts;____

____

____

Home
Seasons
Babies

3 or 10 Today is one of those days when 3 or 10 is a must. So much crazy going on. Busy work and springtime. For months of winter, life is slowed down to a standstill. Too cold, too much snow, icy roads. It is just a fact of North Idaho life. That fact is one of the happiest parts of my life. Four clear seasons. Winter lasts 9 months, and summer is a week in August, but the other 3 months are perfect. Yes, I find that funny. I love my Idaho home. It is a beautiful standing forest of magnificent pine trees. Wildlife around each corner of wagon trails turned into a highway system. Sunsets are so gorgeous, knowing God hand-painted them just for me. Water is so bubbly it gets the name "white water." Elk herds take the breath away, and mountain peaks covered in snow that beauty compares to calendar photos from around the world. I'm so blessed to be "home."

3 or 10 for 4 months, it will be warm enough to be outside. It's funny how little things take up the most space. I put my long underwear away for the season. It is a short season to soak in, but mine to enjoy. It allows me to see baby skunks, raccoons, elk with spots, and maybe a bear cub.

I'm not mean…. I'm just too old to pretend I like you.

Thoughts;____

____

____

Courage
Moral
Rewarding

3 or 10 Some days, ya just have to do what no one else dares to do. The HARD stuff is just that. Hard. And it is so rewarding. I received a decision from a judge that broke my heart. I rolled around with the information for a week. Sad, angry, disgusted, sobbing, no sleep. Well, well, that's stress and depression. NOPE, I DON'T LIVE THERE. So, my choices are to fight back or accept what I know is wrong. Anyone who knows me knows I excel at all things I decide to do. And very rarely am I a quitter. I prayed, and God sent an angel disguised as a community member whose story was similar to mine, with the same current outcome. So, he, too, was angry. And he fought back. His conclusion is yet to be seen. But I rose above WRONG. Yep, sometimes people are wrong. We all know laws are written to protect people from other people. So, I went outside my comfort zone and challenged what I saw because of the laws written; not following them is as wrong as wrong. I might be dismissed again. The laws will remain, and my doing the right thing will continue. Even if nothing changes, I know I did what is right, moral, good, and just. I followed all laws written.

3 or 10 When I decided to challenge the decision made, I felt peaceful, nervous but peaceful, and no matter what was returned, I did RIGHT. Other bad behavior and opinions don't change that fact. Jesus says, "Forgive trespassers," but he also says, "Protect your flock." Even on the Sabbath. So, I gathered together the strength of John the Baptist or David. Goliath and King Herod Antipas remain wrong. John the Baptist died, and David won the battle. One of those two things will happen here. King Herod of St Maries was asked to reconsider a bad opinion. Jerry gave me a high 5, Keith and Joan gave me much-needed support, and I slept peacefully. Peaceful sleep comes from a job well done, knowing good moral choices are my true heart and what I give others. I gave everyone involved a good, loving heart. King Herod lost his way, Goliath lost his battle, AnnetteKaye will win, has already won, and God gave me true courage to stand for RIGHT and to sleep peacefully. I love having David and John the Baptist's courage and conviction. Big smiley face!

**Sometimes you just have to stop being scared and go for it either it
will work or it won't. That's life.**

Thoughts;____
____
____

Faith

3 or 10 Finding happiness because most of the time, it's hiding. Carrying the weight of the world is so hard, heavy, and exhausting. But most of us live there. So happy, grateful, and appreciative of life is sidelined for a lot of moments of the day.

At my funeral, I asked my kids to play "If You're Going Through Hell ' by Rodney Atkins.

[Chorus]

"If you're goin' through hell, keep on going

Don't slow down if you're scared don't show it

You might get out before the devil even knows you're there"

This song dropped me to my knees when Loren was dying. Mom sent me to the store, and it (this song) took me to realize my stepdad was dying, and there was nothing I could do for his pain, mom's pain, my kids, or myself. Thank God I was alone so I could just sit in a parking lot and sob uncontrollably. Realize might not be the right word because we had been battling cancer for 2+ years. It might be better explained by saying, "run over by a freight train." The reason this song is so real is that it is simple and STRONG. No matter what is going on, BE STRONG! Face all things STRONG. Do what NEEDS to be done. As my mom would tell me, "Grab your bootstraps."

3 or 10 It is true when we face HELL, we must keep going. We have no option unless we choose to remain in HELL. I'm going to "Keep on Going." Got a busy day planned? "If you are scared, don't show it." Yep, yep, I'm gonna get busy. "You might get out before the devil even knows you're there"

Psithurism (n) the sound of wind in the trees and rustling of leaves.

Thoughts;____

____

____

Loneliness
Community

3 or 10 Being lonely is a big problem for so many. FB addiction is because of loneliness. Suicide is because of loneliness. Working in nursing homes, I witnessed young deaths because of loneliness. People bully because of loneliness. People marry and divorce because of loneliness. Affairs are usually because of loneliness. So, is loneliness the worst part of our existence? Kind of, yet no one wants to solve the problem. As a kid, the neighbor lady was kinda in charge of "welcome baskets," some jam, bread, cookies, a phone book, information on churches, the butcher, electricity, and phone companies—a WELCOME to St Maries. And the neighbor invited the ladies to her church and her garden. Men of the time met people at work, but the women hung together as a secondary support system. Only southern exposure houses grew beautiful gardens. And northern exposure houses were checked on late in spring cuz of washed-out roads and impassable driveways. Divorce and depression were far less, and loneliness was a choice cuz people cared, worried, and showed up. People were far busier with people, lives, and deaths. I read an obituary this morning, "service at a later date." In other words, no one cares enough to celebrate a life. WTHeck is wrong with our world?

3 or 10 I promise the world a "wake" within 10 days of my death. Yep, we will gather together to give my kids and grands closure, support, kind words, and funny stories to hold on to. A place to cry for a loss and laugh for a life lived, celebrating the very fact that I was here. And made the world a better and more beautiful place for those I will leave behind. But today, mail a thank you, text a friend, or call family. Don't wait for an invite to a funeral to reach out. Grab a basket and fill it with jam, bread, and some good thoughts. Deliver it, and accept the smile as a thank you.

You are not lazy, unmotivated, or stuck. After years of living your life in survival mode, you are exhausted. There is a difference.

Thoughts;____

____

____

Validation
Self Worth
Respectful

3 or 10 I could be having a really bad day. But instead, I'm having a very good day. Yesterday, I got an order from a judge. It was not what I asked for… so I could curl up in a ball and sob. I asked for eleven things. The judge not only found those wrong, she added other things wrong, things she wasn't even asked for a ruling. And entered into her opinion that things were not included in the argument. So, do I hide? Nope… I know for a statistical fact… I was not 100% wrong. How could I fail in things not brought before the court? So, I went and talked to a friend represented by a powerful attorney; he invited me to the Appeals court hearing against this judge. So, this judge has been on the Benewah County bench for a very short time and has already been, appealed. So, because of my stress, I went to prayer so as not to feel so stressed. Anyone who knows me knows that I did not have 100% failure, and I never lied to the judge. So, if I presented somewhat good law and the truth… who did she hitch her wagon to? Not the law, not the truth, not "right," and she didn't rule a winner. She dismissed the case without evidence, testimony, witnesses, cross-examination, or argument.

3 or 10 My failure was trusting the system. I've been pro se in five cases… and this is the only one where I failed more times than I was arguing. All the rest, I've had rulings in my favor. It appears this judge has preferences that are not "the law," "justice," or "the people." So, do I curl up a failure? Not no, but HELL NO! How did I fail at games I wasn't playing? I didn't! So, despite her "opinion," I'm going to carry on and continue telling the truth. Emida got a case dismissed; they did not win and are still wrong. Act II is sure to be next. I best get ready.

Stop looking for validation from people who aren't even valid.

Thoughts;____

____

____

Reap and Sow

3 or 10 No one IS or SHOULD BE 100%. We all rise and fall. We are all sore and resting. We all thirst and are quenched. We all seek knowledge and relaxation. We all labor and toil, yet we all gaze at accomplishing a goal. There are so many writers who explain good behavior and bad behavior. My favorite life quote is from the Bible; examining it answers every life question we could ever dream up. 2 Corinthians 9:6, "Whoever sows sparingly will also reap sparingly, and whoever sows generously will also reap generously."

"You have planted wickedness, you have reaped evil," says the prophet (Hosea 10:13).

"They will eat the fruit of their ways and be filled with the fruit of their schemes," says Wisdom in Proverbs 1:31.

This feeling is what Karma was created to explain.

3 or 10 It is a fact Every Time We "Reap What We Sow." Lots of life's going on have nothing to do with our behaviors. Some STUFF happens. But day to day, we act and create a reaction. Some of it is exhilarating, and some devastating. Always we reap, and always we sow. And always, it is us that face it.

You deserve to be in an environment that brings out the softness in you, not the survival in you.

Thoughts;____

____

____

Woman
Strength

3 or 10 I do love it when men are intimidated by strong women. I am both a strong woman and a proper etiquette woman. I believe the feminist movement destroyed the family, yet I read in the Bible that women have always had jobs. Okay, so I am sorting out those four beliefs to reconcile them. During WWII, my grama was forced to have a baby while grampa was who knew where. She became a postmaster and built a house for her and her son. Did Grama want to be head of the household? I bet she would have rather Grampa had been home and not injured in a British hospital. So, was she strong? Or just a good wife and mother? She had no choice, so she did it. Can you imagine the mid-1800s heading west in a wagon train, having your husband die, you, your young children, a horse-drawn wagon, and no roads to take ya there? Where ever "there" was? Knowing ya couldn't own land or vote.

Do you turn around and head back to Pennsylvania or Illinois, where your father might be? Or do you continue to the Oregon Territory, where you were promised 640 acres to homestead? No home and below zero temps, no farm but mouths to feed, no job but needing money; what does a woman do?

3 or 10 I never wanted to be strong. I wanted a husband to be strong, leading the family. Instead, I married in a church; I believed a man of God, but come to learn, I married Satan. I had no choice: turn back or take the path with no road. I took my wagon, fed the horses, and headed out to raise kids, own land, and vote. Men, if you don't want a strong woman who can do it all by herself, stop forcing us to be stronger than we want. Stop forcing us to survive and learn ways to excel without you. Cuz our brain works to nurture… including ourselves. We make things grow strong. We, by nature, build up our garden… plucking the weeds and throwing them to the pigs. I never wanted to be strong… but I am.

Strong women don't have "attitudes" they have standards.

Thoughts;____
____
____

God
Faith
Hope

3 or 10 This was one of those "click to see" for the most part, they are usually close. This one made me cry. I always question everything. Solving business strategy: My questions are great, with God….but not so much. And in His Fatherly discipline, He always straightened my path. So much stress, and boom, this pops in. There's no need to argue or question this; focus on it. God promises that if you pray for wisdom, it will be given. The part that sucks about that is while using "free will," we fall flat on our face gaining wisdom. It is those bumps and bruises that make us question God.

3 or 10 Yesterday, the judge again "took it under advisement," so 19 days from trial, we are waiting for rulings. Dismiss and whether or not I can use the English word "proprietary." Yes, we had a hearing about limiting the use of a word. STRESS…. Prayer… and a message: "Don't lose hope! If you are confused about how the father loves his children… open your heart cuz it is ABSOLUTE! I needed this message as I'm up against goofy. As the world is filled with Satan, sometimes hope is all we get. "Don't lose hope!" I'm focused… God has this! And he has me!

Dear AnnetteKaye,

Don't lose hope if things seem to be taking longer than expected. Everything happens for a reason, and I'll bring the best things your way at the right time. Keep your faith and trust in me because good things are on their way to you. -God

Thoughts;____

____

____

Thankfulness
Relationships
Hope

3 or 10 So, 3 or 10 was prescribed by a doctor, Marnie, to help me focus on positive and not dwell on the bad. I lived in Lind, so it was before 2013. And look at it now in 2023. It has changed me and helped others.

My forever friend Jo used the 3 or 10 principles in training employees. What? Oh my, I puffed up with pride at this. Her, Lisa, Kayleen, Kieth, Joan Saige, Whisper, and others keep reminding me to get my book published. Kieth tells me I could really help others, so maybe I should start a blog. These compliments always lift my soul.

At times, depression and grief take over my mind.

It is those times that my 3 or 10 are so hard to write, and I know it is precisely those times it becomes a must. Facing trouble is a fact of life. Grief is the worst for me. Finding relief through writing is a long-ago practice. Knowing whether I am happy or sad helps others relate to life, which is priceless.

3 or 10 Marnie planting a seed… others watering my garden… flowers blooming in the summer sun… don't take away depression or grief…. But does relieve some of it! Thank You Everyone

You cannot force someone to comprehend a message that they are not ready to receive. Still, you must never underestimate the power of planting a seed.

Thoughts;____

____

____

Counting Blessings

3 or 10

Three blessings

Jo

Lisa

Friendships

Ten things I'm grateful for

Hard work pays off

It's ok to ask for help

Prayer is always answered, sometimes, "yes."

Crazy people show off

I'm able to help single moms

Pizza is delicious

Marnie Boyer

Little kids make me happy

"Yes." I really like that one

The FedEx guy is funny

Better worry 'bout your own sins, cause God ain't gonna ask you about mine.

Thoughts;____

____

____

Communication

3 or 10 "I" What is so confusing about that word? "I" feel!! "I" want!! "I" need!! "I" like!!

Personally, "I" have had it with people who feel attacked with an "I ' statement. Why do they waste the energy to feel butt hurt because someone made an "I" statement? "I" statements are supposed to be the foundation of conflict resolution.

"I" like pine trees, but it has absolutely nothing to do with anyone else. "I" don't like hot whether... again, nothing to do with someone else.

3 or 10 I love pine trees, and I hate hot weather. I am a redhead, and I hide from sunburns. I am 5 ft 6 inches tall. I love dogs. I love mashed potatoes. I hate talking on the phone. I love visiting with people. I love meeting new people. I hate shoes. Yep, all about me!!!

Evey once in a while someone amazing comes into your life....And here I am. You're welcome. :D

Thoughts;____

____

____

Blessings
God Is Amazing
The Creator (God)

3 or 10 LOOK UP!! As I do this thing called life, I know I am nothing compared to the creator. With that being said, I also know I am everything to that creator. A new friend stopped by; he was here the day I bought this place. He said, "Look what you've done in 2 months? This is really looking nice", he is always kind, but sent from heaven above, people are sent to us. The Alabama song "angels among us" says it all. When we need a boost, it is always provided.

3 or 10 Notice the good in the world. Take time to Look Up And Say Thank You!!!

Thoughts;____
____
____

Family
Memories

3 or 10 Mom's flip-flops. Every morning, I put on my flip-flops and let the dogs out. When my feet get hot, I get in a bad mood. Bundle up with blankets, and my feet stick out a little. Mom was mostly the same; in summer or winter, she wore flip-flops. But I've noticed something now that she is gone. The clicking of my flip-flops reminds me of mom. Flip flop flop-flip with each step, and I think "I walk like mom" maybe? But maybe it is just the sound. It is comforting, Yes, comforting. Losing mom and dad and all others makes a lonely place in our souls. These little memories make us happy. Coffee and cinnamon rolls... the smell always takes me to my grama's table. The cooking of adobo always brings me to family dinner. The smell of fried bread and stew takes me to snowy days in North Idaho. The smell of black velvet takes me to a party in my teens (the first drunk).

3 or 10 the sound of my flip flops is comforting to my soul. Again 3 or 10

The sound of my flip-flops is comforting to my soul.

Thoughts;____

____

____

Death
Heaven
Jesus

3 or 10 Think about how many people you know. Most are good!!! Think about how many teachers you have had. Most of them are good!!! Think of how many dogs you have met. Most are good!!! Think of the last ten people you have interacted with. Most are good!!! As I get older, I realize MY LIFE IS THE LENS I LOOK THRU. When mom was dying, I came to a point where I asked God to end her suffering. I felt guilty, but I knew she wouldn't get better. I knew death was with Heaven. Last night, Monster and I had a detailed heart-to-heart about Jesus, Heaven, and who is there. He thinks Jesus is an angel. I agree.

3 or 10

THE LENS.... Most are good.

My intentions will always be pure. I have no desire to be a shitty person.

Thoughts;____

____

____

Morals
The Bible
God Fearing

3 or 10 You all know I watch the news A Lot. I'm pretty political, and I am God Fearing. The Bible is my rule book. And Heaven is my destination. I'm guided by Angels whose advice/instruction is always from pure love. Most of my failures directly result from not following "The Ten Commandments."

Watching all the chaos in America right now, I'm puzzled as to why Dems can't see every problem comes from a lack of moral fiber.

Looting; Thou Shall Not Steal

Destroying Statues; Have No Gods Before Me

Riots; Turn the Other Cheek

Greed; One of Satans' Tools

Lying; Bearing False Witness

Murder; Thou Shall Not Kill

Bernie Supporters; Spare the Rod

3 or 10 America is in desperate need of MORAL FIBER!!! Those morals are written in a book. Lovingly called "The Bible". More people need to read, and raise the children with GOOD rules.

If someone was there to love you through the times you found it difficult to even breathe, I hope you treasure that person.

Thoughts;____

____

____

Common Sense
Laughter

3 or 10 PEOPLE ARE CRAZY!!! A Lady posts looking for cast iron legs for benches. I have some, so I responded. She only wants to pay $20. So my two sets with all hardware are $25 each. She wants them in Bayview (2 hour drive). I tell her I can meet half way. Then she asked me to take them apart and break loose the bolts so it could fit in a Subaru. NOW I'M done!!!! So I say labor and delivery is an extra $100. Then she has the nerve to say Emida is too far to drive, BUT IT WASN'T WHEN I WAS THE ONE DRIVING....

3 or 10 people stress me out or crack me up.... then.... to get the last word in, she sent another message that she could by them complete for $200... SOOOOO COOL... I'm now cracked up. Laughing and moving on knowing people are crazy.

Photo; Bench $385.85 Bench $648.85

3 or 10 People Are Crazy

Thoughts;____
____
____

Godly
Lies
Satan

3 or 10 What would our world be if people just told the truth?

Yesterday, a man came into my shop and said, "Trump and Putin are best friends. Trump has lots of assets in Russia." What an absolutely stupid thing to say; if Trump really had assets in Russia, all of the media would go wild and tell us that every day. But this man hates Trump so bad that he is willing to stand and say outrageous things. Just lies!! I don't understand why people are deceitful, especially in terms of politics in the media.

And even God, so many people say many things about God that are not true and that is funny. God, put the 10 Commandments as first, and in that, he talks about "bearing false witness." God always wants us, no matter how painful to temper the truth with kindness. God does not want me to tell someone they have an ugly dress or are a bad cook, yet he also doesn't want me to lie. Knowing that it's ok to say "my favorite of your dresses is the blue one", or "last week I loved your soup". Yes; God wants us to be kind and truthful.

3 or 10, Satan gets a hold of little pieces of information and twists them in the mind. We lie to ourselves and others in public, private, and every time, whether in a newspaper article or a coffee with a friend, lies destroy because it is one of Satan's tools; it is the one that Satan uses most often. To loose trust devastates relationship with others and self.

When I get mad at someone, I'm silent. Because if I speak my mind, it is gonna get real.

Thoughts;______________________________________

____

____

Alcoholism
Sadness
Hatred

3 or 10 I'm so incredibly sad that something's going on in life. I've known Jake for over 50 years. K-Garten is where we met. My first kiss!! A girl never forgets that. Teens, 20's, and 40's. Married 36 years after that first kiss.

Dreams come true right? Alcohol and selfishness destroyed a man. A commitment. Till death... and now a lawsuit because I'm the main thing he hates.

His hate for women goes deep. It was the TV show "Law and Order" when this pure hatred was known. I watched him for years degrade women but when Olivia was promoter to Captain, and Jake was so incensed that he would get angry when it came on.

His mother and father taught him this hate... and I believe that is the reason he became a 1/2 rack plus a day drunk.

3 or 10 I look at his life, and I'm sad. Four kids and no relationship with any of them. Sad. Grandkids that he doesn't even know their names... and they live just two miles away. Sad. No friendships. Sad. No making happy plans with family. Sad.

Thoughts;____

____

____

Sadness
Codependent
Divorce

3 or 10 Jake; my husband; He started being a drunk in his teens, and it has destroyed every part of his life, his children, brother and sister, he doesn't even know his grandchildren names. My vows included loving him forever; my sadness proves I'm still doing it. I'm still doing it... the last thing I wanted was a lawsuit, but I provided him with his request as he asked of me. Sad!!! He begged, me to give up on our marriage and refuses to allow me my half of our stuff. Greedy and childish are a part of his alcoholism, I got him sober but he refused to do the work of healing, making amends, personal responsibility.

3 or 10 That sadness proves me a good person. I continue to pray he is still sober. But his being mean makes me think he is drinking again. Sad!!! I hope I'm wrong. Sadness is good at times. Currently, he is making me sad.

(This was written before the diagnosis of cancer and dying in just 2 months)

Life humbles you as you age. You realize how much time you've wasted on nonsense.

Thoughts;_______________________________________

____

____

Healing
Apologizing
Self Perseverance

3 or 10 Well, this set me back on my heels. I'm going through THIS. And I don't know how to deal with it. At what point do we "forget" horrid behaviors? Usually, it is after an apology. But more than not, the apology never comes. I have four people whose behavior toward me is so deplorable that I just turned my back. In the 12 Steps, there is "make amends," and I wait. Maybe I should mail the "Step 9" text, but I know it would do zero good. These four are motivated by selfishness. They lack humanity, empathy, or personal responsibility. I'm forced to accept that. And it sucks to avoid them. So, I resort to avoidance, which leaves me out of family events.

8. Made a list of all persons we had harmed, and became willing to make amends to them all.

9. Made direct amends to such people wherever possible, except when to do so would injure them or others.

10. Continued to take personal inventory and when we were wrong promptly admitted it.

AA.org

Thoughts;____

____

____

Grief
Family
Boundaries

3 or 10 A wise man told me, "Family is Everything," and he, for the most part, lived it. As a child I witnessed true "honor thy mother and father". His mother was not able to care for herself so for a while my uncle lived with her in his teens. And then she was placed in the nursing home. Dementia was part of it. Grampa went everyday to feed her. Yes; even when she didn't know him, he fed her bite by bite. I wish he could hold that truth for others to still attend to family, at times they forget they are members of a herd. I'm a bit bitter about the family that couldn't be bothered with Indy's funeral. My oldest daughter, aunts and uncles, and dozens of cousins could not be bothered with helping my daughter place a tiny little casket in the ground. The only time I have ever fainted, my brother and my son, pallbearers, was busy with their support and a friend caught me whispering "I got you mama, breath, your baby girl needs you". I rested into him until I could get my legs to hold me up. Where were the 200+ family members? Not supporting the worst moment my daughter was forced to face.

3 or 10 Grampa, I miss your instruction, guidance, and sound advice for family ugliness. I'm going to work to put them where they belong. And that is not "me avoiding" all the rest of the family.

I don't forget loyalty and friendship. Nor do I forget betrayal and disrespect.

Thoughts;____

____

____

Denial

Anger

Grief

3 or 10 I appreciate all the calls, texts, and friends stopping by. Grief is a tough one, always. A friend lost her pup, and my comment was, "It is only because of deep love that we go through deep sorrow." Jake died 30 days ago. So the reality is I'm doing good. Yep, work every day, sleep better than 3 weeks ago, and focus on good in the world. Yet, at times in my day, I float backward in healing. When Garrison passed, people would say, "he's in a better place." Please take note that those words do not provide healing comfort. "Heaven gained an angel" only rubs salt in the wound. The most healing were the words, "Do you want to talk?" thank you to everyone who has let me talk. Jake 56 should be planning the next 30 years. Garrison, seven months, would be 4 1/2 now, should be in kindergarten this year, riding a bike, and learning to look both ways before crossing the street. Death sets us backward. Between denial, anger, and acceptance are days filled with laughter and tears. And sometimes both at the same time. Depression and Bargaining are in those five stages as well. Sometimes feeling happy causes guilt.

3 or 10 never scold self for tears that must come. It's okay to feel sad, lost, forsaken. Jake passing at 56 is far different than Garrison at 7 months. With Indy I felt robbed, with Jake I feel as if he should have faced the years of painful sickness before it moved around his body to not be able to be treated. No I'm not blaming Jake for his death I'm sure at diagnosis he felt defeated, yet; I hope he also took personal responsibility. I hope he realized how much he is missed.

Thoughts;____

____

____

Death
Grief
Friendships

3 or 10 I want to pick up the phone and have Jake answer my call. I wish Mom would tell me to get moving. I wish for Garrison to say, "Granny, I love you," but this horrid thing called death and grief is in my way. I'm doing okay... well, at this moment, but at the next, I might need to cry.

3 or 10 THAT IS OK, I'm ok. Grief overwhelming us is 100% ok. At times all we can find words for is to acknowledge and say; Thank You for all the calls and texts and for stopping by. Annette Kaye

Someone out there feels better because you exist.

Thoughts;_____________________________________

____

____

Anger
Protection
Self Aware

3 or 10 I am amazed at times at some things I read. Yep, I'm reading something. This book "The Dance With Anger" has been in my life since 1991, and I have always found "something else" to read. But on page 12, it says, "How does one use this book? Very slowly. No matter how crazy or self-defeating our current behavior appears to be, it exists for a reason and may serve a positive and protective function for yourself or others; if you want to change, it is important to do so slowly so that we have the opportunity to observe and test out the impact of one small but significant change in a relationship system."

Oh My!! Relationship System!!! My Oh My! Married, Mother, Sister, Granny, SYSTEM!

3 or 10 I am, but 50% of every relationship I have. EXCEPT with me!! I am 100% of that one! And I have always known that is the only one I can fix, change, or adjust!!!

Thoughts;____
____
____

Moving Forward

3 or 10 My entire back is in spasm from lifting heavy boxes. Such simple advice!!! Ha, it's not so simple. I'm a Gemini, so worry and fretting are born in, the twins always look at all sides of problems. Last night, I finally gave in and took a muscle relaxer before bed cuz my back is just ridged with stress. Thank God I slept all night!!! First time in a month. So, maybe tonight I can just sleep. Three positive thoughts are easy: my store is doing well. It's not as good as I would like, but it's forward movement every day. Yesterday, I started on emptying the horse trailer... 16X8x6, how many cubic feet is that? Darin or Saige? Ha Ha, is proof that I have peeps to answer the tough questions. So how many cubic feet is 40X8X9? Yep, it's full too!!! Today, I had a return customer who took out three big boxes. Yep, I have shelf space to fill up. So my store is very busy, lots of inventory, and things to do.

So 3 or 10 Sunshine is coming through the door. The cat is soaking it up... in the horse trailer way up front are some lamps that I desperately need... so off my bottom would be a valid plan today!!!

Don't use your energy to worry. Use your energy to believe, create, trust, grow and heal.

Thoughts;____

____

____

Relaxation
Relationships

3 or 10 So I sit... yep, ya can catch me sitting. In 6 months, 11 days... I left my husband. I bought a shop where I'm building a house. I bought a secondhand store with some stuff. I moved a semi-full out of WA, unloaded, and kind of put it away... I moved seven breeding dogs, building them a safe home with dividers and a 1/4 acre play yard... had one litter, and two are pregnant.... sold a house in WA... built an online art gallery... got a 40 ft storage container, purchased an estate and literally filled it to the ceiling.... started my online bookstore again... became a FedEx and USPS shipping station... filed a lawsuit against Jake... Jake died... I took on a wonderful 18-year-old that I adore...I might call him "my kid.".... I've worked hard on an election campaign for a new Sheriff... I met Ammon Bundy... built a couple of wonderful new friendships.

3 or 10 I have a wonderfully happy, sad, exciting, unexpected, busy, crazy, moving forward life, and ya might catch me sitting!

Positive people are not positive because they've skated through life. They're positive because they've been through hell and decided they don't want to live there anymore.

Thoughts;____

____

____

Patriotism
Love
Forgiveness

3 or 10 As I prepare for the civil war, I'm saddened that it is less than three weeks away. I'm not a conspiracy theorist, yet I know conspiracies are a real part of society, so I know they go on in politics. Monster was here this weekend, and when I turned on the news, he piped in, "You know granny Trump is a liar." I asked where he heard that. He said, "The radio." Saige rolled her eyes and said, "Good Lord," with a tone. A funny little moment came, and I pressed him; he said Trump had lied about "the COVID." Monster is seven, so I kept the conversation light. FB, Google, Twitter, and CNN should all be held responsible for the civil discourse. When I was a kid, we had reporters and news. I was terrified of "the gorillas," (1970's wars overseas) and I am not even sure today what army or country they were in. We currently have institutions pushing this civil war. The news should compare. I remember semi-trucks being escorted by the military into Chicago, which was under President Carter!!! In fact, it was an ugly time in America. The LA riots were ugly as well. Ferguson was an incredible display of heathens on the news. The news in the year 2020 has not learned from history, and now it's a bunch of opinion commentary based on personal prejudice.

Yep, "Lemon" is a black man that is a victim first, and he is on the news passing along his prejudices. How did he become a victim in the greatest country in the world? His grandparents told him white people hate him. My family fought in the Civil War and managed part of the Underground Railroad. I was never taught to hate... in fact, I was taught to love, forgive, and patriotism. I was never told people were the color of their skin. Yet, just recently, a white man told me, "Republicans are white supremacists."... I laughed and said, "As a Republican, I have God, Guns, and Guts... and my God told me not to be a white or any color supremacist," But this leaves a mark.... my morals are great and being degraded because of them has created a humbled human to feel angry.

3 or 10 I will stand, I will be humble to all people, and I will shoot back. I'm sad to watch this civil war... how do the words civil and war fit together? They don't!!! There isn't anything civil about war... or "the gorillas."

Social media has made too many

of you comfortable with disrespecting

people and not getting

punched in the mouth for it.

Thoughts;_______________________________________

____

____

Priority
Stress Management

3 or 10 I've missed my daily writing. FB blocked all three of my accounts for weeks. Lots of conservatives got blocked. Wanna know what I did? I posted an anger Management support group in July and a doily (yes, the beautiful crochet doily) in August. Yep, that is how stupid the left thinks. Power and control. Narcissists!!! But Congress called them before a committee. Congress won't involve free speech or due process!!! Congress is about worthless. FB creates anger at their unfair actions. Maybe they should come to my anger management class... haha. The fact that FB won't answer the phone or messages is proof they don't respect Americans. Yep, no respect and that is abusive. Why is America divided? Right and Wrong!!! Maybe I should create an FB account to simply report news articles that are left. Nope, don't have time.

3 or 10 busy days working. Helping a couple that is 88 years old moving. They are so very sweet. Married 71 years!!! Yep, I'm going to focus on that.

My focus shall be on good today!!!

David didn't need to know Goliath's strength because he already knew God's. Pastor Greg Locke.

Thoughts;____
____
____

Stress Management
Organization
Rant

3 or 10 So I went for a mammogram this morning. Dr orders, not there
UGGG. Going in the hospital, a bitchy little girl stopped me at the
door. "Have you come in contact with COVID-19?" Well, I have no
idea. Does protocol change because of the answer? IT IS A
HOSPITAL!!! Hand sanitizer and masks were required....

The sign on the door said "can't visit," so people are dying alone...
what the heck!!! For God's sake!!! Ok, that rant is over.

I do know someone who passed from COVID-19, but I also know of a
suicide in WA (more than likely from the shutdown). This mess in
America is stressing everyone... I haven't missed a day of work; but my
coffee shop sends employees home. UGGG! Ok, that rant is over.

The election is almost over... thank God!!! This crazy news is crazier
than usual. Do you know you can channel surf and find every opinion
known to man??? There are not many facts, though. Ok, that rant is
over.

3 or 10 mammogram is over for the year... 4 phone calls to get orders
that a medical office or hospital lost... ironic!!! During COVID,
someone really dropped the ball...Lord help us... our medical profession
is less on the ball than; the girl that makes my coffee... but it wasn't me
I drug my ass to the appointment on time. My coffee is perfect!!!
Thanks, Little One!!! (Batista nickname) You rock!!! I'm cranky
today... makes the days I do not look better!!! Ha ha, Marnie, I can find
positive in cranky!!! Rant over; see ya all tomorrow.

**There is a 0.01% chance of rain and I'm appalled that nobody
outside is using their umbrella.**

Thoughts;____
____
____

Family
Good Morals
Wisdom

3 or 10 Yep, too old to fight. I've never really been a fistfight kind of girl. Dad used to have Darin and I box each other. I never liked it. But Dad wanted to prepare us for life. I'm pretty balanced because of the lessons important to the people raising me up. Grampa lived patriotism, and we kids just saw his daily doings as important. Dad rose up before the sun and was always out the door to work hard to provide for his family. And we played hard with the best toys money could buy. Mom cooked. She always made sure we were well fed, either canning or Christmas candy. She was dedicated to her family and friends. Yesterday, Keith and Roy built a wall for me. So instinctively, I cooked dinner. Nothing real special or hard... grilled cheese with sausage and Doritos. Yes, 20 minutes to show "I care." thank you, Mom!!! I passed this trait to my girls Saige & Whisper, both are wonderful cooks. Saige drives me crazy cuz she can put out a spread and never get winded. She needs a salt shaker!!! Ha ha, inside joke!!!

3 or 10 My good and bad came from others. Gifts silently!!!! Or curse!!! But I am who I am. There is lots of good going on. Yep, I was raised as a fighter, but now too old to fight. And I've never run a day in my life... another good trait given silently.

PRIVATE PROPERTY

THINK TWICE

PROPERTY OWNER IS

TO OLD TO FIGHT

TO FAT TO RUN

AND

TO LAZY TO ARGUE

Thoughts;____

____

____

Patriotism
God Fearing
Satan

3 or 10 I'm all stirred up. Rumor has it... F off... if I talked like that. But I don't, so KISS MY BUTT... instead of chattering gossip, why not knock on the door and ask. Or invite yourself in (coffee is on) to SEE what is going on!!! Oh heck no, that would be respectable!!! If you did have any self-respect, you wouldn't spread rumors!!! But rumors it is. WTHeck is wrong with people? If you stopped by or took the time to get to know me, you would...

Watch me work 10-12 hours a day

Meet all 7 of my very well-behaved dogs

And one cat

You would see a Bible on the table

You could watch me pray

You would know I'm overwhelmed all the time as I make my way to build another business (YEA 5 to date)

You would be offered dinner with a smile, so I don't eat alone.

You would hear me chat with friends 45 year relationships, as dear to me, grandbabies, and dog owners that I mentor.

You would see me honor the military, America, and family. (Yours included!!!)

3 or 10 KISS MY BUTT if you don't see a really good MORAL person. By the way, in 1969, St Maries became my home. 1981 Emida became home... I married into the military, so I left for 20 years!!!! But I'm back, and YOU will not run me out of town... keep causing trouble...... I'll stand my ground... Or become my friend; you won't find a better one!!! The choice is yours... but the RUMORS have been noted... which one of you is not worth me trusting? Rumors and gossip are Satan's tools... why are you playing with Satan???

No one is harder on me than me. So take your judgment and shove it up your butt.

Thoughts;_______________________________________

____
____

Reflection
Self Esteem

3 or 10 Who really knows me? Some say I'm bold and harsh; some call me Assertive. I'm both! Some know my religion; some say I'm spiritual; some know my Angels; and some know I talk to the dead, and they answer me! Some ask for advice because they know I read it or thought it through; sometimes Darin tells me to "Shut up and listen!!! My dad's best advice!!! My brother repeats!!! I always chatter!!! But at times, I'm silent... usually that's not good.

Some have called me lazy, yet I normally get more done than most. Some say I'm scattered, but with 1.5 million things on my list each day, I've got lots to do, so lots got started. Some call me Mamma (Whisper), and some roll their eyes and say "MOM!!" (with a tone of Saige), but my second favorite is Red or Granny!!! Jake always called me Red, and Monster and Butch call me Granny, and they know I never tell them "no," so that makes me a softie!!! Some call me knowledgeable, and some call me a "know-it-all all." I'm both! Some know I hate the phone, but I love to chat.

3 or 10 I am a sunny day and a horrid storm! I am hard as nails and soft as cotton!! I am a rainbow after the rain. A hot, strong cup of coffee or a smooth cup of chocolate pudding. I'm me, AnnetteKaye, MOM, and Granny!! A little bit bitchy and a whole lot of lover!!!

If you are shocked by anything I say...you obviously haven't been paying attention to who I am.

Thoughts;____

____

____

Blessings
Self Esteem
Relationships

3 or 10 When I took on this new challenge in my life, (I bought a 5000 square ft retail secondhand antique store) I knew I would have obstacles!!! In fact, only hard work pays well. But I didn't know people would jump in to help. Darin, Rod, Jessica, Don, Roy, Saige, Whisper, Keith, Joan, Steve, Loretta, Doug, Jacob, Schumacher Jewelry, Butch, Jackie, Dakota, Kevin, Terrie, Hank, Dave, Mike, Bill, Danny, and all the customers (some repeat!!! BOOYAH). Trailer loading, unloading, moving furniture, building fences, donations, words of support, advice, and just holding my hand while I'm overwhelmed....

3 or 10

Marnie, is that enough said???

One of the hardest pills I've had to swallow was realizing I meant nothing to people that meant a lot to me.

Thoughts;____

____

____

Manifesting
Thankful
God

3 or 10 The more I thank God, the more I'm given. As I look up to pray, question, or even scream, it is true, the more He shows himself working in my life. I'm amazed at what He can do and also amazed when He does nothing. Of course, as a Father, sometimes he tells me "no". Yet, when he says no, he always shows why. I'm like everyone else, and at times, I get frustrated with the no! Losing never feels good. But it is a fact; a perfect life is not possible with Satan running around.

3 or 10 As I look up, I have a choice to count blessings or curse problems. One feels good, the other takes a bad and amplifies it.... I think I like "feels good."

The "main character" in my favorite book dies... but it's okay. He comes back to life after 3 days. I recommend it 100%!!!

Thoughts;____

____

____

Peaceful
Reflection
Family

3 or 10 Stepping Away From Things That Interfere With Peace!!! As I age, I realized that the book "And They Are All Little Things" was an important instrument for good things to read. I am forced at times to reevaluate moments in time. We all are. A gift; I was given, at a young age was common sense; Dad always said, "Think it through" or "If you want to know how it works, take it apart," talking about engines, yet is true for anything... Peace??? Take it apart!!! What is peace to me? What does peace look like? What does life look like when it is peaceful? So, structure those answers into your world. Yep!!! To create anything good, we must "think it through."

Peace looks like;

A job well done. A task completed. Kindness. Standing my ground. Living my beliefs. Respecting myself. Taking time to heal. Giving myself permission to fail. Forgiveness (myself included)

3 or 10 Thanks, Dad, for repeating "think it through" and "take it apart." I still hear the echo of your voice.

Gemini Mantra
Air-Ruled by Mercury

**My cheerful and excited spirit is
my superpower, I bring so much
vibrance to all those around me.
I'm a communicator and good at
expressing messages that people
need to hear. I am dynamic and
curious, always gaining knowledge.
I am here on this earth to experience
and live, nothing can hold me back.**

Sisters Village x

Thoughts;______________________________________

____

____

Mindfulness
Calming

3 or 10 "Negativity" at times is reality. Yesterday, trying to get things done, I needed Stella out from under my feet, so she was outside, BARKING at Lord only knows what. As I kept getting more and more irritated, my internal person became mad. It hit me: "The barking was upsetting my being," so I stopped what I was doing and let Stella in. A sense of calm flooded in me. At times, people say, "Breathe," and it is true. That is very true; just take your temperature.

Today, I have a list of "get done." I must make sure my internal person doesn't get "mad" at my list. It is better to just thump along rather than overwhelm the mind.

3 or 10 Mindfulness is an amazing gift from the creator, and Buddha shared it every day. Quiet the mind and focus on this moment. So, as I thump along today, I'm going to enjoy not vacuuming but doing a task. The dishes will be warm water on my hands. Dogs in and out will be a moment of loving on the kids.

"All negativity is caused by an accumulation of psychological time and denial of the present. Unease, anxiety, tension, stress, worry - all forms of fear - are caused by too much future, and not enough presence. Guilt, regret, resentment, grievances, sadness, bitterness, and all forms of non-forgiveness are caused by too much past, and not enough presence."

Eckhart Tolle

Thoughts;____
____
____

Motives
Happiness

3 or 10 I enjoy it when I create or help people feel happiness. Organizing peeps, a card of thanks, a remembered special day. Happy people make me feel happy. Yet, there is always the flip side of any coin. Angry, mean, and dumb people frustrate me to my core. People who can't hear or don't care to hear irritate me inside. Sometimes I'm able to giggle at their silliness, but sometimes they just upset me!! Motives!!! That is a deep, dark secret in relationships!!! Check the motives. Is the person wrapped up in their own life and can't see the person in front of them? Are they greedy? I always warn my puppy buyers, "Vets make money from sick animals and selling preventative meds a dog doesn't need." It is the same with Walmart; by never having enough checkers, they are forcing us to use the self-checkout, making Walmart more money!!!

3 or 10 I am constantly checking my motives!!! Yep, what is inside me... if I feel happy or sad!!! Am I giving with a pure heart? Or am I mad because someone else couldn't hear? Today, I just want to finish something. Yep, the check mark beside a task is finished!!!

I AM A WANDERER,
Gemini Sun

BUT MY EMOTIONS ARE RATHER COMPOSED.
Virgo Moon

I THINK IN A INTUITIVE WAY,
Mercury in Cancer

BUT EXPRESS MY ENERGY INA PASSIVE WAY.

Mars in Libra

IN LOVE, I SEEK ATTENTION.

Venus in Leo

MY ROLE IN THE WORLD IS THE RULEBREAKER.

Aquarius Rising

Thoughts;____

____

____

Change of Plans
Positive Thinking

3 or 10 This is a point to ponder. I strive to look forward, but life struggles are a fact. The trick I've been taught, by Marnie, is LOOK TO THE GOOD. This morning I have a list of 100 things that are just crap in my life. YET; to flip the coin on everyone, I can opt into the good. Snow!!! I love snow-covered views. As a kid in Idaho, we had a lot of snow days, but today, I have "stuff to do," Butt guess what? It "is" a snow day!!! So here is what I get served with my morning coffee....

I can be mad all day that driving to town for parts is not happening!!! Or, as a responsible adult (haha), I can breathe in this "snow day" and shift my plans. Maturity says "stomping my feet" is not the adult thing to do. But I thought about it. Life always puts stumbling blocks in the way. Oh boy, do they get heavy at times? I think the trick is not moving those blocks around but going around them. Letting them lay!!!!

3 or 10 Where is my snow shovel? Oh yeah, right where I let it lay last time I used it!!!! On a good note, THAT IS WHERE THE SNOW IS!!!! Maybe I'll take a couple of pics and share North Idaho snow days with friends and family!!!

"No one ever injured their eyesight by looking on the bright side."

Thoughts;____
____
____

Peaceful
Loved

Looking around the world and knowing that you have someone willing to move mountains for you is a gift like no other. The peaceful feeling as you drift to sleep knowing you are loved is the greatest of gifts a man can give a woman, no roses, no money, just that precious feeling of knowing love. AnnetteKaye

Thoughts;____

____

____

Honesty

It is my hope today that all are honest, honest in word and deed, those in my tiny little circle and those around the world. Honesty is the only way to show another person who you really are; it is the only form of solid communication; if you said it, wrote it, or expressed it, I hope it was honest. AnnetteKaye

Thoughts;____

____

____

Organize
Clutter

TAKE OUT THE GARBAGE!!!

Sometimes, that includes people; cleaning the closets or organizing a drawer is so freeing. The same thing in life is to throw away that or those that don't serve you. Broken, disorganized, garbage people; it is their choice to be that way. I did this with a woman not long ago, and it feels so good; no more negative or nastiness from her; an email goes to junk and is deleted. IT FEELS GREAT TO HAVE HER "The GARBAGE"; OUT OF MY LIFE, so clean up your life; get rid of the garbage. Life looks better when organized and clean. AnnetteKaye

Thoughts;____

____

____

Suicide

Have you ever had a friend commit suicide? Do you sometimes wonder how sad a person must be to do such a thing? What is it that, as a society, is created to cause or effect such matters? Points to ponder: are you the best friend you can be? Is there someone in the world waiting for your love or respect? Do you need a friend? Are you in pain? Pay attention, people. We, as a group, need each other........AnnetteKaye

Thoughts;____

____

____

Love
Change
Acknowledge

3 or 10 "The fastest way to get your wife to cheat is by continually accusing her of cheating." This has been true for 100's of years. And it's not just cheating; it can be lying, stealing, hiding facts, refusing to help, etc. The more I'm told I'm lazy, the lazier I get; the more I'm told I don't cook, the less I cook; the more I'm told I'm spiteful, the more revengeful I get. YEP, I'M NORMAL!!! Ha!! I never thought of myself as normal. So where is the off switch on people that just degraded another human being? There isn't one!! It's a fact; I do not control others' behavior. I'm only in charge of my actions.

3 or 10 It is my job to recognize ME!!! Fix ME!! Love ME!! Change ME!! And yes, even CELEBRATE ME!!

Thoughts;____

____

____

Anger
Grief
Success

3 or 10 "Anger is a Secondary Emotion." let that wash over you for a moment... yep, as it seems, anger is never the "root;" it is instead the "tree." So our mental health must ask, "What is the root of sadness? Disappointment? Frustrated? Stress? Illness? GRIEF? Yes, I put a huge weight on grief... the reason is it is not talked about enough." Grief could be because of death, but we are not given permission to grieve divorce, a business failure, or even the news. YES, the news. Where do we emotionally put all these shootings, storms, accidents, politics, and abuses? Yep, where do we "put" it? The failure of marriage is another "huge" one that we are not given the tools to deal with. Marriages and family relationships don't just wake up one morning in failure... there are always "root" reasons, but in every marriage or family feud I've ever witnessed, "the end" is anger, anger, ugly!!!

3 or 10 A Milestone!!! Monster has been signing my credit card slips for 6 years now... last year, he signed Jaydon, and granny was filled with pride.... on his trip this week, we learned his phone number (lots of high fives), and I gasped with delight when we had lunch.... look at what "my Monster" did!!!!! Saige, Whisper.

Photo of; Credit Card Receipt

Monster signed for the first time

Thoughts;____

____

____

Understanding
Knowledge

3 or 10 "Some" people just don't understand life's rules. They just don't understand the English language. It is really sad when a person twists words to fit their agenda.

STOP is a pretty simple word.

LEAVE ME ALONE is pretty straightforward.

I DON'T WANT YOU IN MY LIFE is basic.

But there are people that "just don't understand". They are "the last word" agenda, and that is hilarious. Yep, it turns a person's life into a sick and twisted psychology. Funny when I come up against a person with "last-word derangement," I giggle. I find these types of people funny. They force their presents until they are hated. And the last word is "look at the psycho."

3 or 10 Jake and I shared a wonderful weekend with Saige and the boys. A carnival, fireworks, moose hunting, panoramic views from 5000 ft above sea level, food, fun, laughter, relaxing, reading, chatting, 3-wheeler rides, the History Channel, dog kisses, tattoo artists, some volunteer time, breakfast in bed, 6-year-old cooking with granny, and pop hugs, 2-year-old wet kissing, I do love my life!!!

High Score

791

Thoughts;____
____
____

Self Perseverance
Abuse
Satan

3 or 10 I have been faced with many Narcissistic people. They are a sad bunch. I have tears. I feel that some have called me an empath. I feel happy, and at times, I just stand in ahhh at other people being happy... yes, I cry at weddings, sweet 16's, and funerals. Proof that I am not Narcissistic. One of the big parts of the Narcissist is manipulation... this is my downfall in these relationships I'm faced with. I always jump in to help when asked, so the Narcissistic person has me. I am in their sights to get their needs met. Then I realized what was happening and got angry with them and me. Even when they deserve anger, I go through a range of emotions. Guilt is one, but resentment is the one that hurts me.

3 or 10 I have come to realize that narcissistic people are indeed Satan in sheep's clothing. I have also come to know that narcissistic people can't see their behavior as a fact of their own making. They are so blinded by selfishness the pain in the faces, expressions of others can't be noticed. Sad, very, very sad. I will continue being loving, loyal, and living in light. I'm not a Narcissistic Person, but that is a good thing.

No one gets more upset than a narcissist being accused of something they definitely did.

Thoughts;____
____
____

Grief
Lessons
Happiness

3 or 10 I have found that grieving never stops. Loss is 100%, and a piece of the soul is gone forever. Five years ago, I lost Red Puppy and my mother 3 months apart! Crushed by both losses!!! Devastated! But God would teach me.... "this pain is nothing."

"Here, I'm gonna take Indy and show you complete horrific sadness; I'm going to take you to think of suicide and see if you can recover." Well, I'm still here, but I've forever changed! I look back... I ponder their faces, smiles, laughter, and tears. They are never far from my thoughts. And I fight to feel moments of happiness. Yes, I struggle. Did God choose me to struggle to be alive? There is a deep rudeness to grief. As I get older, my friends are dying, and I eat potluck dinners at funerals, not celebrations. This came up today because yesterday Jake said, "What is the big deal? I forgot your birthday." Oh my!!! I'm alive and worth celebrating, not just waiting for a potluck at my funeral.... he is male and just doesn't get it!!!

3 or 10 I beg you all to CELEBRATE AND CHERISH the people in your life... a kind text... a note for no reason... a call to say "I love you," or lunch to catch up, or even flowers delivered at work so the office can see "someone gives a hoot." Sad despair is lurking around every corner.... and even the happiest people need to be loved even more!!!! I hope three friends feel loved today... I hope ten feel appreciated.

I believe the hardest part of healing after you've lost someone you love, is to recover the 'you' that went away with them.

Thoughts;____

____

____

Family
Dedication
Unconditional Love

3 or 10 Saige, Whisper, Bethanie, and Daniel, as your mom, I might be the only person willing to lie down and die in your place. Struggle, stress, frets, fits, and failures... I am the unconditional love that is a God-given gift. Our hearts used to beat together; mine gave you life, and yours is my reason for living. Tears and fights are a part of being a mom, but tears and fights are also the bond of happiness.

3 or 10 Blessed with four, it is just a fact. No, not at all. I'm very "blessed" with four.

Ain't no relationship more important than your relationship with your kids.

Thoughts;____

____

____

Self Aware
Respect
Acceptance

3 or 10 There are lots of things I can't do. State Fairs and Concerts make me nervous and filled with fear. It's ok!!! IT IS OK!!! To have a list of NOPE! I usually say the wrong thing. Not really the words,, but my voice sucks. It's ok!! Loud and harsh. Even I love you comes out wrong. So, the people around me need to think of what I can fix, change, or adjust. Kind of hard to change eye color, height, and voice. I do spend a lot of time reminding people that my voice just is!!! Yes, it is!

But my heart is good.

My words are good. And my intent is good! No one really knows how often I pray about my words and what others hear! Yes, I pray others hear the right words as I intend them. I can't change my voice box! That is a fact.

I can't feel good about living outside my beliefs. I'm going through a complete dilemma right now. My husband wants me to "not" do what is right. It is killing a part of my soul, a bit of my being. It is killing him, too, but in a different way. He knows right from wrong but wants no personal responsibility for the issue. So he is doing nothing, which is causing him anxiety, problems, no sleep, and grouchy; it is causing his self-esteem to take a hit. Sad to watch, but HIS!!!

He wants me to "agree" with him... I CAN'T... Not mine to fix, change, or adjust. HIS!!

3 or 10 Respect comes from Respectable Behavior. Personal Responsibility is integrity, and I can't do State Fairs or Concerts. But it's ok!!! I'm ok! At least I recognize my limits!!! That is good!! I'm good!

Find someone who is proud to have you, scared to lose you, fights for you, appreciates you, respects you, care for you and loves you unconditionally.

Thoughts;____
____
____

Remember
Family

3 or 10 Today is one of those special days that always tug at my heart, both happy and sad. Robert E Lyons was born on 10/15/1916, but to me, he will always be "Grampa." I would bake a cake or a custard pie... and even in the years I was learning to cook, grampa would tell me it was delicious. He taught me many things. He could quote the Bible chapter and verse. And he did often. He was maybe the kindest man I ever met. He taught me more about animals by accident than all books could print. His patriotism was above the fold, but his love for the individual soldier was heart-tugging. Many times, the car stopped; he got out and saluted a flag-draped coffin as it passed. I would ask, "Did you know him?" And would be told, "I fought with him because he fought for us." Grampa was wise beyond his years and quiet.... Until... and when he spoke, we listened. Darin inherited so many traits from Grampa. I often tell DARIN, "You got that from Grampa." Now, as Saige is an adult, I tell her that too. HAPPY BIRTHDAY GRAMPA!!! A custard pie, some cribbage, a nap with the TV on, and I'm sure you kissed Grama at breakfast; I miss you, love you, and honor this day for you.

Happy

Heavenly

Birthday

Thoughts;____
____
____

Intuition
Teaching

3 or 10 At times, we allow people to push their beliefs on us. It usually comes with an internal icky feeling. It is that "icky" feeling that we rebalance to our belief system. That internal conversation is absolutely the most important conversation we have on any day in our lives. Happiness and depression, self-worth and confidence, or insecurity and self-respect are all voices from our internal wisdom. I very rarely live against that voice. Sometimes, it is my Grampa telling me, "The only thing worse than a liar is a thief, and the only thing worse than a thief is a liar," or my dad saying, "If you want to know how it works, take it apart and put it back together" or moms whisper of "You can't make candy when it is raining" some times it is the ten commandments "Don't covenant" or the constitution saying "freedom of religion." Sometimes, it comes from a stranger's smile.

3 or 10 I have a wonderful internal rule system. Sometimes, I fail "it," yet it gently pulls me back to the center. Sometimes, it screams; sometimes, it is a trusted family whisper; sometimes, it is God himself, but it is always a guiding force. Who is watching? From heaven above to Monster and Butch or even me!!!

I thought about quitting, but then I noticed who was watching.

Thoughts;____

____

____

Family
Relationships
Wisdom

3 or 10 Not long ago, Saige and I were chatting and playing a game on the phone, and Saige pipes off with, "You can't play cards you don't have." Well, it made me burst with watching Loren and Mom teach Saige to play cribbage. But it pushed deeper on me, reminding me that Monster and Butch will hear lessons from past people they never even met. But now the words push even harder on me.

YOU CAN NOT PLAY CARDS YOU DO NOT HAVE.

Of course, in any card game, that is a fact. But in any situation, it is also true. I'm struggling inside my own house. A huge life-altering mess. It's so simple to me. No thought, sorting options, or questions to ask, yet no action is moving things forward. So I called my brother; I first said, "I need you to balance me." Darin listened to the facts. And as simple as could be, he said, "People refuse to do what is right because it would require they DO" oh my God "cards I don't have." It is simple to me because I am willing to "do," yet Jake refuses to "do"; his laziness overrides right and wrong. He doesn't want information, he is not going to read a book, he won't take care of business, and he doesn't care that I am losing respect. Cards I don't have! 3 or 10, as I re-hear, my mother generally tells Saige, "You can't play cards you don't have." 15-2 15-4 15-6 Oh my. Mom was teaching a moment and wisdom in her kid, grandkid, and great grandkids; today's cards are 15-31.

Do you ever look at your child and start smiling? Not because your child did something amazing, just smiling because that's who God blessed you with.

Thoughts;____

____

____

Grief
Love
Death

3 or 10 It is "child loss" month! That in itself is sad, but I promise you won't know gut-wrenching lingering grief (PAIN) until ya lose a child (grand). In the first months, I fought God, felt abandoned, and even questioned his love for me. Then I became suicidal quietly; no one knew the tornado that was distorting my soul; it's coming up three years since I fainted for the first and only time in my life. Me and God have reconciled, my heart is still broken, and I focus on Monster and Butch, and I have made the decision to get a memorial tattoo, so I turned to Paul to help me through my tears. I was met with kindness and a loving soul that promised perfection. And I got this picture. And I cry... wipe my tears, and come back to cry again. Saige is getting Garrison's EKG, his heartbeat, birthday, and death date will be included. The infinity loop is a bit long, so I may remove it. One star for each month Indy was with me, "My INDY"

3 or 10; this is going on my forearm because hiding from the world is not why Indy was in my life—Jesus purple "garrison," Kelly Green, "Indy," and yellow shooting stars. And guess what? "Tears" even today, Paul kept his promise. Thank You!!! Whisper, where will you put yours? You will love Paul. Saige, where is yours going to be? Exile Art Collective

Thoughts;____

____

____

Thankful
Praise
God Gifts

3 or 10 At times, silent screams and a moment of solitude become a treasure. Rushing around, I drive past a piece of "oh my" Mountain View. I pull in a wide spot and thank god for his gifts. Just a moment in time, no! Just a moment to treasure and give thanks!

Photo; Mountain View 10 mile wide valley Breathtaking

Thoughts;____
____
____

Self Aware
Thankful

Good Morning! Time to focus on my 3 or 10...

Sometimes, finding three positive thoughts or ten blessings gets overrun by life. My brother posted this picture, which did not make me think of life's injustice. Instead, it made me think of the fiber of my being. I don't invite people to my home, and there is a valid reason. I can only take so much. Little snippets of time, I love the people in my life. But this castle is mine; outside drama is not needed. If you are on the list of people who are welcome, I will get you coffee and cook you dinner. It's a short list. I chat with friends from years gone by. Last night, I was on the phone with a friend from Germany, so thirty-three years of friendship. I have lots of those. I went to coffee with a man who had known me all my life and a friend for just a year. Current events and chat about our fathers working on the railroad. But I got up and returned to my castle with my books, dogs, and a cat that irritates everyone. My best friend and I have been friends for 40+ years. She moved far away, but once a year, she comes home, and I cook for her. (She loves my gravy!) we are lifelong friends because of respect and a deep God connection. Yep, daily, we pray for each other.

3 or 10 I am GOOD! And my internal stuff is good! And my external stuff is good! And sometimes 3 or 10 is just a look at the good, today or 50 years ago.

It's not that I don't play with others......I just don't play well with liars, cheaters, users, thieves, fakes, players, and butts.

Thoughts;____

____

____

Grief
Family
Strength

3 or 10 I told Saige to play "If you're going through hell" at my funeral. It says, "Just keep on going." I love it. Loren was really sick; my stepdad of 30+ years was in pain and dying. My mom was in her own kind of hell. My kids were in pain. My brother would tear up. Believe it or not, I am not strong enough to be all for all! One day, I sent the girls to school and headed to Othello. That song took me from 0 to 60 in 1/4 mile on my way home. I pulled over, lost my mind, bawled my head off, collected my inner strength, wiped my tears, and headed back down the road. "Just Keep On Goin" has been my fight song ever since. There is a lot of "hell" in life.

3 or 10 I own the place.

If your Path demands you to walk through hell. Walk As If you Own the Place.

Thoughts;____

____

____

Self Aware

3 or 10 "What you think of me is none of my business." Fact because when I drift to sleep, I am the only one there! Well, not really, my dogs are there, too!

3 or 10 My peeps know, and they love me!

People may destroy your image and stain your personality, but they can't take away your good deeds because no matter how they describe you, you will still be admired by those who really know you better.

Thoughts;____

____

____

Self Aware
Love Language

3 or 10 I am an "Act of Service" person. I feel love and love, by the "do". "Love Language" might be one of the most important books I have read. What is an act of service? Well, for me, it is "doing" the "stuff", fixing a drippy faucet, or starting a pickup on a cold morning, or burger drive-thru on the days I'm too busy to cook. It sells raffle tickets for veterans or posts motorcycle rides on Facebook. Acts of service cost very little but are truly priceless to me. Whisper called last night for nothing, and it was an hour of good. We solved no world problems; we made no earth-shaking plans. Instead, we chatted about kittens, cooking failures, days off, and Sam Elliot. And life was better because of it. Jake is an "Affirmation" guy. He wants me to boost him up with kind, loving words. He wants me to always agree, even to lie to him about his behaviors. When I disagree, soft-spoken or screaming, I'm wrong! He believes Act of Service means he is degraded as a man. He is giving in to a list of demands from a woman. Oh My! Believe me, those thoughts don't work in life. I will continue to bake for friends for a variety of reasons. I have a friend that I absolutely trust; his humor and advice are always good. When I come up missing in the afternoon, Jake always asks, "How is Dave?" Dave is always good. He always says something hilarious that takes my mind drift away from the struggles and gives my mind a break. So, therapy 101 and Dave are free.

3 or 10 Acts of Service If you want me to feel loved, it is acts of service, the call for no reason, the latte that shows up, the helping me move, the dishes after dinner, the quiet when I nap, or a bouquet that for no reason pops up. And in reverse, if you want to know if I love you, it is raffle tickets I sold, volunteering with your group, baking a cake, doing internet research to solve a problem, folding a basket of laundry, or taking you out to lunch. Do I love you? Did I "do" for you? Do you want me to feel loved? Ask me to sell your raffle tickets or give you a ride because your pickup is in the shop.

The Five Love Languages

Affirmation: Your coffee is delicious.

Acts of service: I made you coffee.

Receiving gifts: Here's a coffee.

Quality time: Let's go get a coffee.

Physical Touch: Let me hold you like a coffee.

Thoughts;_______________________________________

____

____

Respect
Loving

3 or 10 To Respect! This may very well be the most important word in the dictionary. Love depends on it. Friendships count on it. Laws demand it. God and the Bible preach it. Boundaries are set by it. Relationships fail because of it. So, what does it mean to respect? The other day, I was told, "I can't talk to you because you don't agree." I pondered this. To agree and to respect are very different things. A person can respect and disagree. To be asked to agree, has nothing to do with respecting. I completely respect this person; I have done nothing to interfere, stop, or even try to change their mind.

I own dogs; Jake doesn't agree with fences, let them run wild; if they get bred by the neighbor's dog or hit by a car, so be it, there won't be poop by the house. My fencing is leaned up against a wall, and there is enough to fence probably three acres; he refuses to put up a fence, he refuses to allow me to put up a fence, and every time I look at the fence, I am both; angry and hurt because I feel I have no value, I'm not Respected.

My business is not respected, but he gives me bills to pay as money comes in. So, how do I get what I need from someone who doesn't respect me? I can't; because of that, when he says, "I love you," I roll my eyes.

Sometimes, to get to 3 or 10, We must sort out the crap in our lives. To disagree is not bad, to own dogs is not bad, to believe in fences is not bad, to make a living is not bad, and even to roll eyes is not bad.

3 or 10 I am not bad; I respect others, and when I disagree, I have solid reasons for doing so.

Noun: Re-spect

A feeling of deep admiration for someone or something elicited by their abilities, qualities, or achievements. "the director had a lot of respect for Douglas as an actor."

Similar: Esteem and regard.

Due regard for the feelings, wishes, rights, or traditions of others. "Young people's lack of respect for their parents"

Similar: Due regard, Consideration

Verb: Admire (someone or something deeply as a result of their abilities, qualities, or achievements. "She was expected by everyone she worked with."

Similar: Esteem and admire.

Thoughts;____

____
____

Prayer
Grateful

3 or 10 "Pray" so many times we are told to pray. Pray for others; pray for the drunk, pray for the criminal, pray for your kids, pray for your parents, pray to God! My life is proof that prayer works and doesn't work. Proof that at times the answer is yes and at times it is no. "Seek and ye shall find". Look for the good, and you can find it. I'm always challenged to "seek" positive thoughts. I'm always challenged to "seek" gratitude.

So, on this day, my 3 or 10 is to pray for positivity, pray for a grateful heart, pray to feel uplifted, pray for strength, pray for the ability to say "I pressed on", pray for change, pray for others, and pray for myself.

If you rearrange the letters in Depression, you'll get "I pressed on." Your current situation is not your final destination.

Thoughts;____

____

____

Productive

3 or 10 Nervous and Excited! Oh my... yep, I'm stepping out of my comfort zone. I look back on life, and these steps, if baby steps or jumping off a cliff, are always good to make it happen. Sometimes, it was a huge failure, but sometimes, it was a huge uplifting event. When a failure is still perfect, as with any failure their is a learning curve. With learning, the "comfort zone" has expanded. Reading a bad book is reading; the failure of a new recipe makes the perfect so much more tasty. With this gray hair is wisdom; mine is gray, not an attempt to look 20 years younger. I own it.

3 or 10 I'm nervous and excited today, and my plans are all about me. Well, no, not really. I rarely do all about myself, but as the day pushes along, I hope the excitement settles the nervousness.

You have a choice each and every single day. I choose to feel blessed. I choose to feel grateful. I choose to be excited. I choose to be thankful. I choose to be happy.

Thoughts;____
____
____

Patriotism
Beliefs
Tolerance

3 or 10

Sometimes, "drastic" change is needed in life, friends, jobs, and location. I'm one of those people who is excited and enthusiastic about positive change. Starting new projects and goals created in me a passion. I've never been a mundane, stale, or "stable" person, yet stable defines my inner being. But at times, we look at life and "need" to shake things up. In my stableness is a hidden secret of a love for change. As friends and homes are years and years, I also currently have five different businesses going. One thing that feeds my need for change is dog rescue, getting out and "saving" them. Same with pups, I don't know the day they will come, the colors in the litter, or how many, noon or middle of the night. Yet, I owned a microwave on two continents, three states, two husbands, and 15 years. I've been wearing one pair of earrings for 27 years and one necklace chain for 27 and 23 years for the pendant.

3 or 10 Saige and Whisper perfectly represent some of the best parts of me. Saige is so stable, steady, and solid, yet she has a wide variety of things going on. Whisper is always up for a road trip, has a colorful temper, and loves changing her environment.

Both are wordsmiths, hardworking, grounded in the belief of a higher power (they have different Gods, but are 100% dedicated), and love their environment to be home.

I see "me" in them, and I burst with pride; they were certainly watching. They were listening, and I trained in good, solid, stable, drug free, home dedication, and bubbly service to others and the community.

Fact: it is possible to be scattered like crazy and be extremely stable.

Thoughts;____
____
____

Loving
Boundaries

3 or 10 Sometimes, we get pulled in two different directions, which is stressful. Alcoholics and drug addiction are famous for this. Ya want to help a loved one but can't until they are ready. This pull is very real and usually devastating to the relationship.

Sometimes, it is religion or politics. We can't be a part of life choices, squishing who we are.

Abortion is one of those pulls to feel stressed. Criminal behavior also does this.

It looks like disrespect when the reaction is self-preservation. We guard our lives and stress levels to protect ourselves from overwhelming pain.

I'm in a strange cycle right now of tolerance and abandoning issues. I don't want to abandon, but I can no longer be available to live against my beliefs. This epiphany is very painful. I'm hurting in my heart. I'm feeling devastated, defeated, dred. I'm losing someone dear to me.

I've always believed that "our" herd should be filled with like-minded people. A huge failure in our system is tolerance. The Amish and Hutterites have a better system than school busing has created. We should never tolerate things or people that are against our core beliefs. I've been accused of being a racist because I separate from cultures I don't believe in (ya won't find me as a gang banger or drug dealer), and I know it's not racism cuz it has nothing to do with skin colors. I separate from behaviors I don't agree with. There is a saying about "guilt by association," which is normally said to teens who have friends their mom and dad don't like, but it is true for adults, too. This current need to separate is over patriotism, and I promised not to let politics affect our relationship, but it has gone to a level I can't tolerate and I hurt. This is a rough one. But hating America is not ok. She has given so much to us. There will be NO Life, Liberty, or Pursuit of Happiness by hating her. I just can't play in that sandbox.

3 or 10 So I will grieve and know it comes from losing someone I dearly love. He/She is sure to ask about my abandonment, and I hope I'm strong enough to say; no, I didn't abandon you; it's your beliefs and actions I can't have in my life. "Tough Love" was a thing in the 80s and is still a good way to live. Today, I am making sad decisions

because of my core beliefs. I will remind myself that my inner person is good. I am good. I'm solid. I'm steady. I live my life well. And it's been years of hating America that led me to today. But here we are.

Some people will notice your reaction of detachment; yet, never consider how their actions led to that decision.

Thoughts;_______________________________________

____

____

Patriotism
Loyalty

3 or 10 Everything has two sides. Helping is called service, and we are instructed by Jesus Mathew 6.3: "But when you give to the needy, do not let your left hand know what your right hand is doing". But; when living this instruction, we get addressed by persons who take, not; take personal responsibility so we get drug down.

Kindness, politeness, and giving, have to be tempered with boundaries.

It's America season.

Yes, it is an election, and we are commanded to vote for her.

I'm very pulled in two directions because I'm open-minded. I know people in all three parties. But I was also instructed to live my values, moral code, and gut feelings. The election is creating chaos and negativity in my life. Simply for one reason: America could become a 3rd world, socialist, Marxist country in the next three months. I'm terrified for her.

America the Beautiful

Thoughts;____
____
____

Morals
Instruction

3 or 10 The best book I've ever read. I've never sat to read it cover to cover but have jumped around, bible study, topic of a sermon, and to get into a book inside the Bible to just immerse my mind in a title. Job has gotten me through some hard stuff in life; trying times, it is always Job that I turn to. God has explained what "what" that means and what I'm to be doing as a woman and a wife. The Bible has told me what I'm supposed to be as a child (even in my 40s) and has helped me raise my children. It has caused me to feel guilt and shame but has given me the rules to not feel it in the future. But the main thing I've been given, the biggest gift, I got, the way to get to heaven and what heaven looks like. Do you know what heaven looks like? Oh My! Yep, it's in there.

3 or 10 When I fail, when life fails me, when people act out, when life is too much, YEP, there is a rule book on how to play the game successfully.

The Bible doesn't need to be rewritten; it needs to be re-read.

Thoughts;____

____

____

Blessed
Grief

Yesterday, I got my very first tattoo.

52 and my first! It is a memorial to Garrison! Some of you know who Garrison is, and some don't. Garrison is my grandson, my second-born grandchild; he came into the world like an Indianapolis 500 race. I called him Indy; he looked like my dad, and I beamed with pride, meaning he looked like me. He was born 6lb14oz, just like my first baby; he was breach like I was; his birthdate was 31 March, the day before his mom's. His smile lit up the room, and he was always smiling, the happiest baby. He is perfect! I have three grandsons; my second is Indy; he lives in heaven. I am blessed.

You don't know pain until you've sat and begged God to heal your broken heart- Kelly's treehouse.

Thoughts;____
____
____

Patriotism

3 or 10 Ol Glory is her name! As she gets attacked, I am sad. She is a feared, respected part of the greatest nation in the world. America is because of the men and women with "the b@?!/" enough to defend what she stands for. The bloodshed, the tears cried, and the fight fought for me to live a free life to worship, work, and worry as I wish. For "my veterans," I pray for each of you, known or not, you gave me the gift of Ol Glory... THANK YOU! Thank you! Thank You with a knot in my throat, a tear in my eye, and a heart overflowing with gratitude. Thank you!

Red White and Blue

Thoughts;____

____

____

Bonds
Memories

3 or 10 Because I struggle with depression, my 3 or 10 was born. Most days, I have my coffee and try my best to write my 3 or 10. It is hard on some days, but on other days, it is easy. Yesterday, my brother posted a picture of him dozing with his Cat and two grandkids on his lap. My oh my memories of a little girl on Dad's lap on a big D9, with pig tails, and Dad and I smiling (the same smile) as Mom got a snapshot in time. Every day, my brother reminds me of my dad (smile) and my Grampa (mom's dad; smiling). Seeing the best parts of these two great men live on comforts my soul. Yes, I love my baby brother, but more importantly, I value him. I have other family that I have abandoned or have abandoned me. A variety of things cause these decisions. All of them are sad and hurt my soul. But it is a must to let peace be in my life. Yep, with age comes the fact that just because I was born "related" doesn't mean a person adds any positive to my life. My circle is small and tight, and Thanksgiving dinner is a "safe space."

3 or 10, my brother posted a picture, a snapshot in time, that surrounded my soul with 52 years of "oh my," which is the good stuff.

I was asked why I am so quick to walk away from relationships and friendships…I replied as I get older, I have no room for stupidity, ignorance, liars, manipulators, and people who insult my intelligence.

Thoughts;____

____

____

Remember
Heaven

3 or 10 Today is filled with tears; watch as I turn that into a positive one. My brother posted about bringing someone from heaven for one more hug... I love hugs.. and I have so many in heaven that I miss. I wish I could ask my mom for answers to the problems in my life. I wish my dad could remind me to "shut up and listen." I wish Grampa and I could share a custard pie now that the cold of winter leads to baking so we can enjoy the things we don't cook in the summer. I wish my son could hand me a Kleenex today. I wish I could hear Garrison say, "Granny,". But; here is the positive: when I love, it is, to my core, for those on this side of heaven. "If I say I love you, it is deep, sincere, and forever." I know one day I will leave my earth children and grandchildren and cross to my child, grandchildren, Mom, Dad, Grama, and Grampa. Loren and I will be playing crib, and if it is heaven, Uncle Mike will get me to remember "the order of operations."

3 or 10 tears can be 3 or 10! Fact

Some Moms have tattoos, thick thighs, thin patience, and cuss too much- It's me; I'm some moms

Thoughts;____
____
____

Hope
Count Blessings

3 or 10 I got to the news this morning: two new shootings (sadness) and a horrid interview with Jessica about being secular (deep concern for America). FB has blocked me from all my groups; how can FB hate dogs and conservatives so much? (STRESS), Jake cannot figure out how his negative comments (he can not find any positive in the world on any subject; it starts with the weather woman and rolls downhill from there) just wear me out (no hope). By 9 am, I'm already exhausted! Mentally drained! Pooped Out!

So, Three Positive Thoughts

1. It is warm out, so the roads are good.

2. Baby stopped in this morning I love Baby (yard deer)

3. My tattoo stopped itching.

Ten Blessings

1. My kids are brats

2. Monster knows the rule "please"

3. Butch chats on the phone.

4. Pups are adorable (I love my job).

5. Pizza is what is for lunch.

6. A drive to CDA alone will refresh me.

7. 3 or 10 does balance me.

8. The weather woman needs a window

9. FB is goofy.

10. I'm going to have a great day (or else).

If the Bible calls it a Sin, your opinion doesn't matter.

Thoughts;____

____

____

Knowledge

3 or 10 I have a huge problem with wanting to know more about my topics. I am not a know-it-all-all, but if I talk, I have either read it, asked others about it, or given it thought. Yep, it is true I'm an information junkie! I am a bookworm, documentary addict, and a question questioner. I have read half a million books but only one novel (because it was a required book report in a college class), but I turn to literature to ponder the questions of the stars. Yesterday, Whisper, Paul, and I had a conversation about the Bible and tattooing! Slavery and enslaving people, and God stating "you" stop being tattooed, STOP BEING PUT INTO SLAVERY! And the reason Hitler tattooed his prisoners. It was a valuable moment in time because I learned some stuff about what God was talking about! What Paul has studied, his soul also wants knowledge (I like that), and Whisper is now exposed to more knowledge (not from mom because moms don't know).

3 or 10

I love this shirt! X3 + 10

Hang on, let me overthink this (funny Tshirt)

Thoughts;____

____

____

Morals
Enough

3 or 10 Some days, the only option is to demand. This comes after the "I feel" chatter, after the "stop it" requests. The kind, loving mom/wife/friend turns into a raging maniac. Yep, that person I hate inside me gets to a point where I'm all in to stop being taken advantage of.

I hate liars!

I hate drug-addicted personalities!

I hate people manipulating people!

I hate control freaks!

Thieves are a violation of respect,

Chauvinism is the downfall of women!

Tolerating chauvinists cause pain!

Passive Aggressive is abuse!!

Being a criminal is wrong;

I hate the fact that these cancers surround me (and you) and my family!

3 or 10 Yesterday, I lost it! Yep, I unloaded on these traits! And guess what? Each and every one of these people I love blamed me for fighting back. They all blamed me for reaching the point of Oh My God, I've had ENOUGH! I told one of these ass's to ask the question, "What pushed Annette to lose it?" I received a blank stare! Yep, PASSIVE AGGRESSIVE ABUSE! And it is true when pushed, I get angry. Funny, they all forget the 100's of times I've given, the 100's of things I've overlooked, the 100's of $$ I've given, and the core belief that family is everything! The sad thing is their belief that somehow they are "Entitled" to be horrid people, and it's ok! IT IS NOT OK! So, today, I am going to regroup... alone... quiet... crushed by the hurt... and sad at my anger... some days, that's all the human experience is, but the list remains the same. Dogs are the best family members! Dogs are loyal! Dogs love without question!

Without dreams, we reach nothing. Without love, we feel nothing. And without God, we are nothing.

Thoughts;____

____

____

Family
Children
Motherhood

3 or 10 Pushing people past their limits is what starts the fight. We (the family) had a little drama yesterday. I was getting ready to take a nap when a dumb ass decided to start (continue) a fight—threatening me in text. Drugs were involved on his part. Control Freak status kicked in, and his goal was to get even with me (because he's mad, POOR BABY) because I called him out privately for his horrid behavior. Then, he added Facebook as his weapon of choice. (Yes, dumb ass, I read your pity party, and I can tell you "pity parties have very few guests" Maybe your mom showed up!)

Then he made the mistake of degrading and abusing (again) one of my kids. OH MY! So, my reaction was to play his game. I gave him my sheriff's phone number. (I'm friends with most of them, and they have been in my home and know my dogs, but he has never been in my home, so his filing a report is sure to be funny) And I started making phone calls.

His sheriff (I'm friends with them too), his state patrol (I have their private numbers, also), his probation officer (a nice lady), his boss,

3 or 10 Felons committing crimes that are on probation, that are high on drugs, that are driving around uninsured on a suspended license, should not pick a fight with an Irish mom by abusing and degrading her child.

JUST SAYIN!

When the Sheriff called to get a recorded statement about his threatening to go after a sheriff with a machete (because drugs, anger, hating cops, and a machete are not a good mix), I told the cop I pray every day for drug treatment before something really bad happens. (I have in the past gotten him drug treatment appointments, but he refuses to go)

Drugs Destroy People & Families.

I'm hoping today I'm left alone! And my child and her things better be left alone! But if not, I will save all the numbers on my phone so I don't have to look them up again. The pickup is fueled up if I need to go to WA at a moment's notice; SCREEN SHOTS ARE VERY HELPFUL!

I am no longer available for things that make me feel like shit.

Thoughts;____
____
____

Failures
Apology

3 or 10 The angry me sucks! I usually apologize, but one issue is I don't express myself till I am in full mad mode. Then it becomes a win-or-nothing situation, and I crush others to be listened to. This week, I blew, and a year of resentment came bubbling out. The sad part is that the year has been filled with "I will help."

"This behavior is wrong," and "You can be a better person." So, the part that is my issue is acceptance of the other person. Well, there are things I can't accept. Yep, ugly things in life that are not acceptable. I have been told, "Love the person, hate the behavior." Yeah right. But no one has explained how to "love" the drug addict, the selfish, the criminal, the abuser, the liar, the thief, or the control freak. I get lost in their actions!

3 or 10 Usually, I apologize, but sometimes, it falls on deaf ears because the things that infuriate me are horrible. They are failures in the other person's treatment of me, which causes me to fail as a person. This is a nice article about two people's relationships! The part "listen" would be a nice thing in life. But it is a fact very few people "listen." And even fewer people want to fix their failures.

Your Apology needs to be as loud as your disrespect was.

Thoughts;____

____

____

Respect
Self Love

3 or 10 Love me! There is my challenge! I'm so tired of throwing a fit
to get what I need.

Sad that I set myself up to fail,

3 or 10 I have a list of both great and horrible. I'm going to focus today
on my great, even if others can't see or respect it.

**Staying in a relationship JUST because you love somebody is not
worth it. Love is not what you need. Respect is what you need.
Reassurance is what you need. Happiness is what you need.
Knowing every day you're their favorite person is what you need.
Learn to love yourself instead.**

Thoughts;____
____
____

Abused
Self Love

3 or 10 I was listening to the news, and Trump Supporters are now part of a cult! POTUS is accused of controlling my mind. Oh, my people's memories are so short. Obama used the IRS to add me to three watch lists. Tea Party and motorcycle Clubs both became "gang" members; he went to the DMV, and motorcycle endorsement was also a "gang" member; then he went on to Social Security, and anyone with a rep was put on a list to deny gun rights. So, today, I'm part of a "cult." Ha Ha!! It's all good; Christian, Conservative, and Personal Responsibility run my life.

My life is currently in a transition, and I hate it. Change is hard. It comes from the normal crap in life that gets bad. Yes, bad. Relationships either succeed or fail for a variety of reasons. When they fail, pain and sadness follow—self Shatters.

And 3 or 10 become really hard.

3 or 10, I am in a dark place; prayer is not helping, and pain or sadness fills my day. I can say, "I love you," but it falls on deaf ears. I give, and it is dismissed. I give and give and am told I need to give more. I reach out to have my hand slapped. It seems turning my back is basically the only option left. That really sucks.

3 or 10, I have to make changes!

Let me be clear: my love is unconditional, but your presence in my life is not. The moment that you prove that your value of me does not measure up to my sense of self-worth, I'll have no problem unconditionally loving the memory of you.

Thoughts;____
____
____

Knowledge
Acceptance

3 or 10 There are people in the world who don't want to learn, don't want to know more, and don't want to fill their minds with knowledge. WHAT THE HECK. I just don't get it. Yesterday, there was a conversation about Christopher Columbus. I said, "he didn't find the USA." I immediately got the eye-rolling and the "fine"! You know the fine that really means you're an idiot! So you know me, I grabbed my phone and looked up the facts (yes, I like to be right when I speak); he found the Bahamas (year 1492) and was not involved with the Mayflower (year 1620) or Leaf Ericsson (year 985) finding Greenland.

I get so frustrated with people who want to remain ignorant. In the last week, we have had six loaves of cement (bread) that even the dogs refuse to eat, so I get up. No recipe book is involved, and I start putting stuff in the bowl. The refusal to walk 7 feet (yep, his chair and the kitchen counter are 7 feet apart) and learn how to make bread made me do the eye-rolling thing, and when it came out of the oven, I took it to the neighbor, YEP; I DID THAT. Knowing the only way to heaven is through Jesus Christ and a higher power to keep drunks sober; I bought a bible just for those two facts... it has never been opened. Oh my! The rules to life! And it has never been opened! So, while I know what a "good wife" is, ignorance remains. (The Bible was bought 3 years ago, so there has been plenty of time.) In my life, it is the most important book to read. It is a caring, loving gift with instructions on life and eternal life.

3 or 10 I am so saddened that "hating women" is more important than friendship or heaven itself. That is a soul-crushing fact, and I am not big enough to change. Christopher Columbus did not find the USA, and the neighbor liked my homemade bread. Jake wouldn't be there when I got to heaven, so "fine" wouldn't be there either.

Be teachable. You're not always right.

Thoughts;____

____

____

Thankful

3 or 10 I'm not where I want to be. It is sad but true that life is a list of challenges. I'm thankful for some. I regret some. Some I'm forced into. But 3 or 10 is to be about the Thankful stuff. I have a list of friends that make me smile, giggle, and feel loved. I have a brother who is so logical, and he brings balance to any problem. I have kids; they are brats. Yes, BRATS, thank God. I raised them to be adults with their lives, opinions, thoughts, and goals. I have grandkids who are learning to be brats, too. Butch is his mother's child, and Monster is his own little person. I have a business doing business things. I have my pine trees that talk with my soul. I have boxes of books to read. I have words to share and writing to get done. I have poetry in my heart that is waiting to come out. I have 3 or 10 that few read, but it's about me, not them. Happy Thanksgiving, everyone, gobble gobble!

Happy Thanksgiving

Thoughts;____

____

____

Personal Responsibility
Morals

3 or 10 Recently, I've been hit with a list of anger. Some of this reaction is from my actions! Yep, someone is mad at me for something I actually did. That's ok. I did it, I have reasons, I own it, be mad if you like. But there has been an overwhelming anger toward me that includes threats, name-calling, and making up stories about me. What the Heck! I own my behavior, so my part should be done. Oh, Hell No! But as with all people and relationships, it all unfolds in time.

1. It is a fact I give away far more than I keep.

2. Thieves tick me off.

3. Sneaky is a character flaw.

4. Passive Aggressive is abuse.

5. Children pay attention and learn both good and bad.

6. Drugs are bad.

7. Manipulation is a behavior that results from low self-esteem.

8. A mother always protects her young.

9. If you want love, act loving.

10. If you are a turd, admit it.

3 or 10 I'm going to carry on with my day. Protecting myself from the abuse of others... yep, I have a "block" button, and today is a great day to use it.

Don't let someone get over it; help them get through it.

Thoughts;____
____
____

Traditions
Patriotism
Love

3 or 10 Tradition is so very important. When mom died, I lost all the comfort zone traditions she held dear. I miss so much of Mom and Grampa's stuff that just happened. For Thanksgiving, I made Mom's bread... it was delicious... she taught me well. Tears ran down my face as I kneaded it, and I realized I was the last to know Grama Easter's art. My kids are not interested in it. They think kings Hawaiian are fine. Ha, this is not true. My mom whipped up bread with her eyes closed. And I learned by watching. Thank God! Darin does Mom's fudge with his eyes closed. Thank God! Cuz my fudge always sugars!! Yuck!! I kick butt on pies now that the crusts are made for me.

Please grab a box of Christmas cards and handwrite a note to a wounded soldier. Put the 20 cards in a big envelope and make a soldier heal with a little more love. This tradition is Whisper's creation! I hope Saige gets Monsters class to do it, too!

3 or 10 traditions are important

Wounded Soldier c/o Walter Reed 4494 North Palmer Rd Bethesda, MD 20889

Thoughts;____
____
____

Prayers
Personal Responsibility

3 or 10 Hatred is ugly. But more than ugly, it erodes every person's well-being that it touches. "You're mean," "You're pathetic," "You're stuff is a million pounds of shit," "I see, it's about me doing your stuff," "Yes master," "What are you reading," "yea!" "I don't have time to be on the phone all day," "You don't work," "You don't pay bills," "I have to do the dishes." When the tone is ugly, any one of these comments is cut like a long, sharp blade. And when they cut, and the tears come, then it is, "What are you boobing about?" Because being verbally abused by him is just who he is.

3 or 10 I got myself in this mess, and I will get myself out of this mess with my million pounds of shit (business inventory). I'm so sad that he can not find "happy." I'm even more sad that he asked me to build a life, but what that means is "clean my house and shut up." I've asked 3 times for him to tell the child molester to stop coming to my house; the day before yesterday day, I looked in my driveway, and there the child molester stood. This disrespect does not work for me... my castle and there stands a child molester! No, it's not my castle; it's his, and I'm just the bitch, for finding this horrible. The horrible part is, "Why does he find child molesting a forgivable trait?" Friends, I really need prayers for a new home. Yep, positive energy cuz there is none in my house.

I am no longer available for things that make me feel like garbage

Thoughts;____

____

____

Wisdom
Respect
Knowledge

3 or 10 Someone I respect called me "wise." I've had a few compliments I truly value as a "knowing." A high school English teacher knew me in my late 20s long ago and said, "You are non-pretentious." I have always carried that as a compliment. So "wise"?? I am, in fact, wise in some things. And amen, someone noticed. The people I have respected are "wise"; they have a knowing about them. From the Bible or life experience, they are educated on big life questions. I spend a lot of time reading and a lot of time pondering things. And when I think about things without emotional stuff, I usually figure it all out.

3 or 10 Both prayer and goal-setting propel us forward. Selfish people are the saddest people on earth. Rude behavior never has a good outcome. Kindness isn't just words; it is also actions. Mindfulness is a great way to let go of negative emotions. Forgiveness and acceptance are very different. Lies destroy. Respect is a gift of value.

You gotta start romanticizing your life. You gotta start believing that your morning commute is cute and fun, that every cup of coffee is the best you've ever had, that even the smallest and most mundane things are exciting and new. You have to because that's when you start truly living. That's when you look forward to every day.

Thoughts;____

____

____

Truth
Death
Family Bonds
Personal Responsibility

3 or 10 True Words that hurt are still True, even with your bottom lip poking out. Last night a call came in where "honesty" was required. I sat in the living room and chatted; OH MY GOD, feelings got hurt. To flipping bad, but then I was abused because the words were in fact reality. I stood firm in the facts... and politely asked, "If you didn't want me to be honest, why did you put me on the phone?" (Guardian et Litum) Then I followed up with, "If you don't want me to say those things, stop acting like that," but the abuse continued this morning.

3 or 10 When Dad, Loren, and Mom; needed Darin and I to come together... WE DID! There was no laziness, no hesitation for care, no argument over what needed to happen. My brother and I just came together and got through the worst days and months, of our lives. If I needed, I picked up the phone, and Darin answered. Stuff just happened. No one stole from the other, no one denied the rights to the other. We just got things done! My brother knew how important it was to me to be at all 3 of our parent's side when they went to heaven. Yes, I held them as they took their last breath. Not only did he let me do those things, but he also helped me do those things. Our parents knew they were loved and they were not alone as their bodies said "enough." I'm so grateful that on the worst days of my life my brother stood with me.

There were a lot of words last night (an hour phone call), but it was the "this situation is so weird to me; my brother and I stood together, but this family doesn't do that." I know Jakes pain, but I don't understand lazy! I don't get the refusal to "do" for a parent, I don't understand turning back to a parent in need, I don't get shrugging responsibility, I don't understand stealing from a parent or brothers, I don't understand greedy, lying, and neglecting a parent when they need their child the most. TRUE words that hurt are STILL TRUE. Being lazy is a choice, being a thief is a choice, and neglecting a parent is irresponsible! I'm so lucky that my brother and I stood together! "WE" got through it together! I don't know why Jake handed me the phone if he didn't want the court to know the facts. But bad behaviors always lead to the loss of respect. And I said, "If you want me to stop saying "that" stop doing that!" No one can ever say I didn't care for my parents! And no court was involved... my brother and I just got the "hard" work done.

Image; A beautiful big rounded tree with snow ice crystals on all the leaves a blue sky above causing the white to look pure and bright

Thoughts;____

____

____

Morals
Personal Responsibility

3 or 10 I know right from wrong. I'm in a strange place right now with people I love and adore. Knowing I would lay down my life for any of them... Lately, I have needed to stand on the foundation of "right" vs. wrong. People are mad at me! Ha, I don't care. I'm sick to death of the bull! I'm tired of the "but"; there has been no but here lately. I'm so fed up with overlooking bad behaviors. So as I turned my back to "wrong," I was screamed at!! Called names!! And threatened!

3 or 10 "Right" is pretty simple!!! It is easy to behave in a good way. It is easy to flip to see the other person's perspective. Life is kind of easy to evaluate.... "If they did "that" to me, would it be wrong?" I'm crushed by the horrid way some people behave. But I am able to stand firm in "right."

I can't tell you the key to success, but the key to failure is trying to please everyone

Thoughts;____
____
____

Helping
Shunning

3 or 10 People say, "Just let it go," but they only say that about the "bad" stuff, the "disrespectful" stuff, the stuff that stings. Yep, I'm not a big fan of "just let God." Maybe God wants me to remember the cheater, the liar, or the thief; maybe God is showing me the ugly so I recognize it. "Just let it go" bunk... Shunning... yep, God doesn't say "let it go," he says "shun evil." he doesn't say forgive over and over and over... so

3 or 10 Yep, I remember those who helped, caused me to need help, and turned on me. Yep! I remember

I'll never forget who helped me in difficult times, who put me in difficult times and who left me in difficult times.

Thoughts;____
____
____

Grief
Wisdom
Moral

3 or 10 As a young girl, I was blessed with a Grampa who could reflect his moral beliefs in simple kid-knowing wisdom. He said some silly things that were memorable, and today, I still carry them with me. "Jesus is the sage of all man," "God sees you," "God is watching." My Grampa got mad at me when I was about 8. I asked, "Did Grama get to heaven?" Indignant Grampa had an angry tone. He said, "If anyone got to heaven, it was your Grama." I will never forget that. As an adult, I knew he wasn't angry with me; his tone came from his love and respect and deep grief. Our nation was built on these incredibly deep right and wrong core beliefs. This pic is correct. We must rise up and put the greatest country in the world back on track. Killing babies, globalization, stealing tax dollars, defending radical anything, open borders, sanctuary city, and states protecting murderers and rapists, THIS ALL HAS TO STOP. A Dem friend said, "Don't use your bible to write my laws" Knowing she stands to kill babies and let rapists out of jail.... makes my stomach sick. Yep 40 years of friendship is sidelined by YUCK you are a yucky person.

Rise up to make America MORAL AGAIN!

3 or 10, I'm on it!!! I'm doing my part! I'm not killing, raping, or inviting radical ideology into my home.

Meme of President George Washington "If I was alive, I'd bitch slap all of you Americans for allowing this shit. Grow a pair of balls and take back your government!"

Thoughts;____
____
____

Doing Life
Blessed

3 or 10 Wow, it is a day of "doing life" with no parole. I bought myself a 4-wheeler with a snow plow, and it is big enough to take a moose out of the woods. Oh My! I made it to Spokane to have the people I'm meeting find Snowqualimi a slow go, so they are an hour behind! Whisper is 40 minutes late... Saige had a litter of pups born this morning... my oh my! On my way, I was blessed with a huge bald eagle on the side of the road... I was so close I could see his talons! That is close.... he was stunning. The cougar is still at the house, so my deer are hiding somewhere. 3 or 10 JUST DOING LIFE! No parole. While waiting, I got a cup of coffee and pumpkin bread, and they were delicious! So, LIFE IS GOOD!

Thoughts;____

____

____

Rest
Challenge
Courage

3 or 10 When life gives you a list of yuck, ya only have the option to sort and put it in its place. I always have a million things going on. Overwhelmed or just who I am is not important. I have a million things going on. I am pretty good at sorting into lists of important. Lazy at times. Yea, at times, I shut down to read and nap. The point is SHUT DOWN! Kind of a re-start of my thoughts. These restart times are very important to my well-being. My current struggle is not my final destination, but it still needs solving. My self-esteem has indeed been challenged to rise and act. Mom used to call it "which puddle to jump in." I need to jump! Yep, it is time to turn to my problem and face it with all I have.

3 or 10 So far, I have faced all the challenges life offers. Have you been successful? Well, it was not perfect, but I always got through it. And I know I will get through all of this, too. Today is the day I am done with the reading and naps. Decisions have to be made today.

Do y'all remember that before the internet that people thought the cause of stupidity was the lack of access to information? Yeah. It wasn't that.

Thoughts;____
____
____

God Fearing
God Praising

3 or 10 People come into our lives in strange ways. Jo was asking for directions to a bus. That was 40 years ago, and here we are still best! Greg came to me about six months ago because I had lab pups, and his son wanted one! Greg is a pastor; Jo lives a God Fearing life. Funny, it is called "God Fearing" because both of these people in my life are certainly not "afraid" of God. God Fearing? Yes, his wrath can create fear. This morning, Greg posted this poem! My oh my the things we do against God can lead us to a hollow life! I've been there. I might be there right now. As I struggle right now, I keep my eye on Chapter and Verse, yet the words I read sometimes leave me empty, without feeling.

3 or 10 Sometimes, God needs us to struggle; in his wisdom, he sends us the right person to say the right words. Or, on a Facebook post, a poem pops in. Because of Jo, 40 years ago, I made it. She may never know how indebted I am to her love and friendship. On the second worst day of my life, Darin Roger & Karen, Jo Ann , and Kayleen popped in to show me I'm never alone. "God Fearing" no, all these people are "God Praising," and I find comfort and rest in that.

There was a man with hands on head,

"I hated life" is what I said,

Wine and women, song and mirth,

All came to naught and little worth.

He sought with haste a void to fill

But came up wanting and empty still,

The lure of promise, a life of pride

That left him cold and dead inside

Until at length he reached the end

Took up some parchment and a pen

And wrote a message plain and clear

A warning for all of us to hear

"Vanity, vanity!" was his cry

"We soak up life and then we die!"

So when you spend your numbered days

Be sure to invest in eternal ways

Fear God and always do what's right

Live in peace, choose wise your fight

Put on humility, show mercy and grace

Let kindness dwell in vengeance's place

Then, when life is done and through,

And the Father extends His hands towards you,

Perhaps you'll hear, "Well done my child. Now, come on in and rest a while!"

Author Unkown

Thoughts;____

____
____

Wisdom
Knowledge

3 or 10 "Clean Up in Isle 7" dinner with my brother is helpful. Logic is one of those things that emotion can not be a part of. So give him the list of "crap" in life, a calculator, and four options! BOOYAH a plan. Well, maybe not a complete plan, but a to-do list of a plan. But; life went from a scattered mess of "crap" to an "oh my I can do this". So now, let's grab the bootstraps and get stuff done.

3 or 10, I can!

In life, it's important to know when to stop arguing with and simply let them be wrong.

Thoughts;____

____

____

Anxiety
Overwhelmed

3 or 10 There are lots of short readings this week on FB. People are posting little articles. One that struck me was that Saige posted about anxiety. Oh my, we have no health care for this one. It distorts people, lifestyles and health. And the public school system isn't addressing it... so we have violence. The local sheriffs are not addressing it because their favorite phrase is "This is civil," which I believe is "You are interrupting my donut time". Prosecutors are being lazy, so drug charges are really just a reason for judges to say, "released on your own recognizance," Advocates want to squash freedom of speech, religious values, animal ownership, and guns. But want abortions on demand, open borders, and drug cartels. Six people wanting to buy my house don't speak English; how on earth could I enter into a contract with someone so disrespectful to America? I refuse, but that is breaking federal law! Really, I'm supposed to be more than trilingual!

Yep, fair housing laws say I'm supposed to enter into a contract with a person who could be deported. I think I'll stand patriotic, and if you want to talk to me, there's no need to "press 1 for English" I'll leave that to corporate America. Ha, when ya call AT&T, it dials a foreign country anyway. Back to anxiously talking about anxiety! Yes, it is a horrid part of life.

3 or 10 Friends and family, if this holiday season is overtaking you with depression or anxiety, CALL ME! Together, we will talk it out! I might not solve your troubles, but we will laugh a little, cry, and feel better before I say, "I love you! Bye"

Just because someone carries it well, Doesn't mean it isn't heavy.

Thoughts;____

____

____

Bonds
Patriotism
Loyalty

3 or 10 Life, at times, makes no sense. Some people I value have dismissed me because I supported President Trump. Ok, well, that is mean and rude. I miss them, but losing patriotism or the freedom to choose will not happen. So be it! But I'm not the only one, so The Trump Campaign built a web page. America is divided because of the morals subscribed to. As valued friends fall away, it is because they don't value me more than they value them. Ok, well, there is a fix for that! Fall Away! I'm still a great person...

3 or 10 I'm a great friend, family member, mom, granny, business owner, dog mom, neighbour, wife, sister-in-law, daughter-in-law, environmentalist, social warrior, volunteer, scholar, student, researcher, tax planner, IRS fighter, patient, law looker upper, YEP if you threw me away... you lost a diamond in the ruff.

Thoughts;____

____

____

Loneliness
Bonds

3 or 10 Thank God... three positive thoughts and ten things I'm grateful for... during the holidays, this is near impossible, and 2019 was no different. Joy, Happiness, Yule, Mistletoe, Food, FAMILY... yep, the holiday season. I woke up yesterday, and the mean, nasty people of 2019 didn't ask for forgiveness (because I'm always the one wrong), so I was home in my nightgown. I played video games on my phone till it was time to go to bed. Whisper called.... everyone else was busy, I guess. Whisper held tradition and got me a beautiful angel to add to 20 years of tradition. Everyone else was busy, I guess. I planned, shopped, and cooked for six hours, and Jake told me I burnt a casserole. Yep, it is true the green beans were burnt. I told him that next year, he could do the cooking.

I gave gifts; Whisper said thank you... everyone else was busy, I guess A blessing I'm grateful for... I don't have to feel the dread of Christmas for 364 days. New Year's, Easter, Mother's Day, my birthday, or FRIDAY! Nasty people are a fact... they are always busy finding shitty things to do to others. They are busy, I guess, and not productive, loving, or polite. To be honest, Darin invited me to Christmas dinner, but it seems no one missed me. I didn't feel like an 8-hour drive for dinner with people who didn't like me was a good investment of my time. 3 or 10 Whisper remembered me for Christmas.

Hear me when I tell you this: People who ignore you until it suits them to talk to you, are not worth your friendship or your time!!

Thoughts;____

____

____

Sharing

Angels

3 or 10 No one can "do" for anyone else. As I watch people, I love to go through both good and bad with them but " them " have to decide how they "do" life. Me too! I don't always "do" it right. But the good news is I don't always "do" it wrong. My mental health is "mine", and I get to do it as I wish. I know the "rules" they are taught from being a little kid. Yep, in kindergarten, we were taught to deal with our temper, sharing, and disappointment of not being the only one. Before kindergarten, I had a baby brother who was just as important to my mom and dad as I was.

3 or 10 I got this. Yep, I know what I need to do. Now, it is just doing it. My Angels have spoken. They are always right; they have never taken me to places bad for my spirit. My gut! My instinct. The internal me.

Some of the best advice you'll ever get will come from your gut instinct.

Thoughts;____

____

____

Personal Responsibility
Morals

3 or 10 This morning, I got accused of being "passive-aggressive," so you know me, I refreshed my knowledge... "indirect resistance to others DEMANDS... avoidance of DIRECT CONFRONTATION"... well, well... I have yet; not to speak my mind... I've never in my life avoided confrontation, and I have never "indirectly" resisted... if my answer is? Yep, I say it... no one, wondering when I'm happy or mad.. and if I get ticked off, there is a "direct" knowledge of why! Not even a delay! When I get accused of not having "tact," I let it wash over me because I could work on my tact.

3 or 10 If I post on FB and it is about you, I will tag you. Yep, I made it clear that I wanted you to read it. If I post about politics, abortion, abuse... and you are not tagged it wasn't about you... Suppose you feel guilt or anger or are even happy about a post you are not tagged for. In that case, THAT IS ON YOU.... and it does not mean I'm passive-aggressive... it means you need to work on yourself... yep I might think you are a punk, but unless you are tagged, YOU WERE NOT ON MY MIND... that might be because YOU AREN'T WORTH MY TIME... moral of the story... I'm a lot of things, but passive-aggressive isn't one of them. Whisper, I'm gonna respond when Richard attacks me on a public yard sale group with lies and foul language. If he doesn't want me to speak my mind, he should grow up, stop using drugs, treat my daughter well, and be worth my time. He should act better if he doesn't want to be called a punk. If he doesn't want to be a good person, that is on him.

Definition of passive-aggressive in English:

Adjective: Of or denoting a type of behaviour or personality characterized by indirect resistance to the demands of others and an avoidance of direct confrontation, as in procrastinating, pouting or misplacing important materials.

Pronunciation:

Passive-aggressive

Thoughts;____

____

____

Loving
Loyalty
Reep and Sow

3 or 10 FREE!

Yep, let's talk about free. The phone call you didn't make... the art time with kids you didn't do... the apology you never sat to write... the thank you note never sent... the "I'm happy to see you smile" never given.... the piggy bank never deposited... the promises broken... the little simple things never done so another human could feel thought about... loved... wanted. Some will read this and say Annette is passive-aggressive... for those, all I can say is sorry that you have chosen to be rude.... uncaring... disrespectful... But I will not feel responsible for your bad behavior. And all know I have quietly spoken of how I feel when you behave this way or that way. But we, as a "family," always love to tell Annette what is wrong with her.

3 or 10 Hurt by others and becoming quiet is not passive-aggressive; it is "throwing up hands" along with an eye roll. Today, I will not be quiet. If you have refused FREE ways to make me feel good.... deal with me feeling bad. And don't send me a text that you are justified in being a snot.... don't post on Facebook the name calling... fact, if you are a snot, I probably got hurt... reap what you sow.... if you want me to be all hugs and kisses YOU need to be hugs and kisses... "I" "I" "I" Well, so be it. Take your little "one-way street" and go away... but have some self-respect, and don't turn to me for help when FREE is not given to me. FREE! It costs nothing to be a good human and nothing to make another person feel loved.

Whoever sows generously will also reap generously.

Thoughts;____

____

____

Bonds

3 or 10 The other day, we had dinner with the boys, and I had gifts. Monster asked for his package. I said I don't have one for you he looked dismayed and said to his mom, "What did you get?" I giggled and handed him a snack, then I looked at Saige and said "what is the deal?"

She said, "Mom, he knows you always bring him something" She is right! Being GRANNY totally rocks! I'm a trained monkey, I guess!

Kid: Grandma would say Yes!

Mom: Well! It sounds like my mom is cooler than yours!

Thoughts;____

____

____

Self Perseverance

3 or 10 My brother said, "Maybe he asked God for forgiveness" Well, maybe he did. Until the behaviour changes and the hurt is addressed, I'll be protecting myself from more hurt, sadness, and resentment. How are we as people supposed to "let it go" and not get destroyed repeatedly?

3 or 10 drug addicts, liars, and narcissistic behavior are like bullets to our souls. Guard up!

Before you start to judge me, step into my shoes and walk the life I'm living and if you get as far as I am, just maybe you will see how strong I really am.

Thoughts;____

____

____

Loving
Loyal
Caring

3 or 10 When the argument only has one-sided rules, it is no longer debated. 2 human beings, both with hopes, desires, needs, and values! No, not really; I'm currently in three different relationships where I'm being forced to realize "my only value is the checks I can write" How sad is that? Soul-crushing sadness. My failure in it is getting free and wishing. I know my worth, but I feel hurt for those who only see me as dollar signs. Jake keeps saying, "Something is wrong with you!" And this morning, that caused me to blow my top. As if a selfish, dry drunk could evaluate another human being. But I finally turned to it and responded, "Yep, you are right. I got married to a man who said he wanted to build a life; it crushed me to find out he was lying." So Jake is outside for the day. BOOYAH, DON'T tell him the truth; it makes him pout! There is a lot of pouting going on around me. One human who always told me he loved me... now says horrid things to and about me because I responded to his behaviour. His personality flaws finally caught up to me, and I put my foot down. Not being able to control me, he lashes out. Pouting seems to be a common theme. And then person three has decided to withhold others from my value to punish me... yep, if she doesn't agree, I will be punished. But not just me others as well. This is the one that crushes me the most. And she doesn't care!

3 or 10 I'm loving, loyal, giving, caring, and sometimes it is punished. But; it remains "I'm loving, loyal, giving, caring".

Coffee doesn't care if you wear pants. Coffee doesn't wear pants, either. Pants are dumb.

Thoughts;____
____
____

Prayers
Vulnerable

3 or 10 PRAYERS FOR ME TO GET INTO MY NEW HOME! Divorce is ugly, and the reason I haven't been posting. I'm sad, depressed, and overwhelmed! My self-esteem has taken a hit that I made decisions for all the right reasons but with lies being the foundation of information I was given.... that sucks! I FOUND THE PERFECT HOUSE! Four beds, one bath, $90,000, 5% interest on a 15-year contract! $20,000 down! That is where I need help! Please pray for God to provide me with a way! My Lind house sold at my asking price! But down is 6 months out! Ugh! HELP: I need help.... hopefully I find a $20,000 loan, a lottery ticket (I don't play the lottery) or someone who wants to help!

3 or 10 prayers make things happen. Asking for prayers is really hard for me. I hate feeling vulnerable. But; today is an overwhelmed day of realizing this is bigger than "me". I need a home.

Better worry about your own sins because God ain't gonna ask you about mine.

Thoughts;____

____

____

Self Esteem
Acceptance
Differences

3 or 10 Why is there so much hate in America? I have been seriously thinking about all the things that divide us. Back in high school, we had jocks/cheerleaders pot smoking and keggers... we had honor roll and not.... rich and poor.... then I moved to adulthood and found suits and not... army vs navy... enlisted vs officer... management vs. worker... Mormon vs. not... married vs single... over 50, I'm still seeing Division... Republican vs Democrat and Dr. vs. patient rights... humane society vs breeder... gun ownership vs gun confiscation. LGBTQ vs heterosexuality.

Fact; competition is a way of life... to be competitive, a person seeks to be superior... dividing... a cut above, leaving someone behind... when someone is left behind they become determined to be head of the pack... usually the not jock is the drug dealer...that the jock needs! But they can't see it! We must remember the man with the new car also has new car payments, and the poor man is having dinner with his kids... CHOICES!

The division in this country was created by both slavery and abortion... religion and atheism... church and state...

3 or 10 I'm a proud Republican, God Fearing... praying, single woman... if you hate me... that is you dividing our country.

Thoughts;____
____
____

Personal Pain
Life Management
Relationships

3 or 10 Yesterday in class, I asked a question about the material. All of a sudden, I hear a woman screaming at me. So, I clarified my question with quality information. She exploded at me. Her pain and lack of emotional control; she gave the class details of her life that made me feel sad, yet being screamed at, I was also angry. I listened to her for about 5 minutes and then left the class. My question was about fear and personal safety, and her screaming was proof that my fear and need to have personal safety was 100% a real thing.

I sent my book to the publisher and sent "copyright" permission forms out to request permission "to or not" to use real names. One immediately said I don't give copyright. I responded with ok and then said, "I don't give copyright for the "content." Well, that's not how copyright works. I am the writer of 3 or 10, so the fact I "own" the words written. Another one responded with "ok, so if you slander I can sue you," and we had a moment of giggles, I said "well of course." The hilarious part of this is for both I talk in 3 or 10 of wonderful, loving, educational, memories made. So today we have "lessons learned."

3 or 10 It is a fact that in every relationship we are in, people bring their own psychology. Sometimes it's good, sometimes bad, sometimes screaming, pain, and sometimes giggles. And the only part we are responsible for is our actions in the relationship. The other student and I have no relationship and never will. The people receiving "copyright permission" are people that I honor enough to have them in my 3 or 10…. Truly, love each of them enough to note when, where, when, why, and how, they have impacted my journey.

It's already yours-Universe

Thoughts;____

____

____

Family
Events
Memories

3 or 10 Things remembered; we all want to be remembered, and we want moments shared and pleasantly talked about. I'm no different. But different from some, I take time for the late-night marathon calls, make notes, plan events, and keep photos. I commented to a cousin this week about a day trip to Yellowstone that we took together. He was 5, I was 13. He was cute. A little one, toe-head, that was just as inquisitive as he was adorable. Since then, we have both raised kids and have grands (his 1st will be born soon), had successes and failures, and our hair is gray. And one day, we will end this life with a Eulogy read at a day in time for the people who love us to say goodbye.

3 or 10 I told my kids to write my obituary and fill it with the truth. I want it not to be a list of platitudes but a short story about the "real" me. I want my funeral to be a true celebration, a true party of "me," good and bad, greatness, and all the moments I touched the lives of those around me. I do hope my family reads the genealogy that Uncle Ed and Aunt Shirley put in my heart as very important. The 3 of us have worked hard to make it acutely tell our history. And I admit they did the bulk of the work. Why are obituaries, headstones, and genealogy important? If you are Christian and read the Bible, you will see Old and New Testament genealogies that will take us back to Abraham. Why is that important? There is conflicting Google search "info," but Jesus was in Abraham's linage… and so am I. Cool huh?
Very cool

Thoughts;____
____
____

Obstacles
Stalker's
Narcissists

3 or 10 I always have TV or radio on. I don't watch much, but listen. My favorites are documentaries and historical shows. I remember my deep sadness when the biography channel went off the air. This morning, doing my normal busy work, Unsolved Mysteries was on. It ran a full hour of psychopaths. Yeah, the ones we know are like Bundy and Domhar. But, also a bunch I've never heard of. In the end, it said, "Psychopaths are rare, and most of us will never meet one." Oh my goodness, I'm always an overachiever! WTHECK is wrong with me? Who would have thought I would date a single man, for his past to reach out, to be tormented, tortured, followed, and lied about for 14 years and for 12 years after we split up? But here we are!

3 or 10 Some things in our lives are not what we want, not what we cause, and not even our problems to overcome. Some abusers feel joy, which causes sadness, hopelessness, and pain. The only part we can play with is how we rise above these circumstances. I have risen above the bs put in my path. Because of this, I carry and keep perfect records and move forward. I live a life that people know, and I recognize the lies when they come my way.

It's not that I don't play well with others; I just don't play well with liars, cheaters, users, thieves, and fakes.

Thoughts;____

____

____

Little Things
Huge Things
Memories Made

3 or 10 So many people know me or more about me from this picture. When I took it, I wanted to preserve Jake and I's wedding day in time. And that it does yet; it has turned into a bit of ME. And people see this and respond differently.

My follower (yep, her) degrades me over my love for single yellow roses. Yep! Yep! That one is beyond my ability to understand.

I received a message: "I got a friend request, and it had your yellow rose. Is that you?" I had a warm feeling wash me.

My "forever" friend went for a new walking path and took a pic of a beautiful yellow rose, posting it with the words "thinking of you." That bursted in my heart.

The rose has long ago become dry and brittle, put in the garbage, rot, and return to the earth. Yet, it still lifts me. After 42 years of loving me, Jake bought me flowers twice, and both left a mark on my life. But the fact that he normally didn't also leave a pleasant feeling. I adored his frugal management of money. Not once did he go to town, and he didn't bring back a gift. Donuts, huckleberry candy, a Trump 2020 hat, and one day, I truly realized he listened, a farmers almanac because I had said I couldn't find it… he took time to find it, bring it to me, and caused me to say "I love you."

3 or 10 Sometimes, it's the smallest moments in time that take up a huge part of our lives. Those (little) HUGE moments guide our day, our memories, our warm feelings. Since he was two, Monster has used my debit card to pay for things. He scribbled a signature…. I fell to my knees the first time he wrote his name…. I took a picture of it… it pops up in my FB memories, and I feel wonderful. Feelings of a perfect moment in time. I treasure so many (little) huge moments. Because of that, I'm writing a book for my grandson, which contains treasured minutes in this family. Darin sat by Dad, Mom sat closest to the kitchen, and I sat on the back side of the breakfast nook. I was probably 5-6 when I realized, "Mom! It doesn't matter which side of the table I sit on; I'm still left-handed." These little moments need to be noted as memories made, so I'm writing a journal of family members my grands

have never met. I hope they enjoy "memories made." I hope they laugh or cry; I hope they get a piece of my mom, dad, grandparents, great-grandparents, wisdom, and bonds that "moments" make the heart burst or fall to our knees.

The Beautiful Yellow Rose on the Cover is my Wedding Flower

Thoughts;____

____

____

Self Care
Self Love

3 or 10 This is so true. It's a hard lesson in life. But remains steadfast. It is also true that "how we treat ourselves is how we feel about ourselves." I'm in a current negative cycle in my world. No big drastic challenges, but I'm tired. Just absolutely exhausted every day. I write my 3 or 10 and delete it because it's horrible. I've reached out to professional help to realign my world. Yesterday, I got my ass chewed for expressing an opinion. It was an observation of a specific event. I snapped back, and the conversation became two equals, having a rational back and forth. After my "snap," I was relieved to find things we agreed on. But the "need" to snap left me hurt with tear-filled eyes

I am a 56-year-old woman with a loving heart, some bad habits, experiences that have given me wisdom and knowledge, bumps and bruises, excitement, and defeated moments. I have wonderful, great moments in time, along with complete devastation. I have challenges that I work on every day, along with greatness that cannot be denied. I believe I'm a 50/50 person. That is a fact, 50+50=100%; I will not allow my "good" to be trampled on. Denied, dismissed, or ever destroyed. The sad fact in this world is that separation from people is sometimes self-preservation. Because how people treat you is how they feel about you. Period. "2 wolves, one good, one bad; which one becomes stronger? The one you feed".

3 or 10 I'm off to feed my 50% good… I like her. She is special, spectacular, strong, loyal, respectful, deserves respect, loving, giving, knowing, wise, knowledgeable, enthusiastic, stable, and worthy… I shall "feed" her today.

"How they treat you is how they feel about you. Period.

Thoughts;____

____

____

Family
Personal Responsibility

3 or 10 The opposite is also true. Taking personal responsibility and being accountable doesn't mean your behavior is toxic. I always giggle when someone says, "I'm not a control freak." The bad news for them is, "We are all controlling." Toxic is manipulating others, and productive is controlling the "self." I'm absolutely a control freak… I control my housing by owning it, not renting it. I control my money by managing every penny. I control my dogs by training them to have good manners. I control who has access to me. I control repeat business by having a good work ethic.

It's also true that toxic behavior is relative. During family events, there is always a fight/discussion to be won. The referees are the key.

Love my mom to death, but it is a fact she was a chauvinist. Her referee "calls" were based on the sex or age of those involved.

When it came to my aunt and uncle, my uncle was the one wrong cuz he was bullying "the baby." Even when she was 25 to 50. Mom made excuses to reconcile "the baby".

Yet; When my brother and I did the same thing, my brother was correct; girls weren't allowed to do that. My brother and I were both single parents; she did his laundry, ran his errands, and went shopping for his house. For me, she pointed out where I could/should do better. 24 hours a day…My mom made me strong, completely by accident.

Thoughts;____

____

____

Mental Illness
Situational

3 or 10 On the news this morning was an arson; they caught the guy, and his family told the reporter that they "suspect mental illness." Well DUHHH! I'm pretty sure all "bad" behavior is some mental illness. So what is mentally ill, and what does it look like? I think of "The Unibomber" and "Bundy," both serial killers, and from the outside looking in, seem complete opposites. From who they wanted to kill, who they appeared to be, and how they got caught. All very different.

What does the mentally ill look like? Of course, it looks like everyone. Nancy Pelosi and AOC look pretty normal... their thinking does not appear normal at all. It is said our homeless are drug-addicted or mentally ill.

Rapists live in our neighborhoods; the other day at the grocery store, a local child rapist came up in conversation.... I said, "I was shocked because he looked like a nice guy, dedicated to his family, and church."

And, of course, my 14-year history of being abused and watched. She/He looks pretty, organized, and normal. Nothing could be further from the truth. He/She is very mentally ill.

The Green River Killer looked normal, too.

So do we know people that aren't struggling with trauma, depression, rape, discrimination, low self-esteem, PTSD, hoarding, passive-aggressive, domestic violence, etc. very few people have ever experience "nothing." We all have "stuff" that we struggle with.

Even my water issue screams "mentally disturbed." Morally, a business follows its own BiLaws; legally, it follows state and federal laws. And my water and the fight over it was simple: "A control freak found a way to exercise a sense of importance." That is mentally ill. Legally, morally, and ethically, they are complete failures as human beings. But they have control over me. Ha ha, NOPE, they don't! I'm still being a productive, coffee-making, dog mom. With plans, goals, relationships, and happiness.

I listened to Trey Gowdy's interview with Dr Anita Philips.... She said, "Loneliness is as bad physically as smoking 15 cigarettes a day." Well Well! True for sure.

3 or 10 Everyone "struggles," and everyone has "stuff" going on.
Everyone knows people who are thriving or failing. My dearest,
kindest, God-fearing, loyal, dedicated friend… broke her foot so badly
that it required surgery. We chatted because she was stuck, with her
foot elevated, and depending on others. She was sad and somewhat
depressed. And that depression would be labeled as "mentally ill." So I
can honestly say I don't know of UNmentally ill, whether chronic or,
like my saint friend, situational.

It's time to write a new story.

Thoughts;____

____

____

Loyalty
Family
Patriotism

3 or 10 New Year's Day is always a day to "feel" the future. By feeling, I mean we are mainly hopeful. I've been doing my best to sort 2023 and put what it has taught me in its place. The good, & the bad both have solid ground. As I look out, I question, I'm painfully inquisitive. And peacefully look for knowledge. This last week, a weird question bugged me. How can people celebrate Christmas "Christ" and vote for abortion up to birth? How can people "reconcile" wishy-washy beliefs? Child sex traffic and drugs, mostly people think are bad, yet voted for open borders. I need high-paying jobs, yet I shop at Amazon (China) over and over. Why don't our elected officials put America First, sanction or tariff nonAmerican imports? If those tariffs were put in place, Americans would NOT need to pay income tax. Those that are LGBTQIA+, supporting government or terrorists that would murder them in the town square. Colleges with outrageous endowments raise the cost of tuition. Why can't people see that hiring 87,000 employees will create a need to pay them, which will raise expenses? For the IRS to pay more people, tax revenue will need to go up. Call centers are moved overseas to save companies money and non-American wages. Companies have to answer to shareholders and pay dividends, but the government does not. Trump was right to put sanctions and tariffs in place to create America First. Why can't people see America as "family." No one with a good family relationship puts the "family" last.

3 or 10 Wishy Washy… my mom called people that blindly follow the government "sheeple," and this is on my mind… How can we get people to "stand up" for America? Or for Christ? Or for LGBTQIA+ rights? Or for Israel? Or for Family? Harvard is our oldest university and it is supporting Hamas…. Supporting Terrorists… supporting the beheading of babies… supporting Iran as they chant "death to America" if someone wanted to kill your family (Americans) why buy their oil? Why enrich their lives… why make them (Iran) wealthy? Why does Americans use companies that build foreign nations? I'm guilty… I use AT&T, cuz what cell company is American? Things to think about… so I will think!

Throwing me to the wolves doesn't work…..they come when I call-

She walks among the Wolves.

Thoughts;_______________________________________

____

____

Wisdom
Hope
Knowledge

3 or 10

"Pretty is as pretty does,"

"file don't pile,"

"cleanliness is next to Godliness,"

"If you haven't used it in a year, throw it away,"

"ya can't fix the chaos in life until you fix the chaos inside you,"

"if you can't run with the big dogs stay on the porch,"

"listen to hear, not respond,"

"kids are to be seen not heard,"

"mother knows best,"

"a bird in the hand is better than two in the bush,"

"a penny saved is a penny earned," "prayer changes things,"

"idle hands are the devil's workshop,"

"a job done well is a job well done,"

"first we must kill all the lawyers," Shakespeare

"let them eat cake," Marie Antoinette

"don't be a doubting Thomas,"

ETC!

We all have listened to the cliches, which wash over us like a soft rain. Some we put in our soul to make life better. Most of us dismiss it as fitting into a moment in time. Knowing the timing of these little pieces of wisdom means understanding why they were said. We quote Shakespeare, Socrates, Jesus, Queens, and our grandparents. These little "nuggets" of words guide us in our lives. We place them on refrigerator magnets, t-shirts, and 3x5 note cards. And like a soft rain, they are just temporary.

3 or 10 Socrates was 470 bc years before Jesus, and Marie Antoinette was 1765 AD years after Jesus. Shakespeare was born in 1564 and was aware of problems in our current justice system. Douting Thomas was an apostle who went to the "Last Supper." The fact is that history is always taught, but we don't learn the lessons. It continues to repeat itself, over and over, until the lesson is learned. It is the same in our little lives on Earth. As we prepare for WWIII, and I hoard things, history repeats itself. (WWIII is because "our house needs to be put in order") and my hoarding is cuz, well, I'm in chaos… (as always). I always forget the "file doesn't pile." I'm 1967 ad, and I need to learn some lessons… that the wisdom of was already spoken…. "You reap what you sow."

If you do one thing to better yourself every day, imagine where you will be in a year.

Thoughts;____

____

____

Self Acceptance
Personal Responsibility

3 or 10 Do I have positive thoughts today? This is an exercise to "create" positive thoughts in me. Why is it so hard to just "think happy?" For me, my mind races with both sides of any thought. This could be counted as a blessing because, as a college professor said about me, "You have a beautiful way of thinking outside the box." What a beautiful thing "noticed". What a true "curse." I wish I had not considered all the things that could have gone wrong. But planning, preparing, and preventing trouble is a good thing. What to do with a mind that never sleeps? Jake used to complain about not sleeping but would dig at me for medications. He should have respected his being, unique challenges, and body. Every night, to get my mind shut off, I take what I call "sleepy medicine."

It makes Annette sleep. I can stay awake for 36 hours, then nap restlessly, dream, dream, and fight sleep. No one can live like that. So I take my pills, sleep 6-8 hours, and have some sort of normal. When the reality is that the pills were created because no one I know really sleeps. They were not created because of me! But because they were created, I can sleep.

3 or 10 "Normal" that word is not based on a definition that can be grasped. Normal is a scale of "most common traits." Normal… most people are struggling with sleep, 30 lbs they should lose, exercise they should do, grief that needs tears, counseling they need to find, and sadness they need to overcome. Normal is more month than money, struggles with reaching dreams come true, and work hours vs family time. Normal is getting off balance, having to-do lists that are too long, and stress. Normal… I have more "common traits" than not… I am like a large group of disorganized, scattered, and rattled people. Oh my could I be normal? Well I'm in the range.

Sometimes, I just don't like people; they make me want to say bad words.

Thoughts;____

____

____

Patriotism
Community

3 or 10 The end of the year is a stir of looking back and forward. Election year is a stir of so much hate and anxiety. Candidate ads are ruthless and void of facts. Plus, I want to do what I can to get my guys/gals elected. I don't like Haily, and Desantis has failed with his "Spanish-speaking ads. Trump is so busy with all the cases filed… a new one today with Maine removing him from the ballot.

Winter is always "in the house" stuff cuz, at 30* sitting at the picnic table, a glass of wine and a book is no fun.

Spring is right around the corner and my "spring to-do list" is growing. New Year's Resolutions always crack me up. Loose weight, more exercise, saving money, etc… my resolutions are always the same: "I'm not making resolutions to fail to reach."

Knowing the world has gone "mad," I'm not really hopeful about this 2024 New Year's.

The war in Israel is going to create WWIII; Iran has already had 100 attacks on the US Military so far. Yep, lots of my friends don't know that cuz current events are not important to keep up on. Patriotism and Community are not their passion. Defund the police, CRT, and LGBTQIA+, reverse racism, lack of religion, lack of God the creator, and no family loyalty has the world upside down. Poland doesn't accept illegal immigration or refugees…. The most patriotic country in the world. The President of Poland LOVES POLAND…. And I respect him. (Andrzej Sebastian Duda (/ˈɑːndʒɛj ˈduːdə/ AHN-jay DOO-də; Polish pronunciation: [ˈandʑɛj ˈduda]; born 16 May 1972) is a Polish lawyer and politician who has served as president of Poland since 6 August 2015.) I don't respect Biden Harris because they hate our beautiful Americans. I bet none of my peeps know of Poland's policies. Well, maybe Kayleen and I would love to spend our time talking about history.

3 or 10 New Year's is to be hopeful, sending 2023 to the past and "ringing in" 2024. It's an election year… I'll pray for America every day like always… hopeful it becomes better. I'll pray for our police… to get the staff they need to make our neighborhoods safe. I'll stand against CRT, reverse racism, and drag Queens reading to children.

I'll tell everyone about my relationship with Jesus. I'll make way for LGBTQAI+ to live peacefully when they use good manners. And I'll call out grooming, pedophiles, and sex trafficking. I'll be vocal that "transition" chemicals and surgical procedures should wait until the age of 21. And I will pray, and pray, and pray that everything upside down turns right side up.

You can delete me, block me, unfriend me, or even unlove me, but you can never unmemory me.

Thoughts;____

____

____

Good
Happiness
Thankful

3 or 10 A funny meme, but anything funny always has some truth to it. Comedy comes from teasing life, life events, and even science. Why? Cuz we need laughter and tears to have a complete life. Yep, without one, the other one will consume us. No one wants to be consumed by sadness, so we add humor to our lives. All things are a pendulum; love people and need solitude. Love family closeness needs some superficial relationships. Love holiday celebrations are made better by the sad funerals we must go to. The soft caress of a cat and the hard touch of the dream corvette. Oil paint; add black to white to create every shade of gray…. Life is black, white, and a million shades of gray.

3 or 10 Thank God for the pendulum so we know sadness and can feel good, happiness, content.

3 or 10 We can't escape the black, to only have a life of white. The reason is pure white is hard to find sustainable. Yesterday, I stopped and got a latte, the first drink, hot, rich, refreshing, was perfect. It made the drive to town rewarded with a perfect; moment. Fact; if that was every cup of coffee it would loose it's moment. A pure white minute in time… made pure white by all the gray, and even that gulp of coffee, cold, nasty, bitterness, black. Seek the white; enjoy the gray; know that the black is the pendulum swing, but usually, it doesn't last long.

Be the reason someone smiles today. Or blocks you. Whatever.

Thoughts;____
____
____

Finding Hope
Happy
Thankful

3 or 10 I've written and deleted 3 or 10 twice this morning. Proof that I "have" to do it again, getting it right today. Some days, it is a really hard task. Sometimes, ya just don't "feel" not good or bad, just nothing. Melancholy. I've never used that word before. Thank goodness my phone knows how to spell it. Ha Ha! I am surrounded by both good, great, and wonderful things, and I also have a list of failures, dislikes, and want to change. So how will a day like this become three positive thoughts and ten things I'm grateful for? Sometimes, "simple" is best.

1. My coffee was hot and full of flavor.

2. I'm not frozen cold.

3. I'm not 100* hot and couldn't sleep.

4. I'm in fair health.

5. My back is loose, not a spasm.

6. I got stuff to do.

7. I'm hopeful for the new year.

8. I have check marks on yesterday's to-do list.

9. Today's tasks require me to be out of the house.

10. I'm going out to lunch.

11. I've been sorting out 2023 to get it closed on time for the IRS.

12. I have people that count on me.

13. I can delete 3 or 10 when it's not really 3 or 10.

2024 is just around the corner.... That only means I will fix writing 2023… ha ha at least I can laugh at that for a month.

3 or 10 Sometimes, 3 or 10 are written and deleted. Sometimes, I just can't write a positive thinking post. And then some days it is so easy.

Happy just comes to the page. Why? Cuz the brain is, in fact, hope for the future but sometimes dwells in the pain or past.

Thoughts;____

____

____

Purpose
Content

3 or 10 It is to look for happiness in life. Today is a good morning. Not
because the pups playing woke me up an hour before my alarm, but
because the pups were playing. For me, as they growl at each other,
learning how to be polite with each other is indeed music to my ears.
Oh yeah, they are loud, bark when I'm on the phone or play rough in
the 30 seconds of the news I wanted to hear. People don't understand
me. That's ok! I'm surrounded by complete unconditional love. Being a
mother is so ingrained in me that I remember the day and the moment;
it all started, like it was yesterday. I was about 5 or 6, and at the
babysitter, a newborn was brought in the house; I was mesmerized:
Mrs. Lugenbule sat me on the couch and placed the baby in my arms;
she put my hands where the baby was secured in my lap and arms. My
heart exploded with love and purpose! And there we have it....
Annette's heartstrings were set.

A Mommie was all I wanted to be. I sat holding the baby every minute
that I was allowed. It was a perfect moment in time.

3 or 10 Kids, grandkids, and dogs all take tender hours of the day.
They all take dedication and patience. They all have individual
personality quirks and excel, personally to themselves. Watching them
grow and knowing I am part of their "grown" upbringing is a little
perfect. More than a "little bit" perfect. I do love my titles…. Mama,
Mom, Mother, Granny, Grandmother, and from my furbabies… "Hey,
human; don't leave the room." Yea they don't talk much… except to
each other at 5:30 am. 😄 😄 😄

**I love it when my pets sigh… Like what ails you, my little
unemployed freeloaders?**

Thoughts;____
____
____

Praying

3 or 10 "When people tell you who they are, believe them." I believe this is a quote by Dr. Phil. I ponder it often. When I married Jake, he had stopped drinking. He was an alcoholic, drinking daily into a stupor for 30+ years, and he just December 7th, 2016 stopped drinking. I had prayed for it for 25+ years. He didn't tell me he was going to quit; we didn't talk about it; after all my years of nagging and begging, poof, he just stopped. Frankly, he didn't change much. Yes, the stupor, blackout hours, of not knowing what he did stopped. The drunk temper tantrums stopped, but the tantrums continued. All of his "good" continued, same as December 6th. But it didn't get better or more often.

3 or 10 Sober is better than drunk but the personality is the same. When I prayed for him to stop drinking I sincerely thought his thinking, and habits would improve, they did and didn't. There is a term "dry drunk" and it is a real thing.

Thoughts;____

____

____

Worth
Self Abuse

3 or 10 "You are WORTH more than second thoughts and maybes!" How powerful is that? How many of us live it? Why is it a struggle to convince others of it as a fact? I've noticed that the people who deny this fact demand it for themselves.

I'm very good at letting people I value know it as a fact. I check in, text, call, message, tag, give, and listen; I always take their calls. I'm not good at phone calls… but I am good at reaching out.

I'm currently in a war of…. Boundaries! I've asked for help, paid for help, and offered to pay others for help. I've stated what I can and cannot do. And in all fairness, I've had some show-ups, honored the relationship, and put some elbow grease into my life. Those are the ones that keep me feeling loved. I treasure them!

I'm in a strange cycle with some right now. It's mostly my fault. The first thing I did wrong was not stop this cycle sooner. The choice in life is a doormat or "you are being mean." I'm normally the doormat; some people not only count on that but also use it to benefit themselves. After a while, I become "mean" when I put my foot down and say ENOUGH! Then "they" pull their love, respect, moral responsibility, or even what is paid for. This sucks!

3 or 10 Doormat Syndrome is usually to keep the peace and is always taken advantage of. It also has the bubbling effect of resentments built over time. I know this but I am sure to be a doormat again, seems to be my MO. I spent Christmas with Mark Furman Diaries, and my dogs. My brother called and we chatted for an hour. I received a text from 1 child, "Merry Christmas." With predictive text that took 1.5 seconds. 1 aunt texted a bit. I didn't let anyone know about the surprise exam. Grades were given out at about midnight. "I" am WORTH more than second thoughts and maybes." I will focus on this fact, even if others disagree.

You are worth more than second thoughts and maybes.

Thoughts;____

____

____

Change
Personal Responsibility

3 or 10 One thing that lots of people forget is that our life is 100% our own doing, aside from things outside our control: deaths, trauma, and tragedy. Yet, the day-to-day life we lead is our own doing. I've been deep in thought of my life, both things I adore and hate. Learning from mistakes and celebrating triumph, this life of mine is.... my doing. I'm not in control of how others behave, and there are even horrible circumstances that I have nothing to do with, but I have options to rise or fall. THAT FACT IS POWERFUL! Regrets and guilt sometimes run the motor of that power. Sometimes, complete life-changing motivation is the power itself. Transitions and change are hard, sometimes paralysis, sometimes transformation, but always hard.

3 or 10 I need a call from heaven; my mom always motivated me. That's not possible, but her words echo in my head. Two facts: those echoes are a reminder of her love, and they lead me to good places.

Thoughts;____

____

____

Self Care
Personal Responsibility

3 or 10 I signed the contract to publish. I received an invoice from a company, not the name of the person I contracted with. So I went to task to investigate. It was a British corporation. So, I asked my contact, Max, about it. He said they use different finance departments. He would send me a different invoice. So, I went to their website, and at the bottom of the page was a different company. It was a British corporation with two members who had the same name, and she was Pakistani. They incorporated June 2023. So, I contacted my contact, and he had the same story about "the finance department." But he sent an invoice in the company name that I signed with. The next day, the company on the website was removed from the bottom. Therefore, I clicked on the 5-star reviews posted by Trust Pilot; they were beautiful reviews. So, I went to a different computer and went directly to Trust Pilot. Found the company, and it had no reviews at all. The contact info was the same phone number as Max's and the website's, but the name is Kevin.

3 different contacts, all with the same number… um, that is suspicious.

3 or 10 It's sad that there are scams and scammers everywhere. Why would a USA company use a British company owned by a Pakistani? Why would TrustPilot not get involved in 5-star reviews? Max said he's American with a British father. This popped up when I said, "You speak British, not American." The company is not licensed in New York or New Jersey, but the phone area code is American (New Jersey), and the sales tax is (New York). Tracking down and analyzing all these Things is hours invested. No wonder so many people get scammed. It's too good to be true… but the facts don't match. Max was good… but Annette is better. I am still looking for a publisher, UGGG.

I texted Hello, but what I really meant was, "You crossed my mind, and I paused."

Thoughts;____

____

____

Grief

3 or 10 December 23rd was a regular day for many, but it became one of my happiest days. I didn't know that it would also be one of my saddest. How did it happen? Well, it is an "anniversary" of a happy moment in time that becomes a reminder of grief. We all have these moments in our lives. A birthday, an anniversary, a beautiful day, followed by a complete sad loss. I'm not special or unique; I'm normal! Yeah, crazy me is….normal. Ha ha, when they say "time heals all wounds," they are just minding their manners. We have lots of phrases that are platitudes, not truth. After Indy passed, an unexpected thing happened that changed my world forever. Someone said, "He's in a better place." Those words are mean! And I've never used them since. As a writer and a reader, I can honestly say, "Words are more powerful than a bow and arrow."

"Words build and destroy."

"Words are more abusive than a beating."

"Words heal or kill."

"Words rejoice or educate."

"Words are a weapon or a bittersweet truth."

3 or 10Today is Jake and my wedding anniversary; his death makes this a sad day in time. Not because it was a perfect day once, but because he's not here to celebrate. It is also the anniversary of buying this property. Which is perfect; it gives me hope and security. Which is the future, yet knowing Jake is the past. Words: I have my wedding vows printed; I can read them and have the warmth wash over me. I can look at the escrow statement and see I'm gaining ground. Both documents are very powerful…..words, are never "Just Words."

It's perfectly Ok to talk to yourself and it's perfectly Ok to answer yourself. But it's totally sad that you have to repeat what you said because you weren't listening.

Thoughts;____

____

____

Advice
Self Care
Health

3 or 10 Free advice is a specialty of mine. I got my vision back today. Free advice: If you think you should go to the ER, you should! So, I had eye buggers; when I rubbed my eye, it started to hurt. For three days, I told myself, "It will get better," but it didn't. Finally, my eyes swelled up, and it completely shut down on day 6 (Monday). I headed to urgent care, but I wasn't sure I could drive with just one eye. I'm an independent woman who certainly never needs help. Well, it was an interesting challenge. The doctor numbed my eye and then strained it. He called it "A divot!". Well, I haven't been playing polo or golf, so there is that. And my drive home was a little crazy. So, eye drop antibiotics. Still, a lot of eye boogers and pain. But on Tuesday, I called the office to report that I was a little better. This morning, I woke up thinking I should go back to Dr. Tylenol. I had coffee, which would upset my tummy.

My dogs and I later woke up at 11:30 am and poof! All the eye boogers were gone. No eye boogers and swelling went down enough to see the TV. It was 4 pm now, and I could see. Oh my goodness! Still watering and hurts but not ER status. I think I might be on the mend.

3 or 10 A divot! A divot! How on earth does that happen? And how long do divots take to heal? For my medical friends, is "divot" even a medical term? For all my other friends, Do Not Get A Divot. They hurt like hell, and it ruined plans for days. Day eight arrived, and I started to feel much better; thank Goodness! Next challenge: how long does it take to grow back eyelashes?

Things I'm Super Good At:

1. Forgetting someone's name 10 seconds after they tell me.

2. Buying produce and throwing it away two weeks later.

3. Digging through the trash for the food box I just tossed, because I already forgot the directions.

4. Making plans qnd then immediately regretting making plans.

5. Leaving laundry in the dryer until it wrinkles. Then turning on the dryer to dewrinkle. Then forgetting it again.

6. Calculating how much sleep I'll get if I can just "fall asleep right now."-3am thoughts

Thoughts;____

____

____

Acknowledgment
Self Aware
Self Love

3 or 10 I'm taking a class to "be a better me." It's a hard class cuz so much of the homework is about "others," whether it is work, family, friends, or community. Very few things in the world are not hinged to other people. Happy or sad usually involves others, and work and play usually involve others. Even Stress or relaxation usually involves others. Today's question was "Getting what you want" and all the things I'm "not" supposed to do. My answer was ACKNOWLEDGED. Who in life doesn't want to be acknowledged? From walking into a business or being a business, having lunch with family, or having a stranger open a door, a birthday card to a Pulitzer Prize, all humans seek acknowledgment.

The sad truth is that building oneself is mainly an on our own list; the world is filled with impersonal experiences, rude, narcissistic, controlling, self-absorbed, and interactions. Judgmental and disrespectful are no-nos to healthy relationships with everyone, even with ourselves.

3 or 10 Wanting to be acknowledged is a human need. Praying and Faith are what God says is acknowledging him. But; he also asks for testimony, whether a song of praise or sharing his "word." Praise and worship but also the way we present ourselves to the world. Acknowledging a person prevents loneliness, low self esteem, and depression. As everyone knows I have a relationship that I don't want; sometimes (lots of times) she requests, that I apologize, hear her side of the story, and acknowledge her greatness. If that would work to end the relationship, I would gladly do it, yet; her refusal to acknowledge me, my requests, or respect my boundaries means the relationship will continue to be horrible. I'm gonna work on "", put out what you want to be returned, "Acknowledgement," every chance I get, can create or push for. I'm gonna "Send out" acknowledgment. Like The Secret says, "What you want, give away."

You will inspire some and annoy others. Do it anyway.- Here's to sassy living.

Thoughts;

Evolving
Change
Content

3 or 10 As I get older, I'm losing my drive for a few things and gaining it for others. It is said that our taste buds "e" every seven years, so we should always sample foods we may not have liked. It's true that I now eat ketchup, which I did not like as a child. In life, good and bad, our taste evolves, and so do we. My books, decor, and clothing are all different. Sleep and resting styles have also changed. Faith and knowledge. I remember a girl mesmerized about my future is now settled into hating change. I used to need to "go," and now I dread "public." Some of these changes are physical; I now need to go home before dark, as I prefer to see the elk on the road. And I play "Where are my glasses?" all day.

3 or 10 Evolved? Life always changes. My first grandbaby was born perfect. The cutest baby I had ever seen is now ten, and I see a young man evolving. He wears pants the same size as me. Oh my! 56 is closer to 70 than 40, and 100 is closer than 21. This is a bizarre thing! I'm currently closer to 100 than 21. I miss the energy of 21 and love the knowledge I'll have of 100. 21 was fueled by drive and fearless; this 56 thing seems to be about a good finish. 21 was no fear of dying, and 56 is fear of dying alone. Change is both feared and inevitable. I now put ketchup on my fried potatoes, and I love it. I look in the mirror and see wrinkles on my face, but my beautiful red hair is gray. I giggle cuz I sparkle when I know where my glasses are; without them, the wrinkles are a blur. The best part of age is becoming humble and humble does feel good.

How can you stop a determined woman?

You can't

Thoughts;____

____

____

Evil Abusive
Satan
Manifesting

3 or 10 I believe we all have negative traits and things that we justhate. I'm blessed that there are only three people I've ever hated. Mainly, I'm a loving person. I scold myself for hating and would love to be able to let it go, yet these three refuse to leave me alone. They love the control they believe they hold and refuse to act in a good or healthy way because of their need to lord over me. I'm constantly looking over my shoulder. They don't only target me; they target everyone around them. To me, the three relationships are very different. And I'm even told by some family members that my "feelings" are wrong. These family members have never lived through what I have, so the advice is from no "experiences."

I love being told, "Maybe they asked Jesus to forgive them." If that were true, the behaviors would change, and healing could begin. When salt is rubbed into a wound, it does not heal; it burns and becomes bigger. As I live in terror, watching, waiting, knowing terrible will come from these 3, I also know it is all because of their broken psychological mind. The abuse they enjoy inflicting is pure evil. A healthy, content mind never produces such freakish behaviors. Being continually stalked by unhealthy psychology is horrible. I don't fear for my life because to kill me would cause them to lose the pleasure they receive from the torture.

3 or 10 It helps me with these three. Asking Jesus to forgive my hate helps me. Praying for these three comes with each attack, so I'm confident I'm doing my part well. I could offer forgiveness when the bad behavior changes, and until then, I will continue with the good in my life, not in spite of them but in lieu of them. They don't realize they have no true control. I carry on, I smile, I build, I have endurance, and I succeed. So, those wishing I fail, I am unhappy, or have become a loser. Good Luck, Satan, cuz you are not a successful evil in my life. BOOYAH, I win! Knowing they spend their time on me is knowing they have no time to receive good. They rob themselves; some call that Karma. Some call it "reaping what they sow." Some say it's what is put out that is returned. I'm exhausted by their toxicity, but only for a moment. They hate themselves but take it out on me; I win cuz I love me.

I am in charge of my happiness.

Thoughts;____

____

____

Family
Loyalty
Loving

3 or 10 "I'm watching." I don't share or speak of all I see. So many things are not easily put into words. But, face it, things that matter are set in our hearts. Because I'm always watched and attacked for just being me, I'm constantly looking over my shoulder. The pain and heartbreak that stalkers create is real. Self-esteem gets shattered when lies are told and believed. Being stalked is shattering. Yet; my self is risen from knowing both my truth and hers.

But; triumph is achieved when things get crazy because knowing who we are is realized. This family of mine has so much wonderful "stuff," and some of it comes from the fire burning to complete failures. Ashes are the foundation from which to build. Those ashes turned into the mortar holding the bricks together.

Know I'm watching…

The alcoholic that no longer drinks, druggies that beat their addiction, family feuds that turn into unbreakable bonds, children growing, teenager mistakes are made, and learned from, babies that grow into young people, and "homes" built from failure to success as a family.

Know I'm watching.

To rise above where failures once lived.

3 or 10

Know I'm watching even when I don't say it.

Know, I'm praying even when not asked to.

Know I'm rooting for you to succeed even when it seems there is no hope.

Know, I notice each heartbreaking step it takes.

Know I'm here, always.

Know you are not alone.

Know that my quiet isn't me being blind.

Know that I wait to be told I'm needed.

Know that when asked about your battles, we can win the war.

Know that if we lose the war, we will still be family-strong.

3 or 10 But I was the "E before I"

family member. The creative left-handed, outspoken, bold, talkative,thoughtful, loyal, watcher.

I BEFORE E

EXCEPT WHEN YOUR FOREIGN NEIGHBOR KEITH RECEIVES EIGHT COUNTERFEIT BEIGE SLEIGHS FROM FEISTY CAFFEINATED WEIGHTLIFTERS.

WEIRD.

Thoughts;____

____

____

Memories Made
Treasured Friends
Growing Up

3 or 10 A couple of weeks ago, someone dear to me commented about me, as far back as sixteen. I kept re-reading the comments as they could have been meant as a joke, or a little dig, either way, it doesn't matter as a negative. First, I've far outgrown the 16-year-old girl I once was; second, what others think of me is none of my business. But the interaction made me think I always have options.

1. I could giggle at a joke!

2. I could take it as a dig, feeling hurt.

3. I could remind them of their teen behavior.

4. I can blow it off.

5. I can ponder and

6. write a beautiful ending.

Thoughts;

3 or 10 Well, here we go.

I don't have many close friends from my teens. I have lots of Facebook friends from as far back as kindergarten, but we aren't close to each other. I have so many fond memories with so many of them, and they mostly don't participate in my trips down memory lane. I have eight from high school, and I still adore our interactions. I have one who calls me a "forever friend," Jo will always be a part of both the past and future. As an Army wife, I had people I counted as close but have since fallen away. Jake was from kindergarten, 52 years, and had so many wonderful moments we share. I would have held his hand in death, but he didn't want me to. The first kiss to death was 42 years ago. As my first kiss and his last lover, we have a story to tell. I have a novel to write but secrets to keep. I'll assume the comments were loving jokes, and I'm valued. Options lead us to be happy or unhappy; the part that is ours is "the reaction." I'm going to react, haha, it's too funny! That 16-year-old girl is treasured; she was beautiful, strong, loving, and lovable! She was loved! Even by him.

Thoughts;_______________________________________

____

Self Awareness
Self Worth
Self Esteem

3 or 10 Depression, loneliness, sadness, and stress are facts of life. But so is happiness, fulfillment, rest, and relaxation. I'm in therapy because I'm struggling with some stuff. I'm in DBT training 2 days a week, and something popped up this week that got me thinking. The statement was "Getting the other person to do what you want." The exercise was about "my" part. My first thought was "manipulation". My second was, "Ya can't force others to do what you want". Then I thought of college "stuff" building self-worth. Personality testing, work preference, and relationship-type tests made me think of results. A therapist uses the DSM to come up with a diagnostic psychological problem to solve. So my "type A" personality then needs to be fixed cuz well fact is the therapist could care less about the good tests results, cuz fixing, improving the way people are is not the point, getting insurance companies to pay is the point.

3 or 10 the DSM never looks for good. It doesn't have a diagnostic list of positive productive traits to acknowledge and enhance. It's a really sad book. Thank God in college I got "the good stuff" testing.

Thoughts;____
____
____

Happiness

3 or 10A lot of stuff in life goes around in a wiggly line, not in a full circle. I look out and know very few always "happy" people. Very few that don't suffer from anxiety, sadness, displeasure, or loneliness. I know very few people without big problems. And some of these people must have happy, content, and joyful times. Wiggly lines are trying to come full circle. Mistakes, trials, triumphs, great days, happy thoughts, angry moments, grief, beautiful. A thing called "doing life". I'm busy today "doing life."

Poetry is there if you can see it:

just because someone carries it well doesn't mean it's not heavy

Thoughts;____

____

____

Family
Children

3 or 10 I'm very guilty of trying to steal God's pen. In my first marriage, I had to work and be a full-time mom and wife. It was too much. Three full-time jobs (job, wife, household, and children) robbed us of the special time I needed to excel at one. Lots of women do it, and we are all tired. But because we are women, we handle it as best we can. God designed the "family" with a logical man and a nurturing, emotionally balanced woman.

The WWII and the feminists took the woman out of the house, placing them in corporate America. My mother always had a beautiful garden that had produce for our family. She nurtured it almost every day. Because of her divorce, she was pushed into a full-time job at 1% of Dad's wages; our family shifted negatively.

I've always worked, not because it was best for the family, but because it was required for the family to survive. Taking away God's pen. An 8-hour work day is 10+ hours. I was blessed in 2001 to step out of corporate America. I was told I couldn't switch my lunch hour to attend Saige's first school play. I thought, "Who will be at my funeral?". I left for my normal lunch hour and never returned. Saige was adorable. I can't even remember my boss's name, but Saige received higher self-worth forever.

3 or 10 "God's pen" is a real struggle when we are trained by society to get it done, to shift priorities away from his perfect plan by design, to social demands. God says, "Be still." Society says to drive faster cuz you are always late. God says, "Fear not." Society says to live in fear. God says, "Reap what you sow," society says build corporations' earnings. God says, "Give Caesar his due." Society says we will steal your money, joy, and time. God gave us the instructions (the Bible) to find "joy"; society says no joy for you. God promised "rest," but society says you don't need sleep. I think it is time to give God back the pen!!!

God is still writing your story; stop trying to steal his pen.

Thoughts;____

____

____

Prayers
Faith

3 or 10 Still trying to figure this out. My math is not working right. Math sucks; sellers are demanding 25% down... oh my! Prayers: I still need all my friends to lift me in prayer. Life is crazy at times. Mostly, in fact! Maybe God's answer is just "NO". That leads to more depressed feelings. Sad frustrated, and it's been a year to find perfect. My child is causing me trouble and also causing me feelings of hurt, but Marnie Boyer says I still have to do my 3 or 10; yep, practice, she wants me to practice.

3 or 10 The snow falling energizes me; my pine trees covered in the snow show me God's perfect plan of seasons, watering His garden and giving me a shady place to rest. Yep, the snow falling is one of his gifts to ME! The cold of winter is solace for my soul. As God took time to "Feed my soul," I must trust that he has a plan for a home! Maybe not this one, but a plan, I'm sure. I need to trust; that's my issue.

Realtor ad for a perfect home

Thoughts;____
____
____

Patriotism
Community

3 or 10 My Patriotism is strong and creates a complete gut-wrenching reaction to those in government trying to destroy America. I'm really upset by the people running or voting to take the Founders' values away.

This coronavirus is going to hit the undocumented and the homeless. THEN WHAT? I'm saddened that people will die in mass numbers. And it is a product of the local governments, run by Dems.

WA is a sanctuary, which will create mass numbers of people infecting others. But Patty Murray won't face the fact that she helped to make WA a 3rd world country. When the virus gets to Othello and Mattawah, it will be a rapid-fire of events. And it will be 100% the fault of the laws not being enforced. Yep! No deportations for the last 50 years have created pockets of people who won't get medical attention.

3 or 10 I've been watching America get destroyed from within. How stupid is that?

God Shed His Grace On Thee

Thoughts;____

____

____

Patriotism
Community
Health

3 or 10 I had a friend who was running for the State Representative I want conservative government values and have stood with him until this morning. He freaked out about ID not allowing Hemp, but last year and this one, he has grown in WA but still flipped out. "The government can not regulate agriculture; it's not in The Constitution." Well, thank God the government controls drugs!

Yes, Hemp, just like tobacco, aspirin, and poppies to produce heroin and pot, all need to be controlled. Some of the control is keeping drugs out of the wrong hands, some is to control demand so prices stay up, but mostly, the government controls quality. I'm a weirdo in his mind that I don't want wheat with ergot! Yep, the mind going crazy from Ergot caused the killing of the girls at the Salam Witch Trials. I want my government involved. So, he called me a Socialist, and his friend asked if I "Was from CA." When I asked him if he could list three things that were important to me in voting for him, he told me my wants from a rep were not important because only The two Constitutions matter. What? The voter doesn't matter? Ok, well, I re-evaluated our relationship when he said, "Take your meds."

My oh my! So I'm some psycho because I want USDA, DEA, and FDA not to allow "snake oil salesmen" to grow drugs. However, his wanting pot listed as an herb that everyone can grow would align him with Bernie Sanders. His (correction Hari states no felony convictions) felony arrests and running from warrants make him like so many politicians.

He Doesn't Think Rules Apply To Him.

3 or 10 Not from CA, not a socialist, not psycho, not Voting For Him!

He won't make it to his wanted seat because my wants don't matter, and his 60's attitude is outdated. Maybe I should run against him to create school choice, balance the state budget, fix roads, and stop Idaho from taking in more refugees.

Snake Oil

noun

INFORMAL NORTH AMERICAN

noun; snake oil; noun: snake oil

**a substance with no real medicinal value sold as a remedy for all
diseases.**

**A product, policy, etc., of little real worth or value that is promoted
as the solution to a problem.**

"the new tax plan was denounced as snake oil."

Thoughts;____

____
____

Boundaries
Knowledge

3 or 10 I'm a thinker! It's a fact! I think things through. I look for info, read, research, chat with others, listen, and then form opinions. I solve problems and am a "Think outside the box" person. I've been thinking a lot about people. I stay away from politics. Extreme! Those are the ones I have been getting rid of on both sides. Bernie is so far away from logic that he irritates me. Raise Taxes! Open Borders! Late-term abortion! And yesterday, I got rid of a No Government at all. Extreme sucks the life out of any conversation.

I'm sad that these people can not hear! And they have no respect for others. CA and NYC are so extreme that life there must be stifling. Can you imagine living in NY? Or CA? I have a neighbor; she is over the top in her demands on everyone on my mountain. Everyone hates her! Yep, hate her! The places she works lose business because you either agree with her extreme or she verbally attacks you. It's sad for people forced to be there. Where is she from? CA. She moved here from CA with her two best friends. Yep, from CA. I'm a thinker, but not extreme at all. I can hear others' opinions and agree or disagree. But facts drive my mind; research is a must. My feet are firmly planted in a couple of things: abortion, family, lying, criminals, and drugs, all thought through before I made a stand. North Idaho has Wolf tags. People from CA pack up, destroy anything in their path, kill for fun, leaving carnage. No government creates chaos, hurts the vulnerable, leaves the weak and disabled to starve, increases abortion and drugs, killing productivity. Bernie's bros will steal from the productive, taking liberty out of America and letting her suffer a slow, painful death. North Idaho has wolf tags, and we should be allowed to use them.

Thoughts;____

____

____

Family
Bonds

3 or 10 this pic popped up. Very few people tell others the real thing, the core, the truth. Me and you included. Not many people have a clue what is going on with me. Because; I don't trust them, it is none of their business, or maybe I don't know for sure. I have a list of people that mean the world to me, I try hard to let them know, but, some people can't see the gifts of love. Yesterday my brother and I shared a milk shake, oh yea no big deal right!!! Wrong!!! For 51 years we have shared a milk shake... $3 for 20 minutes of chatting... and a milk shake. We chatted about all kinds of things; we hit all the big topics... kids.. grandkids... brats... plans... the next month... but we also hit Tradition!!! A moment of childhood!!! Memories of mom making us milkshakes... a little gift in a busy day, week, life.

3 or 10 today I ponder this pic... yep not many know what is going on with me.

Why you should be gentle with people

What you know about it (*****)

Someone's Life

(**********************************)

Thoughts;____

____

____

Motivation
Self Acceptance

3 or 10 Sometimes, it is a "grab your bootstraps" kind of life. It's not a get comfortable and relax; it's a get up... "pull wisdom teeth" kinda thing. Change is good! I'm a Gemini! Yep, change is normally okay with my inner being. So, the question of the day!

3 or 10 Where are my "bootstraps?"

I said to myself "self", (and I knew it was me because I recognized my voice and I was wearing my underwear). "today is going to be a good day!"

Thoughts;____

____

____

Giving
Loving
Self Acceptance

3 or 10 Here we go again. I'm so saddened by our mental health treatment in the US. What to do when another person can't stop bad behavior? They shatter relationships, self worth, and energy. I'm absolutely exhausted by narcissism. Most people are at some point abused, manipulated, or harassed, by another person needing to be center of attention. Yet; the ones in therapy are not the narcissist... the one begging God for relief is not Satan... Today's challenge, my phone. Jake has books, magazines, newspapers, a calendars, a clock, an alarm, and talks on his phone for hours at a time. But; my phone is the problem in the relationship??? No!! His ME ME ME is the problem!!! But I'm the one looking for solutions, support, changed behavior. Am I an idiot? I can't change another person... I'm not jealous of his books, magazines, newspapers, calendar, clock, alarm, or talking to his family FOR HOURS. This is not my problem... I'm not the narcissist!!! All this overwhelming feelings come as another narcissist turns up again. Yea, I had hoped it was over... oh hell no!! Of course not. Dec will be 10 years. Oh My!!! 3 or 10 if you are selfish... I'm exhausted. If you want to harass me, I'm numb. If hurtful makes you feel powerful, I know a therapist that maybe can help you. EAR PLUGS are in my future, so I can read a book (on my phone) and not be irritated by babbling, ME ME ME!!!

Before you fake your lifestyle on Facebook at least block the people that know you in person!

Thoughts;____

____

____

Blessed
Health

3 or 10 STRESS did you know the birth of a child and the death of a parent have the same stress level. Happy or Sad stress is STRESS. I ponder stress a lot!! Some is worry, some anger, some is happy, some is loss, and some is control. I have an MD in a federally funded clinic. His appointments are over booked, clinic organization is lacking, follow up does not exist, and a phone call is almost always, to the wrong persons voice mail. So my health has been declining, the main treatment I need is for my sleep problems. I don't sleep!!! And without medication when I doze I either have night terrors or weird dozing that is not restful.

My MD is not listening to Annette as a whole person. I knew for about 6 months I was in trouble, but winter, selling and buying a house, and divorce I kept blowing it all off, until a week ago... I returned to my old Dr, Marnie. .. she said something that was a lightbulb moment.. "Annette doesn't do well with medication stacking!!!!" And she pulled me off 2 meds... LAST NIGHT I SLEPT 8 HOURS NO DREAMS NO NIGHT TERRORS AND I FELT GOOD WHEN I WOKE UP AT 8 a.m.!!!!!

3 or 10 Marnie is the best dr... I'm blessed to know her and have her take ME, the whole me, into account when I pop in to see her!!! Marnie I SLEPT 8 hours!!! SLEPT not just twisted in a bed!!! Not a quiet time cuz it's dark outside!!! I SLEPT!!!

A strong woman has faith that she is strong enough for the journey, but a woman of strength has faith that it is the journey that she will be become strong. www.spiritusilentrium.com

Thoughts;____

____

____

Angels
Loved Ones

3 or 10 Tears... yep tears are a sign that my angels are chatting and I'm to be listening. My faith in my angels is absolute.

Giggles lift the heart...

A hug can sooth the soul...

A peaceful nights sleep refreshes.

A smile from a stranger is still a smile.

The laughter of a baby in church deserves a Hallelujah, Amen.

3 or 10 "Chris Young, Voices" is a beautiful song that always gives me goose bumps. To listen to the words ground me to loved ones I miss. Happier times.

My inside Annette is so stressed. Going through stuff, is just that, but I'm promised "rest" if I just stay in "faith". It is hard sometimes.

But it IS!!!

So on this day I've just got to stay in the Moment.

Listen.

Be Assertive....

Stand My Ground.

Thoughts;____
____
____

Prayers Answered
God Is Faithful
Home

3 or 10 Oh My Today I Really Need My 3 or 10. I need my friends and family to give me a boost of mental health. God showed up and provided me a home in Idaho. Yep, with prayer, dedication to his path, I'm not being forced to return to Lind. Oh my... every penny will need counted, sorted, and placed in the HOME account. But; oh my moving. One more trip to Lind, load up the semi... I already paid the driver, so that is a blessing. Then a trip for the 5th wheel and I'm done with the move. But; then the move here inside Benewah County. Normally I would have money to pay for help. But I bought a house this month, so money is all gone....

3 or 10... oh my I bought a house... so PEACE is coming. 3. Peace... peace... peace. 10. Blessings... if I work really hard in 10 days I will wake up in a different space.

Thoughts;_______________________________________

____

____

Rest
Blessings

3 or 10 I'm in my pajamas playing solitaire today because I'm absolutely over whelmed.

Bought a house, a new business, a new horizon.

I got the keys yesterday. Oh my!!!

I sold my house in Lind... glad it's in my rear view mirror and

I'm terrified.

Owning outright vs payments.

Such a blessing to a new family that is excited to have goats and chickens. I worked on the contract yesterday and today. I'm beat up.

Snow, rain, sunshine, snow again, big black clouds. Idaho is not cooperating with me moving.

So I did 8 hours today and went for a nap that I did not get.

3 or 10 overwhelmed is ok.... when it is with a goal of making life better. Please say a little prayer... me and my dogs need it.

Thoughts;____
____
____

Family
Love
Motherhood

3 or 10 today is my RooRoo's birthday. But because she didn't like me living my beliefs, she blocked me. So here I sit thinking of her, but really don't feel like going out of my way to find her work number to call. I haven't seen the boys since the first week of November, yep I feel a little upset about that. I got a "stop fighting" talk, but it isn't me that did the blocking, the lack of holiday, or the fight (name calling), I'm supposed to be "the bigger person" ha that is funny. Begging to be respected isn't in my list of "stuff I'm gonna do". So I sit here this morning wishing I could be a part of celebrating her birth, her very being, and her as a gift from God.

I'd give anything to have lunch or a phone call from my mom, I guess Roo doesn't feel the same way.

3 or 10 27 years ago, April Fool's Day, I called my mom to tell her I had a baby girl. 7 lb 4 oz, healthy and I was amazed at how beautiful she was. This will heal in time but today I miss my baby RooRoo

Thoughts;____

____

____

Family
Bonds
Missing

3 or 10 for a couple months I've been looking for a psychic. This has caused people to pray for me, worry about me, and send me strange messages.

But; Lott, Moses, Mother Mary, and Sarah all spoke of communication with the other side so I think I'm safe to follow the lead of the Greats that made it into The Bible.

My family is filled with "knowing" so wisdom and knowledge have always been a part of my world.

My search lately is because since Indy died I've been blocked from my gift of "knowing".

A lady messaged me and told me she wasn't psychic but she was "knowing". Her gift was to help with trauma. And then she started typing.

She knew of Indy and his reddish hair. She talked of my mother smiling and then mom scolded me "you were raised better" "jump in feet first without thinking, just get it done" she told me I was wearing moms rings. She then said your mom wants you to go garden, but she is laughing. It must be an inside joke. I was giggling and crying at the same time. Mom loved her garden, I did not; but I loved mom so I spent a lot of time weeding.

Then I asked the looming question.

Were the twins boys or girls? Boys and your mom calls them Adam and Jack. One has fiery red hair. Your mom sings to them. Then the lady said 3 not 2. I said "yes I have 3 grandchildren in heaven". She said "2 are in a lot of pain". I said "yes they were murdered". Then she said "your mom has them, she is teaching them silly stuff" sometimes comfort comes from strangers.

3 or 10 my twins are boys and their names are Adam and Jack and one of them has the Herreid red hair. My mom has them, and she sings to them. And I feel comforted.

Knowing

Mother's Intuition

Angels

Thoughts;____

____

____

Forgive
Honesty

3 or 10 Happy Easter HE HAS RISEN!

I always love these tap here to see that! (Facebook game) And how close they are some times.

My brother tells me that I need to forgive people for bad behaviors. He is right I need at times to let go. And for the most part I do.

I remain friends for 40 years with people that have broken me, I stay in touch with past lovers, I care for people far to busy or selfish to care for me. For the most part I'm a good person.

I usually say the wrong thing, at times in the wrong tone, and when I'm angry my words get away from me. But let's face it... "When people show you who they are, BELIEVE THEM" Dr Phil.

People that suck... suck. I try hard to just avoid them. This little test popped up today. I think it is pretty close. I am indeed "brutally honest" a down fall when people want you to lie about deplorable traits. I hate liars and thieves. They Suck. Ugly Boots are ugly, and I don't feel the need to say "oh how cute". But I do recognize some people like Ugly Boots!

3 or 10 HONEST... in good and in bad, it is true I don't have the trait of lie to people, because it's nice!!! It is not nice to be a liar!

Thoughts;____

____

____

Sharing
Caring

3 or 10 This is so true on every level a relationship can have. Sharing!!! When given a baby brother I learned to share my mom... When I got to k-garden I learned to share color crayons, the merry go round, and stand in line to wait my turn. When I opened candy or potato chips I was required to share with everyone in the room. When Christmas came my Grampa got in his wallet and shared his blessings with Boys Town. I was taught to share everything from books to bicycles, knowledge to wealth, poetry to faith, I'm so blessed to be humbled at all things in life, bigger and smaller than my self. I am the one that visits the sick, gives to the poor, and talks to the child.

I'm in the midst of a divorce, I feel a failure, but the fact is one of my core beliefs and strengths is SHARING. Jake cannot share. His or not. Even as it's time to fix plates for dinner he can not share the hussle in the kitchen. Money is an all out war of greedy. "We" do not have a drill for the house... it is "his" and I must ask permission to use it... (I bought the drill). We have no mutual friends, goals, or property. We make no plans, or share responsibility. By not being able to share he took love and turned it to resentment, he took a home and pitted it against itself, the REMOTE... can you believe a married couple could fight over a remote... yes after he would go to sleep I would grab the remote, he would wake angry taking the remote putting it on his nightstand, needing the remote I would reach across him, and the fuss would begin that I woke him. This hostile environment created a stress... HIS REMOTE... since I couldn't read, (the light bothered him), and I couldn't watch what I wanted while he was asleep, I reacted. I unplugged the satellite receiver and hid the power cord. Yes; I got bitchy... and he learned nothing.

3 or 10 I'm so blessed to have been taught, expected, and required, TO SHARE!!! If you need help with a flat tire call me... Jake won't answer the phone, he will not come help you, and you can't use his jack... call me... I can't fix a tire but I will sit with you while "we" wait for a guy to help, and we can share my coffee!

Sharing is Caring

Thoughts;____

____

____

Motivation
Knowledge

3 or 10 What creates a person to refuse to be better? No goals, no plans, no reading for knowledge, no learning from another, no answers to the question "why?", no motivations to make life better or easier. Within minutes of getting out of bed I'm reading, planning, setting up goals, motivated to become better than yesterday. This is my person. I fail a lot but never can someone say "she didn't try". People call me all the time with weird questions. Yes; I read IRS law cuz well "I need to know", I read newspapers from around the US, yep there are things going on in the world... and I need to know, WHY? So when someone calls I know some stuff. HaHa

3 or 10 my kids and I played Trivia when ever we were in the pickup... 40 miles to moms house and "we" were better people when we finished the drive. My kids "knew" more stuff, and now all grown up they are Smart Ass's, haha but they must look back and admit, "mom taught us the weird stuff".

Knowledge is a wonderful gift, We Give Ourselves

Thoughts;____
____
____

Praying
Jesus
Selfishness

3 or 10 I'm lost this morning. How on earth is it that people say "I love you" when really what they mean is "I love you when you are doing things my way" or "I love you when you are giving to me". Yep, yep, some family and friends treat people like crap, over and over. Why?

I think of my kids when I think of love, I would literally lay down and die so they could live. I think of Lloyd... he was always happy to see me, tease me, joke around, and smile. I think of Skip and his insistence that my kids would "have" all they worked for. I think of my brothers crazy house, from 3 to 90 years, all come to the table. Then I think of Jesus, how can he forgive ALL? But he does.

Then the "takers" come to mind... they suck. It is the "takers" that make life hard. It's the "I love you's" with conditions that drain the mind. It is the ones that don't show for the work or the hard times, that make life lonely.

3 or 10 the song "Jesus Take the Wheel" by Carrie Underwood is my motivation at this point. As I took on far more than I can do myself, and I'm overwhelmed. I have been spending a lot of time reminding, begging, my mom to guide me (her advice still lives on). I've been asking Jesus to help me forgive so many. And I'm trying to understand why? Why are there so many empty "I love you" people in the world?

I'm glad I'm not one of them.

I'm praying for them.

Thoughts;____

____

____

Faith
Blessings
Change

3 or 10 THE BIG PICTURE!!! At times in life we get so wrapped up in the little stuff, drama, stress. We surround "us" with a list of stuff that doesn't even matter. But; it is the BIG picture that defines the future. Kids turning to adults and having kids of their own. Parents passing. Building our home. Gaining that degree. TURNING TO GOD. Faith is a little step to the big picture. I know in my heart I have a future but today I just need to move. I know I'll get thru anything given me, but oh my where to put a coffee pot is literally making me crazy, ya know water and power, convenient, out of the way, safe for kids, WTHeck this is making me crazy. So a deep breath, it's a coffee pot for God's sake.

3 or 10 I have a future... with a coffee pot some place. I have a house to turn into a home. I have neighbors to meet and friendships to build. Life is... THE BIG PICTURE!!!

Guide removes people from your life because he heard conversations that you didn't hear

Thoughts;____

____

____

New Beginnings
Change
Grief

3 or 10 Building New!!! Yep; we need both headlights and a rear view mirror. Going thru divorce is hard... all that is lost. BUT... I'm "building new" I've given myself permission to grieve my marriage, it's absolutely ok to feel sad, angry, hated; hateful, BUT.... it's ok to look forward and even feel excited for "the new".

This is silly but I bought a 5000 sq foot shop turned into a home with no heat... what on earth was I thinking? No heat vs staying married... a no brainer. That tells me how bad I feel about my marriage. That is sad; really sad. But very REAL.

3 or 10 best get off my bottom and get heat in my home!!!! And doors, windows, and a floor, not cement. And, well, life is busy… ALWAYS... headlights not rear view mirror.

"The secret of change is to focus all of your energy, not on fighting the old, but building the new" Socrates

Thoughts;____

____

____

I am

3 or 10 I'm definitely a dog person. I have a wonderful witty humor. I'm a Gemini. (That's why I "get" President Trump) I multitask very well. Some call me scattered. My house is a complete disaster of 100 projects going on in various stages, but none are put away. My mind covers a million different topics. I get scolded all the time because my pickup floor is covered in trash. But; I make a choice, clean pickup or read a book!!! Ha I'm reading a book.

3 or 10 Dogs don't care about my "stuff" "my scattered" because they get to eat my cooking mistakes, I'm willing to open the door a 100 times a day, and my split personality, either one of them, is fun.

Them; are you a dog person or a cat person?

Me; all I can tell you is I'm not a people person

Thoughts;____
____
____

Success
God

3 or 10 bold, brash, never feared confrontation or consequences for standing for my beliefs.

My Grampa used to say "God seen that" that is a pretty good way to teach a kid to behave. Yep, even all alone, God seen that.

When I get to the pearly gates will judgement go smoothly? So many want to blame, point fingers, name calling, threats. For the most part I let it roll off me like water on a ducks back, but sometimes I can't. Sometimes it pushes on me, sometimes I get completely overwhelmed. Sometimes I'm a complete failure. "God seen that". Sometimes I'm a complete success. "God seen that". But it is true the things that haunt me, are the things I haven't let go.

3 or 10 sometimes I'm a complete success!!! "God seen that" Period

sometimes your worst enemy is your memory, let that go!

Thoughts;____
____
____

Knowledge
Learning

3 or 10 when I'm trying to learn new things life gets crazy.

I like my normal I like things to stay the same I like it when I have control of my environment.

But there's times we have to do things we don't want to do but they're a must.

So I bought a new house and it has a ramp not steps so to get upstairs I walk a ramp which is great but there's a space in my butt muscles that are sore, so I was trying to figure out what I was doing to make a knot in the muscle of my buttocks, guess what… it's the ramp. So I'm wondering now is my butt muscle getting exercise or getting bigger? Haha It probably doesn't matter because I'm not going to build steps.

I'm also trying to learn a Android tablet which is crazy because for 10 years I have been iPhone.i think Android is right-handed haha yet; I will learn this also.

3 to 10 I have a ramp. I have a two-story house. I have butt muscles. I am sore.

Me, shutting down is far worse than me blowing up I promise

Thoughts;____
____
____

Common Sense
Knowledge

3 or 10 I get cracked up at times that people listen to the media without thinking. We all recognize Trump derangement syndrome. It's just a fact in society but this week I seen a news post that says "the government will allow people to buy beef from the farmer". Oh my, this is hilarious that people can't think. Americans have always been able to own cattle, butcher cattle, eat cattle, but this week there's an article in the paper that says "Americans can buy meat from the rancher". Now; seriously think about that. Americans have now been given permission by the media to do something they have always been able to do and Americans fall for it so this week you have been given permission to talk to a farmer and buy produce and buy meat and buy eggs and get milk.

The media has you snookered. 50% of education is being able to sort information and think about it. I had a business teacher that always said "think outside the box". He told me in front of the class that this was easier for me than for others because I was older and life was different when I was in grade school and the fact that I'm left-handed helped me in sorting information into logic. I cannot believe that the school system is failing our kids… it's sad

3 or 10 in America you can buy beef from a rancher!!! for over 200 years now!!! but they just notified us in the paper. I hope friends and family that are young will choose to think Logically!!!

Grace is when God gives us good things that we don't deserve

Mercy is when he spares us from bad things we deserve

Blessings are when he is generous with both

Truly we can never run out of reasons to thank him

Thoughts;____

____

____

Divorce is hard but the months before you know it's time to leave, they are the hardest

"you can't force someone to see that you are a blessing, you just gotta let them miss out"

Patriotism
History

3 or 10 I got to Germany in 1986 and lived there till 1990! It was a wonderful life experience. I was a good Army wife. I totally embraced the entire experience. From eating the food, krankenhaus baby delivery, watching the wall come down, to speaking German and Italian. I look back to see what a blessing it was. I went to Hitlers Eagle's Nest and Dachau. He was indeed a twisted soul. History shows us lots of twisted souls in power. My experience in the world and today's current events... I'm watching and I want everyone to open their eyes. China has a twisted soul. HEADS UP Nancy Pelosi and Joe Biden are friends with China and have billions of dollars invested in that relationship. I'm not a conspiracy nut but I am an eyes wide open kind of person. COVID19 was no accident. It was no natural Act of God, Most don't know but Hanford WA in the 1940's released "stuff" to test it in Warfare. We won WWII but many people are now labeled Downwinders. So I'm a Downwinder, I walked where Hitler walked, and COVID19 now has me sheltering in place.

3 or 10 power and control is not good for a government, whether China communist party, Hitler, or even Governor Inslee. I'm going to clean house, haha if you know me you know I'm fibbing.

The Nazis had a phrase which covered all abuses by the state

"Fur Ihre Sicherheit"

....

It's for your safety

Thoughts;____

____

____

Blessings

3 or 10 oh my so my store was open today, 4 elders, came to help and in 3 hours we unloaded a 40 ft semi, separated to yard, upstairs, and down stairs. I played with the dogs. Port has decided hiking his leg in the house is fun till I see him then he drops his head knowing mom is mad. It was 70 today so I actually got to take my coat off. I know my mom had a hand in my new house. I bet she is laughing her head off at me, character I think is her plan. It is kicking my butt yet is coming together, even tho it feels like I'm falling apart. The list of done gets longer each day.

3 or 10 I hurt from head to toe, but it's good to be on my feet.

Maybe life isn't about avoiding the bruises. Maybe it's about collecting the scars to prove we showed up for it.

Thoughts;____

____

____

Personal Responsibility

3 or 10 I went to get a load of stuff from Jake's. Oh he is mad... I abandoned him. Today I found out I stole "his" Tahoe!!! I bought a Tahoe before we got married.. I made all the payments... I paid all the insurance... I paid for most of the repairs... he bought the radiator because he wanted to drive it... and it was broke down, and I refused to fix it for him to tell me over and over I contributed nothing to the family. He hates woman, and I abandoned him. Why do woman always abandon and cheat on him... because he hates woman. "But I'm the problem". I never cheated but "all woman" cheat. And last week that came up.

3 or 10 I can't change or fix "being a woman" nor would I want to. I completely understand why the women in his life get so sad and lonely that they cheat, they look for value and friendship away from him. I left with only 1/2 a pickup load because the stress had me in tears. I am enough... it is Jake that cant see why I left, (abandoning him)!

I am Enough

Thoughts;____

____

____

Resilience
Courage

3 or 10 I want things done!!! But I keep adding to the list of goals. So really I want to accomplish things. I want to feel good about reaching a goal or finishing a project. Yesterday I got 40 ft of walls. Oh yea right!! No really I got walls. Today's goal is heat. So electric, propane, or wood? All come with expenses. So what is the plan? I'm thinking! I promise. I think I'm gonna install the pellet stove.

I'm in a lot of pain as I work muscles that for the last couple years I haven't needed. It is getting better. Did you know walking a ramp either up or down uses leg muscles ya didn't even know ya had. Yep it's true.

3 or 10 divorce takes your feet right out from under you. I laid on the ground floundering for far to long. But; I'm up, and running. I'm on my feet, setting goals. I'm getting stuff done... yesterday I got 40 ft of walls... so heating 5000 square feet is now down to heating 1000 square ft. It's a good day!!

If you kick me when I'm down, you better pray I don't get up

Thoughts;____

____

____

Self Aware
Stand Your Ground

3 or 10 what the hell is wrong with people. I put 3 dogs out. Maybe 5 minutes I hear a bark so I go look to see what's wrong. The DRUNK neighbor is screaming at my dogs, flapping his arms, and squirting them with a hose sprayer for high pressure. I scream at him to stop it. So he continues and is now screaming at me. So that sets my dogs in a stance to protect me. So I head to the other door to let the dogs in. The idiot goes in his house comes out and starts doing it all again. So I bring the dogs in. This exchange might be 10 minutes but probably closer to 7. So I get the dogs put where they belong. Because in their fenced yard with tarps blocking their view is not safe. I go upstairs, the phone rings, I answer and hear "Annette? Annette?" From downstairs inside my house. Yep Mr Shitfaced is now inside my house. I yell "get out" and to my phone call I said "stay on the phone and listen" for Mr Shitfaced to get in my house he went thru his gate, opened and walked thru my gate, came thru the yard and my back door. So I'm now officially hostile angry. But Mr Shitfaced wants to talk... I am in awe struck by stupid and say "don't abuse my dogs" "don't squirt my dogs" " don't flap your arms at my dogs" don't tease my dogs" "don't threaten or scream at me" "and get out of my house" so then he rambles on about my dogs barking all night... I said "you are a liar cuz my dogs are in my bedroom all night" so finely he leaves. I go back to my phone call. We chat, he said "what is his problem?" I said with a giggle "he hates my Trump 2020 hat".

3 or 10 it is so sad that people (Dems) will do anything to get even with Trump supporters. (Yes Mr Shitfaced has screamed at me about how horrid #MyPresident is) Who divided this nation? HATE.. whether for a President, a race, a gender, murdering babies, or high taxes. The beliefs we carry dictate who we like. Mr Shitfaced will like the bailiff bringing his lunch if I find him in my house again.

Thoughts;____

____

____

Goals
Plans

3 or 10 kind of a strange picture!!! Yep, well I've been living in a parka yep a parka over 2 sweat shirts. I've been sleeping with 4 comforters, even over my head. And yes it has been better than being married, last Thursday I got 40 ft of walls... TODAY I GOT HEAT INSTALLED!!! It's such a good day!!! But my WA family and friends are 70+ and I am 40... yes my beautiful Idaho... still snowing in the mountains. I'm on one of those mountains. I AM ON ONE THOSE awesome views, breath taking, elk walking by, mountains... 3 or 10 life is good!!!

Picture of a pellet stove

Thoughts;____
____
____

Regrets
Mental Health
Motherhood

3 or 10 A friend was murdered this week by another friend. A guy that never showed me any violent behavior, took a long gun and murdered a sleeping man. COVID19? Stress? Drugs? PTSD? We will never know Why? But this proves 2 things to me. We NEVER know when our last breath will be. And we DON'T know what is in other people's minds or hearts. I'm terribly sad by the events that went on, yet in a way I get it. I hate to enlighten some but Satan, sadness, and NO HOPE, are all man made. Our society is not forgiving, loyal, or at times kind. I have been to the depths of suicidal, I have been so crushed I've stayed in bed for days, and I have lashed out at people I love. I have been bitter, and even unforgiving. It does not make me good yet admitting it makes me better. Better than yesterday. I have a child I haven't spoke to in years. What broke us was not me, her behavior led to guilt and her stubbornness has distanced us. She has demanded I agree with her. Well that's not going to work. She asked me once "when are you going to accept" I responded with "I have accepted, I still can't condone" her path is a hard one, she can never change what happened, and I do believe she wishes she could. She has given me 2 grandkids that I have never met, she didn't even tell me they were born. So bad behavior continues. And needless to say I gave birth, loved with all my heart, yet have removed 2 children from my will. I bet when I die she posts to Facebook for sympathy.

3 or 10 call a friend, send a text, write a letter. Tomorrow might very well be too late.

When I'm dead, please don't post on my timeline saying you wished heaven had a phone. I have a phone now and you don't even call.

Thoughts;____
____
____

Motherhood
Unconditional Love

3 or 10 love this t-shirt but I have girly girls that wouldn't ware it. I have 2 of the most beautiful young women. Saige just taller. Whisper is me, with a little more fire. Yes; she has a bit more fire!!! Or I'm getting too old for the fight so I'm quieter. I know it was my job to raise them, but fact is they taught me the important stuff. They made me be better everyday than I was the day before. They forced me to my feet on the days I wanted to sleep in. They made me sit through sports (yuck). But one of the biggest gifts was they made me look at the world, not about me!!! But about them. Selfless!!! Is indeed a quality worth having. Selfless... vs self. I am indeed nothing without them. Yesterday I called the bank where Saige works and I told the man "look at Saige and say hippopotamus and see if she smiles" I hear in the background "LIONESS" life is indeed THOSE LITTLE MOMENTS... one word.. that makes a smile burst forward.

3 or 10 I'm a mom... really with all the things I value and am good at, MOM is the most important. I've done well at that job... both of my girls are bratty, have fire in their belly, know what hard work is, and will fight me at any moment, (yea I taught them to always stand for what they believe in). Saige is the quiet fighter, Whisper is the loud and proud. But both welcome the struggles, that lead to the rewards.

Thoughts;____

____

____

Self Awareness
Manifesting
Faith

3 or 10 so most of my friends know I fall into the category of "a bit eccentric" "maybe crazy" and certainly a little "weird". I am "one of a kind" for sure. So I own a second hand store and I told my Angels I need a glass case. I started my search, marketplace, went to all the second hand furniture people in the area, stopped by the local jewelry store... I found big and little, over priced, and out of budget. So I was watching one that just tugged at my being. $200 so I said I'll wait and see how business goes. So I'm stalking a glass case. Yep!!! BOOYAH he dropped the price. Not a little, he got right with it and dropped the price.

3 or 10 have faith in the process, and know you don't need to worry because once you ask your Angels for help... THEY GET BUSY to do good in your life. This prayer took them a month, but look!!! Is it just perfect? Keeping faith patiently is hard for us mere mortals. Yet if we open our eyes and hearts to "something" bigger than ourselves!!! They, My Angels, will show themselves everytime.

Thoughts;_________________________________

____

____

Acknowledgment

My dear children Bethanie, Daniel, Daniella, Saige, and Whisper you all always kept me going. Each brings with you your sparkle and success. All the challenges we faced, for me, were an unbreakable bond. Thank You for picking me to be your mom.

My beautiful grands, Monsters, Indy, Butch, Munchie, and two in Iowa… you added a feeling that no one else ever has. That feeling is the greatest (and the saddest) but is so deep in my soul. Bubbling up to be pure bliss.

To Mrs Sharp, that fed my history bug, building me up one assignment at a time, to take on the world. You were the first to teach me I could read and comprehend, and my value wasn't how fast I finished the assignment, but I was of value even when I didn't. You influenced every day of my life.

To Lisa, Jo, Keith, and Kayleen, thank you for the little push to complete this manuscript. Each of you are my cheerleaders, giving me my own cheer section, my own rally, and my own moments of doubt you refused to let define me. Pushing or praising, I'm not sure, but it is a gift from your heart.

Tonya (therapist), I know you can't admit it, but thank you for acknowledging my good. On days I came in, you lifted me simply by saying, "How is your 3 or 10?" "That is beautiful." "You truly think about things." I know you can not admit to knowing me, but I can admit you are in my cheering section.

Marnie, not sure why you just saw in me more than I did, but what a heaven-sent blessing after a psychiatrist tried to destroy me. Look at all the years, milestones, challenges, and friendship. You are an angelic being that God placed in my life; Thank You, Lord Above, for Marnie.

Most importantly, my mom told me to be a journalist or attorney!!! You said it not once but often. You published first, which pushed me. Your love and a kick in the butt made me a better everything. I hope from Heaven above you are proud of me cuz of all the people along the way; you being proud is for sure "a feather" in my cap. I'm sure you have more life advice cuz I can still hear your voice in my day. I did it Mom; I hope you are proud.